READERS LOVE TERRY LYNN THOMAS

'I flew through the pages of this well-crafted historical thriller.'

'I am hooked on historical fiction, especially women in World War II. This book includes all the intrigue of espionage, secrets, German paperwork – and of course, murder. It was just what I was looking for!'

'*The Silent Woman* will keep you turning pages long into the night, and eagerly awaiting the next installment of Catherine Carlisle's story.'

'I highly recommend this book to both lovers of historical fiction and those that have an interest in pre-war Europe as a whole.'

'This one is a page turner. Couldn't put it down! I highly recommend this book, and I can't wait until the next one.'

'You are transported to another time and lifestyle in such a way you feel you have lived it.'

'Will certainly read the next book with these characters.'

'I thoroughly enjoyed this historical novel.'

Terry Lynn Thomas grew up in the San Francisco Bay Area, which explains her love of foggy beaches, windy dunes, and Gothic mysteries. When her husband promised to buy Terry a horse and the time to write if she moved to Mississippi with him, she jumped at the chance. Although she had written several novels and screenplays prior to 2006, after she relocated to the South she set out to write in earnest and has never looked back.

Now Terry Lynn writes the Sarah Bennett Mysteries, set on the California coast during the 1940s, which feature a misunderstood medium in love with a spy. *The House of Secrets* is a recipient of the IndieBRAG Medallion. She also writes the Cat Carlisle Mysteries, set in Britain during World War II. *The Silent Woman* is the first book in this series. When she's not writing, you can find Terry Lynn riding her horse, walking in the woods with her dogs, or visiting old cemeteries in search of story ideas.

Also by Terry Lynn Thomas

The Drowned Woman

The House of Secrets

A Family Secret

The Silent Woman

Terry Lynn Thomas

ONE PLACE. MANY STORIES

HQ
An imprint of HarperCollins*Publishers* Ltd
1 London Bridge Street
London SE1 9GF

This paperback edition 2019

19 20 21 22 LSC 10 9 8 7 6 5 4 3 2 1
First published in Great Britain by
HQ, an imprint of HarperCollins*Publishers* Ltd 2018

ISBN: 9780008328658

For more information visit: www.harpercollins.co.uk/green

Printed and bound in the United States of
America by LSC Communications

For Doug, with all my love.

Prologue

Berlin, May 1936
It rained the day the Gestapo came.

Dieter Reinsinger didn't mind the rain. He liked the sound of the drops on the tight fabric of his umbrella as he walked from his office on Wilhelmstrasse to the flat he shared with his sister Leni and her husband Michael on Nollendorfstrasse. The trip took him the good part of an hour, but he walked to and from work every day, come rain or shine. He passed the familiar apartments and plazas, nodding at the familiar faces with a smile.

Dieter liked his routine. He passed Mrs Kleiman's bakery, and longed for the *pfannkuchen* that used to tempt passers-by from the display window. He remembered Mrs Kleiman's kind ways, as she would beckon him into the shop, where she would sit with him and share a plate of the jelly doughnuts and the strong coffee that she brewed especially to his liking. She was a kind woman, who had lost her husband and only son in the war.

In January the Reich took over the bakery, replacing gentle Mrs Kleiman with a ham-fisted Fräulein with a surly attitude and no skill in the kitchen whatsoever. *No use complaining over things that cannot be fixed,* Dieter chided himself. He found he no longer had a taste for *pfannkuchen*.

By the time he turned onto his block, his sodden trouser legs clung to his calves. He didn't care. He thought of the hot coffee he would have when he got home, followed by the vegetable soup that Leni had started that morning. Dieter ignored the changes taking place around him. If he just kept to himself, he could rationalise the gangs of soldiers that patrolled the streets, taking pleasure in the fear they induced. He could ignore the lack of fresh butter, soap, sugar, and coffee. He could ignore the clenching in his belly every time he saw the pictures of Adolf Hitler, which hung in every shop, home, café, and business in Berlin. If he could carry on as usual, Dieter could convince himself that things were just as they used to be.

He turned onto his block and stopped short when he saw the black Mercedes parked at the kerb in front of his apartment. The lobby door was open. The pavement around the apartment deserted. He knew this day would come – how could it not? He just didn't know it would come so soon. The Mercedes was running, the windscreen wipers swooshing back and forth. Without thinking, Dieter shut his umbrella and tucked himself into the sheltered doorway of the apartment building across the street. He peered through the pale rain and bided his time. Soon he would be rid of Michael Blackwell. Soon he and Leni could get back to living their quiet life. Leni would thank him in the end. How could she not?

Dieter was a loyal German. He had enlisted in the *Deutsches Heer* – the Germany army – as an eighteen-year-old boy. He had fought in the trenches and had lived to tell about it. He came home a hardened man – grateful to still have his arms and legs attached – ready to settle down to a simple life. Dieter didn't want a wife. He didn't like women much. He didn't care much for sex, and he had Leni to care for the house. All Dieter needed was a comfortable chair at the end of the day and food for his belly. He wanted nothing else.

Leni was five years younger than Dieter. She'd celebrated her fortieth birthday in March, but to Dieter she would always be a child. While Dieter was steadfast and hardworking, Leni was wild and flighty. When she was younger she had thought she would try to be a dancer, but quickly found that she lacked the required discipline. After dancing, she turned to painting and poured her passion into her work for a year. The walls of the flat were covered with canvases filled with splatters of vivid paint. She used her considerable charm to connive a showing at a small gallery, but her work wasn't well received.

Leni claimed that no one understood her. She tossed her paintbrushes and supplies in the rubbish bin and moved on to writing. Writing was a good preoccupation for Leni. Now she called herself a writer, but rarely sat down to work. She had a desk tucked into one of the corners of the apartment, complete with a sterling fountain pen and inkwell, a gift from Dieter, who held a secret hope that his restless sister had found her calling.

Now Michael Blackwell commandeered the writing desk, the silver pen, and the damned inkwell. Just like he commandeered everything else.

For a long time, Leni kept her relationship with Michael Blackwell a secret. Dieter noticed small changes: the ink well in a different spot on Leni's writing desk and the bottle of ink actually being used. The stack of linen writing paper depleted. Had Leni started writing in earnest? Something had infused her spirit with a new effervescence. Her cheeks had a new glow to them. Leni floated around the apartment. She hummed as she cooked.

Dieter assumed that his sister – like him – had discovered passion in a vocation. She bought new dresses and took special care with her appearance. When Dieter asked how she had paid for them, she told him she had been economical with the housekeeping money.

For the first time ever, the household ran smoothly. Meals were produced on time, laundry was folded and put away, and the house sparkled. Dieter should have been suspicious. He wasn't.

He discovered them in bed together on a beautiful September day when a client had cancelled an appointment and Dieter had decided to go home early. He looked forward to sitting in his chair in front of the window, while Leni brought him lunch and a stein filled with thick dark beer on a tray. These thoughts of home and hearth were in his mind when he let himself into the flat and heard the moan – soft as a heartbeat – coming from Leni's room. Thinking that she had fallen and hurt herself, Dieter burst into the bedroom, only to discover his sister naked in the bed, her limbs entwined with the long muscular legs of Michael Blackwell.

'Good God,' Michael said as he rolled off Leni and covered them both under the eiderdown. Dieter hated Michael Blackwell then, hated the way he shielded his sister, as if Leni needed protection from her own brother. Dieter bit back the scream that threatened and with great effort forced himself to unfurl his hands, which he was surprised to discover had clenched into tight fists. He swallowed the anger, taking it back into his gut where it could fester.

Leni sat up, the golden sun from the window forming a halo around her body as she held the blanket over her breasts. 'Dieter, darling,' she giggled. 'I'd like you to meet my husband.' Dieter took the giggle as a taunting insult. It sent his mind spinning. For the first time in his life, he wanted to throttle his sister.

At least Michael Blackwell had the sense to look sheepish. 'I'd shake your hand, but I'm afraid ...'

'We'll explain everything,' Leni said. 'Let us get dressed. Michael said he'd treat us to a special dinner. We must celebrate!'

Dieter had turned on his heel and left the flat. He didn't return until late that evening, expecting Leni to be alone, hurt, or even angry with him. He expected her to come running to the door when he let himself in and beg his forgiveness. But Leni wasn't alone. She and Michael were waiting for Dieter, sitting on the couch. Leni pouted. Michael insisted the three of them talk it out and come to an understanding. 'Your sister loves you, Dieter. Don't make her choose between us.'

Michael took charge – as he was wont to do. Leni explained that she loved Michael, and that they had been seeing each other for months, right under Dieter's nose. Dieter imagined the two of them, naked, loving each other, while he slaved at the office to put food on the table.

'You could have told me, Leni,' he said to his sister. 'I've never kept anything from you.'

'You would have forbidden me to see him,' Leni said. She had taken Michael's hand. 'And I would have defied you.'

She was right. He would have forbidden the relationship. As for Leni's defiance, Dieter could forgive his foolish sister that trespass. Michael Blackwell would pay the penance for Leni's sins. After all, he was to blame for them.

Leni left them to discuss the situation man to man. Dieter found himself telling Michael about their parents' deaths and the life he and Leni shared. Michael told Dieter that he was a journalist in England and was in Germany to research a book. *So that's where the ink and paper have been going,* Dieter thought. When he realised that for the past few months Michael and Leni had been spending their days here, in the flat that he paid for, Dieter hated Michael Blackwell even more. But he didn't show it.

Michael brought out a fine bottle of brandy. The two men stayed up all night, talking about their lives, plans for the future, and the ever-looming war. When the sun crept up in the morning sky, they stood and shook hands. Dieter decided he could pretend to like this man. He'd do it for Leni's sake.

'I love your sister, Dieter. I hope to be friends with you,' Michael said.

Dieter wanted to slap him. Instead he forced a smile. 'I'm happy for you.'

'Do you mind if we stay here until we find a flat of our own?'

'Of course. Why move? I'd be happy if you both would live here in the house. I'll give you my bedroom. It's bigger and has a better view. I'm never home anyway.'

Michael nodded. 'I'd pay our share, of course. I'll discuss it with Leni.'

Leni agreed to stay in the flat, happy that her new husband and her brother had become friends.

Months went by. The three of them fell into a routine. Each morning, Leni would make both men breakfast. They would sit together and share a meal, after which Dieter would leave for the office. Dieter had no idea what

Michael Blackwell got up to during the day. Michael didn't discuss his personal activities with Dieter. Dieter didn't ask about them.

He spent more and more time in his room after dinner, leaving Leni and Michael in the living room of the flat. He told himself he didn't care, until he noticed subtle changes taking place. They would talk in whispers, but when Dieter entered the room, they stopped speaking and stared at him with blank smiles on their faces.

It was about this time when Dieter noticed a change in his neighbours. They used to look at him and smile. Now they wouldn't look him in the eye, and some had taken to crossing the street when he came near. They no longer stopped to ask after his health or discuss the utter lack of decent coffee or meat. His neighbours were afraid of him. Leni and Michael were up to something, or Michael was up to something and Leni was blindly following along.

During this time, Dieter noticed a man milling outside the flat when he left for his walk to the office. He recognised him, as he had been there the day before, standing in the doorway in the apartment building across the street. Fear clenched Dieter's gut, cramping his bowels. He forced himself to breathe, to keep his eyes focused straight ahead and continue on as though nothing were amiss. He knew a Gestapo agent when he saw one. He heard the rumours of Hitler's secret police. Dieter was a good German. He kept his eyes on the ground and his mouth shut.

Once he arrived at his office, he hurried up to his desk and peered out the window onto the street below. Nothing. So they weren't following him. Of course they weren't following him. Why would they? It didn't take Dieter long to figure out that Michael Blackwell had aroused the

Gestapo's interest. He had to protect Leni. He vowed to find out what Michael was up to.

His opportunity came on a Saturday in April, when Leni and Michael had plans to be out for the day. They claimed they were going on a picnic, but Dieter was certain they were lying when he discovered the picnic hamper on the shelf in the kitchen. He wasn't surprised. His sister was a liar now. It wasn't her fault. He blamed Michael Blackwell. He had smiled and wished them a pleasant day. After that, he moved to the window and waited until they exited the apartment, arm in arm, and headed away on their outing. When they were safely out of sight, Dieter bolted the door and conducted a thorough, methodical search.

He went through all of the books in the flat, thumbing through them before putting them back exactly as he found them. Nothing. He rifled drawers, looked under mattresses, went through pockets. Still nothing. Desperate now, he removed everything from the wardrobe where Michael and Leni hung their clothes. Only after everything was removed did Dieter see the wooden crate on the floor, tucked into the back behind Michael's tennis racket. He took it out and lifted the lid, to reveal neat stacks of brochures, the front of which depicted a castle and a charming German village. The cover read, *Unser Schönes Deutschland*: Our Beautiful Germany. Puzzled, Dieter took one of the brochures, opened it, read the first sentence, and cried out.

Inside the brochure was a detailed narrative of the conditions under Hitler's regime. The writer didn't hold back. The brochure told of an alleged terror campaign of murder, mass arrests, execution, and an utter suspension of civil rights. There was a map of all the camps, which – at least according to this brochure – held over one hundred thousand or more Communists, Social Democrats, and trade unionists. The last page was a plea for help, a battle cry calling for Hitler and his entire regime to be overthrown.

Dieter's hand shook. Fear made his mouth go dry. They would all be taken to the basement at Prinz Albrecht Strasse for interrogation and torture. If they survived, they would be sent to one of the camps. A bullet to the back of the head would be a mercy. Sweat broke out on Dieter's face; drops of it formed between his shoulder blades. He swallowed the lump that formed in the back of his throat, as the fear morphed into blind, infuriating anger and exploded in a black cloud of rage directed at Michael Blackwell.

How dare he expose Leni to this type of danger? Dieter needed to protect his sister. He stuffed the brochures back in the crate, put the lid on it, and pushed the box back into the recesses of the wardrobe. There was only one thing for Dieter to do.

Chapter One

Marry in haste, repent at leisure, says the bird in the gilded cage. The words – an apt autobiography to be sure – ran round and round in Cat Carlisle's head. She pressed her forehead against the cold windowpane and scanned the street in front of her house. Her eyes roamed the square, with its newly painted benches and gnarled old trees leafed out in verdant June splendour. A gang of school-aged boys kicked a ball on the grass, going out of their way to push and shove as they scurried along. They laughed with glee when the tallest of the group fell on his bum, turned a somersault, popped back up, and bowed deeply to his friends. She smiled and pushed away the longing that threatened whenever a child was near.

She thought of the time when she and her husband had loved each other, confided in each other. How long had it been since they'd had a civil conversation? Five years? Ten? How long had it been since she discovered that Benton Carlisle and Trudy Ashworth – of the Ashworth textile fortune – were involved in a long-term love affair? Ten years, two months and four days. For the record book, that's how long it took for Benton's love to morph into indifference and for the indifference to fester into acrimony. Now Cat and her husband rarely spoke. On the rare occasions when they did speak, the words between them were sharp and laced with animosity.

Cat turned and surveyed the room that she had claimed for her own, a small sanctuary in the Carlisles' Kensington house. When she and Benton discovered she was with child the first time, they pulled down the gloomy wallpaper and washed the walls a charming shade of buttercup yellow, perfect for a child of any sex. But Cat had lost the child before the furniture had been ordered. In an abundance of caution, they hadn't ordered furniture when Cat became pregnant for a second and third time. Those babies had not survived in her womb either. Now she had claimed the nursery as her own.

It was the sunniest room in the house. When Benton started to stay at his club – at least that's what he told Cat; she knew he really stayed at Trudy's flat in Belgravia – Cat moved in and decorated it to suit her own taste. She found she rather liked this small space. A tiny bed, an armoire to hold her clothes, and a writing table – with space between the pieces – were the only furnishings in the room. She had removed the dark Persian rug and left the oak floors bare, liking the way the honey-toned wood warmed the room. She had washed away the buttercup yellow and painted the walls stark white.

'Miss?' The maid stood in the open doorway of Cat's bedroom. She was too young to be working, thirteen if she was a day, skinny and pale with a mousy brown bun peeking out from the white cap and sharp cheekbones that spoke of meals missed.

'Who're you?' Cat asked. She forced a smile so as not to scare the poor thing.

'Annie, ma'am.' Annie took a tentative step into Cat's room. In one hand she carried a wooden box full of feather dusters, rags, and other cleaning supplies. In the other she carried a broom and dustpan. 'I'm to give you the message that Alicia Montrose is here. She is eager to see you.' She looked around the room. 'And then I am to turn your room.'

'I'll just finish up and be down shortly,' Cat said.

The girl hesitated in the doorway.

'You can come in and get started,' Cat said.

'Thank you, miss.' The girl moved into the room and started to work away, focusing on the tasks at hand. 'Do you mind if I open the window? I like to air the bed linens.'

'Of course not,' Cat said.

She reached for the box that held her hairpins and attempted to wrangle her curls into submission. Behind her, the child opened the window and pulled back the sheets on Cat's bed. While the bed linens aired, Annie busied herself with the dusting and polishing.

Cat turned back to the mirror and wondered how she could avoid seeing Alicia Montrose. She couldn't face her, not yet. The wounds, though old, were still raw.

The Montrose family had always been gracious and kind to her, especially in the beginning of her relationship with Benton when she felt like a fish out of water, among the well-heeled, tightly knit group who had known each other since childhood, and whose parents and grandparents before them had been close friends.

Many in Benton's circle hadn't been so quick to welcome Cat into their fold. Not the Montroses. They extended every courtesy towards Cat. Alicia took Cat under her wing and saw that she was included in the events the wives scheduled when the husbands went on their hunting and fishing trips. Alicia also sought Cat out for days of shopping and attending the museum. And when the Bradbury-Scots invited Cat and Benton for dinner, Alicia swept in and tactfully explained the myriad of customs involved.

'They'll be watching you, Cat. If you hold your teacup incorrectly, they'll never let you live it down. And Lady Bradbury-Scott will load the table with an excess of forks and knives just to trip you up.' Alicia had taken Cat to her home every day for a week, where they dined on course after course of delicious food prepared by the Montroses' cook. While they ate, Alicia explained every nuance to Cat – *speak to the guest on the right during the first course. Only when that is finished can you turn to the left.* The rules were legion.

Cat credited Alicia's tutelage for her success at the dinner. She had triumphed. The Bradbury-Scotts accepted her, so did Benton's friends, all thanks to Alicia Montrose. One of these days Cat would need to make peace with Alicia, and talk to her about why she had resisted Alicia's overtures. Cat didn't expect Alicia to forgive her. How could she? But at least Alicia could be made to understand what motivated Cat to behave so shabbily. But not today.

She plunked her new green velvet hat on her head and pinned it fast without checking herself in the mirror. As she tiptoed downstairs, she wondered if she could sneak out the kitchen door and avoid the women altogether. With any luck, she could slip out unnoticed and avoid the litany of questions and criticisms that had become Isobel's standard fare over the years.

'I think the chairs should be in a half circle around this half of the room.' Alicia's voice floated up the stairs. 'A half circle is so much more welcoming, don't you agree?'

'Oh, I agree.' Isobel Carlisle, Cat's domineering sister-in-law, a shrewish woman who made a career of haranguing Cat, spoke in the unctuous tone reserved for Alicia alone. 'Move them back, Marie.'

Poor Marie. Isobel's secretary bore the brunt of Isobel's self-importance. Cat didn't know how she stood it, but Marie Quimby had been Isobel's loyal servant for years. Cat slunk down the stairs like a thief in her own home.

'But we just had them in the half circle, and neither of you liked that arrangement,' Marie said. She sounded beleaguered and it was only nine in the morning.

'There you are, Catherine. Bit late this morning.' Isobel stepped into the hallway.'

Catherine,' Alicia said. She smiled as she air-kissed Cat's cheek, while Isobel looked down her nose in disapproval. 'How've you been, Cat? You're looking well. We were worried about you. Good to see you've got the roses back in your cheeks.' Alicia was resplendent in a navy dress and a perfect hat.

'It was just a bout of influenza. I am fully recovered,' Cat said. 'And thank you for the lovely flowers and the card.'

'Won't you consider helping us? We could certainly use you. No one has a knack for getting people to part with their money like you do.'

Cat smiled, ignoring Isobel's dagger-like glare. 'Maybe next time. How're the boys?'

'Growing like mad. Hungry all the time. They're excited about our trip to Scotland. The invitation's open, if you'd like to join?' Alicia let the question hang in the air between them.

'I'll think about it.' Cat backed out of the room, eager to be outside. 'It's good to see you, Alicia.'

'Come to the house for the weekend, Cat. If the boys are too much, I'll send them to their gran's house. We've some catching up to do.'

'I'd like that,' Cat said. 'Must run.'

'Perhaps we should get back to work?' Isobel said.

A flash of sadness washed over Alicia's face. 'Please ring me, Catherine. At least we can have lunch.'

'I will. Promise,' Cat said.

'Isobel, I'll leave you to deal with the chairs. I'm going to use your telephone and call the florist.'

'Of course,' Isobel said.

Once Alicia stepped away, Isobel stepped close to Cat and spoke in a low voice. 'I do not appreciate you being so forward. You practically threw yourself at Alicia. Don't you realise what my association on this project could do for me, for our family, socially? This is very important, Catherine. Don't force me to speak to Benton about your behaviour. I will if I have to.'

Cat ignored her sister-in-law, as she had done a million times before. She walked past the drawing room, where Marie was busy arranging the chairs – heavy wooden things with curvy legs and high backs. Marie looked up at Cat and gave her a wan smile.

Isobel, stout and strong with a mass of iron-grey waves, was the exact opposite of Marie, who was thin as a cadaver and obedient as a well-trained hound. Marie's wispy grey hair stood in a frizzy puff on her head, like a mangled halo. Cat didn't understand the relationship between the women. Isobel claimed that her volunteer work kept her so busy that she needed an assistant to make her appointments and type her letters. Cat didn't believe that for one minute. Cat knew the true reason for Marie's employment. Isobel needed someone to boss around.

Her sister-in-law surveyed Cat's ensemble from head to toe, looking for fault. Cat dismissed her scrutiny.

After fifteen years of living in the Carlisle house, she had become a master at disregarding Isobel.

'What is it, Isobel? I really must go,' Cat said.

'Before you go, I'd like you to touch up the silver. And maybe you could give Marie a hand in the kitchen? I know it's a bit of an imposition, but the agency didn't have a cook available today. I'm expecting ten committee members for our meeting this afternoon. I wouldn't want to run out of food. I need these committee members well fed. We've much work to do.'

'I can manage, Izzy,' Marie said.

'I've asked Catherine,' Isobel said. 'And those chairs won't move themselves.'

'I'm going out.' Cat paused before the mirror. She fixed her hat and fussed with her hair, taking her time as she drew the delicate veil over her eyes.

'You should be grateful, Catherine. Benton has given you a home and a position in society. You've made it clear you're not happy here, but a little gratitude wouldn't go amiss. You and Benton may be at odds, but that doesn't change things. You'd be on the street if it weren't for us. You've no training. It's not like you are capable of earning your living.'

'I hardly think any gratitude I feel towards my husband should be used to benefit you. I'm not your servant, Isobel. I'm Benton's wife. You seem to have forgotten that.'

Isobel stepped so close to Cat that their noses almost touched. When she spoke, spittle flew, but Cat didn't flinch. She didn't back away when Isobel said, 'I suggest you take care in your dealings with me, Catherine. I could ruin you.'

Cat met Isobel's gaze and didn't look away. 'Do your best. I am not afraid of you.' She stepped away and forced a smile. 'Silly old cow,' Cat whispered.

'What did you call me?'

'You heard me.' Cat picked up her handbag. 'I don't know when I'll be back. Have a pleasant day.' She turned her back on Isobel and stepped out into the summer morning.

She headed out into the street and took one last glance at the gleaming white house, one of many in a row. Benton's cousin, Michael Blackwell, Blackie for short, stood in the window of Benton's study, bleary-eyed from a night of solitary drinking in his room. Blackie spent a lot of time in Benton's study, especially when Benton wasn't home. She knew why – that's where the good brandy was kept.

Blackie had escaped Germany with his life, the clothes on his back, and nothing else. A long-lost cousin of Benton and Isobel, Blackie turned up on their doorstep, damaged from the narrow escape and desperate for a place to live. Of course they had taken him in. The Carlisles were big on family loyalty. Now Blackie worked at a camera shop during the day and spent his nights sequestered in his room with a bottle of brandy and his memories of Hitler.

Cat often wondered what happened in Germany to frighten Blackie so, but she didn't have the heart to make him relive his suffering just to satisfy her curiosity. He saw Cat, smiled at her, and held up a snifter of Benton's brandy, never mind that it was only half past nine in the morning. Everyone knew Blackie drank to excess. They didn't care. He was family. Cat waved at him, anxious to get as far away from the Carlisle house as fast as she could.

***

Thomas Charles watched the watcher, sure now that the woman who had been lurking outside the Carlisle house for the past week was Marlena Helmschmidt, aka Marlena Barrington, most notably known as Marlena X. He thought back to the last time he and Marlena had been face to face. He thought of her husband, dead from a bullet. He thought of Gwen, his colleague at the time, huddled against a wall, a knife in her chest, clinging to life, and ultimately losing the battle.

Marlena X specialised in espionage. She was an extremely competent typist and secretary. She spoke French, German, English, and Swahili. It was rumoured that she could take shorthand just as fast as someone could speak. The last time he had dealt with Marlena, she had insinuated herself into a high-clearance position working for the navy. God knows what information she had accessed. Her bosses sang her praises.

When Thomas told them their darling was a spy, they shunned him, dismissed his accusations, and sent him on his way. Until documents went missing, and they came crawling back. Thomas never said I told you. That was most certainly not his style. Marlena was tough. She had the personal qualities of a well-educated sophisticate, but underneath the polished veneer, was a woman who knew her way around bombs and could street fight as well as any man. Her lithe and supple frame allowed her break into the most challenging locations. She also had a quick hand with locks.

Her appearance at the Carlisles' was not a portent of good things. What the devil was she up to? He stepped close to the oak tree in the garden square, keeping himself hidden, as Marlena arrived to sit on the bench, just as she had done every day for the past week. His orders were clear – watch her; do not approach her. Find out where she is staying, who she talks to, anything about her day-to-day activities, and report back.

He'd been watching her for a week now. Her routine never varied: arrive at the Carlisle house and sit on the usual bench, the one that afforded the best view of the house, one of a neat row that had its own garden square.

Thomas had wanted to approach her, finish the business between them, but he knew better than to let his personal feelings interfere with his work. He sunk further out of sight and watched. Marlena reached into the large bag that sat next to her and took out a ball of yarn and knitting needles. She started to knit, her hands industrious as they wove the yarn over the needles.

Soon a girl in a maid's uniform came out with a bucket of hot steaming water. She spent a good fifteen minutes scrubbing the front steps and polishing the brass plate on the front door. She made quick work of it and did a thorough job. Thomas watched as the girl went down the steps and stared up at the front door from the vantage point of the pavement, scrub brush in hand, surveying her work. She nodded, picked up her bucket and went back into the house. Still the woman sat on the bench.

At nine a.m. a long black saloon crept to the kerb. A burly chauffeur hurried around to the back of the car, surprisingly nimble for a man so large. Thomas noticed the driver's meaty hands and the way his eyes roamed the area as he held the door for Mr Carlisle. Thomas had been briefed on Mr Carlisle's firm and the work they were doing for the Air Ministry: something to do with detecting enemy aircraft, technology that would help England win the inevitable war. The chauffeur was more than just a driver.

After the car pulled away, the woman checked her watch, took out a tiny notebook, and wrote something in it. Yesterday she abandoned the bench after Mr Carlisle's car pulled away. Not today. Another car came, a taxi this time, and an attractive blonde dressed in a navy blue suit alighted and went up to the front door. The woman on the bench didn't even look up.

She's planning something, Thomas thought. *And it has to do with Mr Carlisle's work for the Air Ministry.*

Soon the redhead – Mr Carlisle's wife, according to the dossier – came out of the house, just as she had done yesterday. Thomas watched as she pulled the door behind her and walked down the nine steps to the street. Even from a distance Thomas could tell that Mrs Carlisle was a beautiful woman: tall, slender, and with a mass of red hair. She moved like a dancer. Today she wore a green suit with a matching hat, a tiny thing with a sheer veil that covered her eyes. She stopped outside the front door and pretended to fiddle with the clasp of her handbag while she studied her surroundings, as if looking for someone.

Thomas stepped back behind the tree so he could watch Marlena X. If the German agent followed Mrs Carlisle, he would follow as well. The bench was empty. Marlena X was gone.

Damn.

Mrs Carlisle turned right and headed towards the high street, where Thomas knew she would enter the garden square, just as she did every day. Thomas followed, staying far behind so as not to draw attention to himself. He nearly missed Marlena X, who seemed to appear out of nowhere as she followed the redhead, keeping a safe distance between them, taking her time. Thomas tailed them both. Marlena kept the perfect distance from

26

Mrs Carlisle so as not to arouse suspicion. Marlena knew her job.

Mrs Carlisle stopped at the gate to the entrance of the square. She pushed the veil up and tipped her face to the sun, as though she were making a wish or an offering of some sort. The angle of her face gave Thomas a clear view of her profile. He took in the well-shaped nose, the perfect cheekbones. He couldn't help but notice the full lips and the woman's long white throat. He wondered – once again – what she was up to, only to realise too late that he had been so focused on Mrs Carlisle he had once again lost sight of Marlena X. *Never mind. She's here. I can feel her.*

***

The sun warmed Cat's back as she walked, her tension easing with each step that led her away from the house. Benton would be furious if he knew what Cat was up to. He had wealth untold, but he was stingy with Cat's pocket money. On more than one occasion over the years Cat had approached her husband about getting a job, but he forbade her. 'A man in my position cannot have a wife who works.'

At one point, Cat volunteered at the hospital. She spent her day doing mindless things like arranging flowers, sorting books, and delivering magazines to the patients. The work hadn't been challenging, but it gave her something to do and an excuse to get away from the house.

She came to a standstill as she stepped through the gates of the wooded garden square that had become her private sanctuary, a place to escape Isobel's prying eyes and Alicia

Montrose's relentless pursuit to rekindle their friendship. She stood in the sunlight for a moment and tipped her head back, not caring that the sun would cause her skin to freckle. She said a silent prayer, *I want to live my own life, be independent. How do I do this? Give me a sign.*

She saw Reginald just as she stepped onto the sunny green in the middle of the garden square. The old man smiled and waved a hand at her. They had first met at this very spot on a spring day in 1932, when Reginald approached Cat out of the blue and said that he had known her father during the war. Over the next five years they bonded while cajoling the squirrels to take the food out of their hands. Reginald regaled Cat with stories of her father – a cryptographer, who worked for MI5 and served valiantly – and Cat's mother.

Cat savoured those conversations about her parents, who died tragically in a motorcar accident in 1917 when her father was on leave. Now she considered Reginald a trusted friend, a small thread to a tapestry that didn't involve her husband and sister-in-law.

For some reason, today Cat noticed the hand that grasped the walking stick had grown more gnarled, the hump between the shoulder blades more defined. Sir Reginald's eyes hadn't changed a bit, cornflower blue with a penetrating gaze that missed nothing. But his body had aged.

'What's wrong? You're wound tight as a spring,' Reginald said.

'I'm a thirty-seven-year-old woman who cannot have children, lives in a loveless marriage, and sees no escape.'

'Catherine –'

'Sorry. I didn't come here to discuss my problems. How are you? Lovely day.'

'Can you not leave? Surely your aunt and uncle will help?'

'I need to sort this out on my own.' She didn't give voice to her true feelings: *I am terrified to leave him. What am I, if I'm not his wife?* She put on a brave face and turned to face Reginald. Out of the corner of her eye she saw a woman on a blanket, her child in her lap. Near her, two blonde-haired girls chased each other, their dollies sitting on the blanket.

'I'm grateful to you, Reginald. The work has been a great help, but I'd feel better if you told me what I was delivering and why everything is so secretive. Am I in danger?'

'No danger that I know of,' Reginald said. 'I'm sorry. You're going to have to trust me. Just know that you're helping in ways that you will never understand. Keep your eyes open. If you need to reach me, just follow the instructions, call the number and use the code word.'

'St Edmund's pippins,' Cat said.

'Just use it in a sentence. I'll be there.'

'All this cloak-and-dagger intrigue is affecting my judgement.'

Reginald rifled through the briefcase that rested on the bench between them. He pulled out an envelope and handed it to Cat. 'This needs to be delivered today. Hamer, Codrington, and Blythe again – same address as last week. The secretary will let you in and excuse himself, claiming an important meeting. You're to go to the same office and insert the envelope on the top shelf, just like last time. There's nothing to pick up today.'

'Will they let me in the door today?' Desperate for income of her own, Cat had accepted Reginald's offer of easy employment – delivering packages and on occasion accepting something to return to him – without question. The work was easy, the money a boon. The Carlisle name allowed Cat access to the finest dressmakers, spas, hairdressers – any luxury she could imagine – but other than a small allowance she received from her parents' estate, Cat had no money of her own. She hated being dependent on Benton, especially since he was so stingy. Her work with Reginald remedied that. The money – which she saved in an envelope hidden in her room – provided the promise of freedom.

The courier work had been easy enough, and Cat hadn't experienced any difficulties, until last week. Her instructions had been to deliver a similar innocuous-looking envelope to the firm of Hamer, Codrington, and Blythe. By prearrangement, Cat would be let in the building and left on her own. She was to walk down a hallway to an empty office and deposit the envelope on the top shelf of an out-of-the-way bookcase.

Instead of being given entrance to the building, a new secretary – a supercilious young man who needed to be slapped – had ushered her out into the street and had asked her question after question, interrogating Cat and growing more and more suspicious when she refused to answer his questions. He wouldn't even let her into the office. Luckily, after fifteen harrowing minutes, Mr Codrington's secretary had intervened on her behalf and brought her into the building. As planned, he excused himself, leaving Cat to carry out her assignment.

'They're expecting you. There won't be any trouble this time.' He pulled out another envelope, this one smaller and full of notes. 'This is for you. You did well last time. Codrington's secretary told us that you handled the situation like a professional. There's extra in there for your efforts.'

'Thank you,' Cat said. She tucked the money in her handbag.

'Your father would be proud of you, Catherine. Never forget that. You're doing a patriotic service for your King and country. Caution is the operative word, my dear. I'll have something else for you in a few days. Look for my ad.' Reginald stood, his arthritic knees popping from the effort. 'Not as young as I used to be. I'll do anything I can to help you get sorted, Catherine. I mean that. *Not all women are destined to do what society expects of them.* I'm sorry that you and Benton weren't blessed with children, but that's not your fault, my dear. And there's certainly no shame in it.' He touched a gentle hand to her shoulder.

'I know. Thank you for that.'

She sat on the bench in the warm summer sun and watched Reginald walk away. He was keeping something from her. Every fibre of her being sang with that truth. She wondered where he went when he wasn't meeting with her. He told her over and over again – more so during the past six months or so – that another war was coming. Hitler was rearming, while France and England were sitting by, doing nothing.

Cat wondered why there was no mention of war in the newspapers. She'd never been interested in politics until she met Reginald. Now she scoured the newspapers, looking for any hint of the things Reginald told her about during their meetings in the park. Cat had been too young to do anything important in the last war, and it had resolved by the time she could make some contribution. But she had seen the soldiers coming home from the battlefield with their arms and legs blown off. She had seen the women who had lost husbands and sons and soon came to recognise that look of sorrow and emptiness.

Cat had arrived in London as a seventeen-year-old country girl, with a northern accent and all the wrong clothes. In the beginning, she tried to embrace her new life. Moving from a small village in Cumberland to London required a bit of adjustment. Lydia took her shopping for the latest fashions and dragged her along to art openings, plays, and writers' salons. Cat tried to fit in. Aunt Lydia went out of her way to help Cat find a set of like-minded friends, but the death of her parents had ripped a hole in her heart. Cat preferred spending time alone with her grief.

And that was why – Cat realised from the Olympian vantage point of one who looks at the past with a critical eye – she married Benton at twenty-two, when she was young and naive and thought that the passion he stirred in her was the type of love that would withstand time, the type of love her parents shared. Cat knew now that her judgement about Benton – and about love in general – was gravely flawed.

She shook her head, chastising herself for her sentimentality. This was not the time for wistful dreams of days gone by. Full of purpose, Cat set off at a brisk pace, her heels clicking in time to the beat of the city. She blended in with the foot traffic, savouring the feeling that she was part of something bigger than herself, that she was doing something productive. Every now and again Reginald's words would pop into her head. *Not all women are destined to do what society expects of them.* She certainly hadn't disappointed on that score.

As she walked, her thoughts turned – as they often did of late – to her relationship with Alicia Montrose. Cat and Alicia became friends the minute they laid eyes on each other. Benton's work schedule allowed Cat plenty of freedom. He approved of Cat's friendship with the influential Montroses, and didn't seem to care when they went on holidays to the sea, skiing in Switzerland, and to Alicia's country house. Sometimes they would travel in a large group of women – Alicia Montrose had a large circle of friends – sometimes Cat and Alicia would travel alone.

The women were overjoyed when they became pregnant at the same time. But Cat had lost her child, while Alicia had given birth to a healthy boy. Reeling from the loss, Cat had slowly stepped away from society in general. She lost her desire to travel. She had no interest in anything. Over the next three years Alicia gave birth to two more children, while Cat suffered three more miscarriages.

Now the sight of Alicia Montrose caused an unbearable ache in Cat. She felt guilty for it. She knew that she had turned her back on a good friend. But she simply couldn't face Alicia and her children, and the painful reminder of how things could have turned out for Benton and her.

Time changes friendships. Alicia was busy with her children. Cat involved herself in the fundraising work and charity balls that were the centre of her sister-in-law's life. She found she had a knack for it, so she threw herself in, using the exhausting work as a psychological crutch. She and Alicia crossed paths and were polite to each other, but the sister-ness between them – a word coined by Alicia – had left. Cat lived a whirlwind of committee meetings and fundraisers, which she managed and oversaw with great success. The charity balls she organised grew exponentially each year. She was creative and hired lavish entertainment.

She worked herself to exhaustion, and would have continued to do so until a bout of influenza almost killed her. She had been in hospital for a month, and then at a luxurious spa for a rest cure for three months after that. During this time, Cat had re-examined the choices she made and had found herself wanting.

During Cat's hospitalisation Alicia had visited her regularly. When Cat requested the nurses turn Alicia away, Alicia sent flowers and books. To this day, Alicia – with the tact and social grace that was her birthright – still made an effort. She had proven to be a true friend, and Cat had shunned her for her efforts.

She walked amid a throng of people, past the tobacco shop, a tea shop, and a dress shop. The woman who ran the haberdasher's stood outside, surveying the street as though it were her personal domain, a faraway look in her eyes. Cat nodded to her as she walked past.

She needed to make things right with Alicia, but she had no idea how to go about doing so. The foot traffic diminished as Cat approached the block that housed Hamer, Codrington, and Blythe. She passed an insurance office and a watch and clock repair shop. What if she could just start over, someplace where no one knew her? She could adopt a child … She almost snorted with laughter. What would she do with a child? How could she possibly cope with a child by herself, with no job? She was snapped out of her reverie when someone grabbed the strap of her bag and yanked hard.

Cat cried out as pain wrenched her arm and raced up to her shoulder, like electricity travelling up a wire. The force stopped her and yanked her around, forcing her to come face to face with what at first glance appeared to be a small boy. On closer inspection Cat saw that her assailant was a woman, lithe and spry as a dancer, and very strong despite her size. The woman had clear skin, devoid of any cosmetics, brown eyes, and a thin mouth pursed in a line of determination.

'Let go of my purse!' Cat cried out.

The woman yanked on the bag. When that didn't work, she reached inside, her fingers grasping Reginald's envelope. Cat pulled her bag close to her chest and held fast. Her attacker persisted, but Cat held on.

'Give it to me,' the woman said.

'Let go of me,' Cat said.

'You there!' a man called out from down the street. He took off at a run towards Cat and her assailant, his tie flapping in the wind.

'Just give me the envelope and you won't get hurt,' the woman said through gritted teeth.

With one final pull, Cat jerked the bag free of the woman's grasp. The woman growled like a dog. The punch came hard and fast, like the strike of a snake. The woman's fist connected with Cat's cheek, knocking Cat's head back. Stars swam before her. Her knees started to buckle. She clung to the bag as she sank to the hard pavement. Once she was down on the ground, she sat dazed and unable to move. Through the crowd of legs that stood around her, she recognised the scuffed brown shoes that belonged to the woman as she walked away, her gait sure and steady.

'Call the police,' someone said.

'Is anyone a doctor? I think she's in shock. That boy tried to steal her purse!'

The pavement seemed to roll like the deck of a ship.

'Maybe we should move her,' another voice said.

Cat's vision blurred. Blood pulsed into the skin near her cheekbone and her eye. Fluid pushed its way into new places, causing the skin to tighten with swelling. *How will I explain this to Benton?* Cat thought.

'Move aside. Move aside, please,' Cat heard a man's voice say. 'I saw everything from down the road. Move, please, and let me get to her.' The crowd parted and the man squatted near Cat and studied her face. He was very tall, with dark hair worn a bit longer than was fashionable. The strong line of his jaw was covered with the dark stubble of a beard. His intelligent grey eyes peered at Cat. Are you all right?'

'Not sure,' Cat said.

'What is your name?'

'Catherine.'

'Do you know what year it is?'

'It's 1937. I'm not concussed,' Cat said. 'I've just been attacked.'

'Can you stand?' The man stood and held out his hand. 'Take my hand, and I'll help you up. Careful now. If you're dizzy, just lean on me.' She took his hand, and he pulled her to her feet. The man turned to the crowd. 'All is well now. Carry on.'

Cat allowed the man to lead her to a bench in the shade. He helped her sit down before he went into the closest shop and returned with a glass of water.

'Drink this. It will soothe you.'

Cat obeyed, letting the cool water run down her throat. While she drank, she noticed the man glance up and down the street.

'I dare say she won't come back.' He studied Cat's face. 'I'm afraid you're going to have a black eye. Do you want me to take you to hospital? Maybe you should have that seen to.'

'I'm fine,' Cat said. She brushed off her skirt, dismayed to see the large rip at the elbow of her new suit. Her hat had come off and now rested in the street. Cat watched, helpless, as a lorry drove over it, mashing it beyond repair.

'May I escort you home or at least arrange for someone to come and get you?'

'No, thank you. I'm fine really. I need to run an errand and then I'll see myself home.' She forced herself to sound strong and sure. 'You've been very kind. I've an appointment just down the street. I know I must look a fright, but I'm all right, really. When I'm finished, I'll go and have a cup of tea to settle my nerves.'

'We really should call the police,' the man said.

'I'll go directly there and make a report in person,' Cat lied. She had no intention of going to the police.

'Here's my card. You'll give that to the police? Have them call me. I got a pretty good look at her.' He reached into the pocket of his suit and handed Cat a card printed on thick milky paper. *Thomas Charles, Historian*. There wasn't an address, just a telephone exchange. She thanked him, took the card, and said her goodbyes, setting out once again to fulfil her obligation to Reginald. With each step, the anger that had saved her – and prevented the theft of Reginald's documents – was replaced by a relentless knot of fear.

Fifteen minutes later she dropped off the envelope in the appropriate place. The secretary met her directly and – according to plan – excused himself and left Cat to her own devices. She was in and out of the building in less than five minutes. She resisted the urge to buy a new hat to replace the one that was damaged and turned her attention to more important matters, such as how she was going to explain her bruises to her inquiring sister-in-law and insolent husband.

***

Thomas took a taxi to an antiquarian bookshop in Piccadilly, lodged between a tailor and an estate agent. A rack of old books stood in front of the shop. A man browsed through the titles now, his hat pulled low over his head. As a precaution, Thomas walked past the estate agent and circled back. When he returned, the man was gone. He stepped into the shop and breathed in the smell of the old books.

He loved writing almost as much as he loved reading and books in general. He travelled Germany under the guise of being a writer, a cover that allowed him to move around without question. On a whim, Thomas decided that he would write a compendium on historical churches, a travel guide of sorts, in order to lend credence to his cover story. Thomas actually started the process of writing, jotting down a few paragraphs about the churches and sights he visited. The enjoyment he took from the process surprised and delighted him.

When he submitted the book to a publisher, who snapped it up in exchange for a hefty fee, Thomas was surprised. He studied craft, read how-to-write books, and even took a correspondence course in writing professionally. His career flourished. His books were met with critical acclaim.

The shop's purveyor looked up from behind a desk and nodded, while Thomas continued to browse along the rows of the old books with their cracked leather spines and unique mustiness. He picked up a fine first edition of *Ivanhoe* when the bell jangled and Sir Reginald came in. Thomas tucked the book back on the shelf as the old man turned the closed sign to face the street and locked the front door. The proprietor nodded at Reginald and headed up a rickety flight of stairs at the back of the shop. Neither Reginald nor Thomas spoke until a door at the top of the stairs shut and footsteps creaked above them.

'Were my suspicions correct then?' Sir Reginald asked.

'It's Marlena X,' Thomas said. 'She's been watching the house for the past week.'

'Someone in that house is working with her,' Reginald said.

'Agreed.'

'But you've never seen her make contact with anyone?'

'No, sir,' Thomas said.

'And Mrs Carlisle?'

Thomas turned to face Reginald. 'Marlena made a run for the papers she was carrying, just as you expected.'

Reginald took a deep breath. 'And?'

'Mrs Carlisle managed to thwart her by sheer willpower. She clung to that purse as though it were a lifeline. Marlena hit her. Mrs Carlisle fell to the ground, nearly passed out, but clutched at that damn purse.' Thomas looked at Reginald. 'I hope you know what you're doing, putting an untrained woman such as Mrs Carlisle out in the field against the likes of Marlena X.'

'I'm taking a risk, I know,' Sir Reginald said, 'but I'll stand by it. Finish your report.'

'I made contact with Mrs Carlisle, gave her my business card.' Sir Reginald faced him, staring at him with that penetrating gaze that had brought many a man to his knees. 'As far as she's concerned, she'd been mugged.

A crowd had gathered around her. I had to get close to confirm the documents were safe.'

'Understood,' Reginald said. 'Watch her. See that she doesn't come to harm.'

'What about Marlena X?'

'Leave her be for now. Let's give her a nice long rope, shall we?' He stared at Thomas. 'Is this too personal for you? This is not time for vengeance. Gwen's death was a tragedy, but you must not let it sway you. Not now. Too much is at stake.'

'No, sir,' Thomas lied. He knew full well what was at stake. But he had a score to settle with Marlena X, and he intended to do so, with or without Sir Reginald's approval.

Sir Reginald unlocked the door, turned the sign back around to open, and without a backward glance, stepped out into the June afternoon.

Chapter Two

One week had passed since Annie Havers had run away from her mother and lied her way into a service job in the posh Carlisle home. Timid Annie Havers had faced Isobel Carlisle and had told her that she was an orphan who needed a job. The minute she spoke the words, she expected the heavens to open and lightning to strike as punishment for her falsehood. At the very least, Annie expected Miss Carlisle to laugh in her face and send her back to Bermondsey.

But Miss Isobel Carlisle had not laughed in Annie's face. Instead she stared down her long nose and asked a handful of questions relevant to housekeeping. Did Annie know how to dust? How would she go about cleaning a room? Could she cook a bit?

Annie answered all the questions truthfully. She knew how to keep house. She'd been helping her mum for as long as she could remember. She enjoyed it. She appreciated the satisfaction of a job well done. She didn't tell Miss Isobel that the best part of domestic work was that it gave Annie time to paint pictures with her mind. She didn't tell Miss Isobel that while she swung the broom back and forth, she imagined the brushwork necessary to capture the crashing waves of a seascape or that she could figure out which colours to mix to develop a shade of deep red as rich as blood. But this was the

Carlisle house, and Miss Isobel Carlisle was looking for more than an uneducated girl. 'Can you read?'

'Yes, ma'am,' Annie said. 'I can do sums as well. I am – was – a good student, ma'am. I also draw. My dad was going to let me go to art school.' Annie looked out the window. She could tell a partial form of the truth about this part of her life, for her father was indeed dead, and he had promised art school before the accident that had taken his life. 'But he and my mum died. There was no place for me to go, and now I need a job.'

Miss Carlisle stared at Annie, judging her. Annie met her eyes and smiled. 'I'm a good worker, ma'am.'

Miss Carlisle nodded her head and crossed her arms over her stout bosom. 'I usually wouldn't ask a girl with no experience about cooking, but our cook is taking care of her husband who has been ill. I'm looking for a temporary replacement, but have yet to find one. It's usually just me, Marie, and Mrs Carlisle. We dine properly when my brother is home, which isn't very often. He has a very important job that takes him out of town on a regular basis.'

Annie waited, not quite sure what to say.

'Very well. You can start today. Marie will see you're situated.'

The tall woman who sat next to Miss Carlisle during the interview stood up. She hadn't spoken since she ushered Annie into the room, and Annie had all but forgotten she was even there. Now she noticed the crown of downy white frizz and the cadaverous frame. The woman's clothes were rumpled, the hem of the skirt uneven. The white blouse she wore under the navy cardigan had a tiny stain on it. When Miss Marie smiled at Annie, a genuine smile that lighted her whole face, Annie liked her right away.

Unable to believe that she had gotten away with all the lies, Annie grabbed the valise she stole from her mother and hurried after the woman. She felt guilty about taking something so dear from her mum, but Annie couldn't run away with her possessions in a paper bag. She vowed to repay her mother once she established herself. The bag now carried all of her worldly goods: a tattered copy of *Through the Looking Glass*, a picture of her grandparents, her good dress, her Sunday shoes, her nightgown and underclothes. She'd left her good winter coat at Harold Green's house, but now at least she would have enough money to buy one before the summer weather turned.

The woman didn't speak as Annie followed her to the back of the house and up a narrow staircase off the kitchen. Annie's room was on the second floor, tucked into an out-of-the-way corner. The woman opened it, allowing Annie to step in first.

'Welcome to the Carlisle house, Annie. I hope you'll be happy here.'

The room was small and bright. A wooden bedstead was tucked in the corner, its crisp white linens frayed at the edges. On the opposite wall was a washstand, with a floral print pitcher and basin. Next to it lay a stack of flannels. The window was covered in muslin curtains embroidered in scarlet poppies and blue forget-me-nots.

For a moment Annie missed her real room, the room that she lived in before her father died and before her mum married Harold Green. That room was big, with well-worn rugs and large windows that flooded the room with light. At night, Annie would crawl into the high canopy bed that belonged to her gran, snuggle under the eiderdown, and fall asleep without a care in the world.

One corner of the room held her easel, a box full of paints, and a set of real mink brushes. She spent hours painting. When she wasn't pretending to be an artist, she spent her free time playing in the garden with the children from the neighbourhood. She longed for the life that had been so cruelly taken away from her. When her dad died, the house they lived in had gone to her uncle. He had his own family to support, and although he offered Annie and her mum a room for as long as they wanted to stay there, Annie's mum moved into a house that she couldn't afford. To save themselves from poverty, Annie's mum had married, and now here Annie was.

'It's all right, my dear. Things will be fine,' Miss Marie said, as if she read Annie's thoughts. 'It's been a little difficult since cook left. Her husband had a heart attack and she's tending to him. The agency has been sending over replacements, but Isobel has yet to find one that's satisfactory. With Benton – that's Mr Carlisle – working so much, we've just been making do. You'll be helping me in the kitchen until we can find a cook that Isobel likes. Come down when you're settled, and I'll give you something to eat. Miss Isobel is very particular about how she wants things done. I've much to show you.'

Getting the job was one thing, but doing the daily work to Miss Carlisle's satisfaction was another thing entirely. Annie discovered that Miss Marie's real job was to serve as Miss Isobel's secretary. Annie wasn't really sure what that meant, except that Miss Isobel bossed Miss Marie around and Miss Marie said, 'Yes, Isobel,' and did as she was told. Sometimes Miss Marie called Miss Isobel 'Izzy' when no one else was around, which surprised Annie.

Miss Isobel had high expectations indeed. Miss Marie explained the best way to use the lemon oil to polish the furniture, and how to use the soft cloth to wipe the oil off and buff the wood to a high gloss. She explained how to wind the clocks every three days, and which vases Miss Carlisle liked to use for which flowers. Marie taught Annie the proper way to set out the towels in the bathroom, how to make a bed, and how to tidy the bedrooms and close the curtains at night. Mr Carlisle liked a carafe of cold water in the morning, while Miss Isobel liked hers at night. The house ran like a well-tuned engine, and it was Annie's job to see that things went as smoothly as possible, especially on the rare occasions when Mr Carlisle was home.

Mrs Carlisle was a mystery to Annie. She smiled at Annie and spoke to her as though she were a friend rather than a servant. Only yesterday she offered to get Annie a cup of tea. Miss Marie was kind and gentle-natured, but Annie liked Mrs Carlisle the best. Mr Blackwell, a distant cousin with a tragic past, also lived in the house. Blackie was a sad old soul who had seen better days. He drank too much and often snuck Mr Carlisle's good brandy of a morning, pouring it right into his tea when no one was looking. Annie had the impression he was scared to death of something or someone, but she was too busy to wonder what or who frightened him so. Annie didn't see much of Mrs Carlisle or Mr Blackwell. The bulk of her work catered to the cares and demands of Miss Isobel Carlisle.

Annie had been nervous at first, afraid that some strange set of circumstances would allow her mother to find her. She scrubbed the front steps and polished the brass kick plate on the front door of the Carlisle home with one eye trained towards the square and the pavement, half expecting her mother and stepfather to come stomping up, demanding that she return home at once.

She didn't want to think of the scene that would follow. Harold Green would act righteous and assert his influence as Annie's stepfather, while her mother would nod in the background, afraid to disagree with the new husband who offered her financial security. They would insist Annie return home. A well-bred lady such as Miss Isobel Carlisle would have no choice but to give way to Annie's parents. The thought of it brought Annie to her knees with fear.

But the days went by and Annie's mother never appeared. As Annie settled in, her worries started to slip away. She took to her new job. She liked being busy. She polished and scrubbed and scoured and served until she fell into her tiny bed at night, exhausted from her efforts. She slaved her days away to forget the life she left behind, a happy life with her mum and dad and their lovely house.

After the first week, Miss Marie was so pleased with her work that she wrote up a list for Annie in the morning and left her to work on her own. Annie liked the idea that Miss Marie trusted her enough to let her work unsupervised. She did the tasks that she was assigned, and did other chores without being told to do so. Annie carried out her tasks while remaining appropriately in the background, unseen and unheard. None of this effort was lost on Miss Isobel or Miss Marie, who gave Annie a rise in salary after her third day.

By the end of her first week, the worry that her mother and Harold Green would find her started to fade. Annie's mind was now free to notice things. And notice she did. With the artistic talent that had shown itself when Annie was a young child, she noticed the sunlight coming through the window in the entry hall, and the way the beams lit up the cut crystal vase that held the elaborate spray of roses. She noticed the long, dark shadows in Mr Carlisle's office as she dusted, and the way the darkening shadows brought out the jewel tones in the thick rug that covered the floor.

She noticed the relationships between the members of the household. Miss Isobel bossed everyone around. She was especially bossy to Mrs Carlisle, who seemed to ignore Miss Isobel as though she weren't there. Annie learned quickly to run the other way when it looked like the two women would meet.

On this particular day, Annie finished washing and putting up the breakfast dishes by eight a.m. She packed the wooden box that was kept in the cellar with a fresh bottle of lemon oil and a bundle of clean rags. She intended on polishing the wooden surfaces in Mr Carlisle's office while he was at work. Annie opened the door and stepped into the room, surprised to find a camera in pieces along with a glass of brandy on Mr Carlisle's desk.

'Hello?'

'Oh, Annie,' Mr Blackwell – who was down on his hands and knees, out of sight, behind Mr Carlisle's desk – struggled to his feet. 'I've dropped a tiny screw to my camera.' He nodded to the camera that lay on the table with the back removed. Three tiny screws rested on Mr Carlisle's desk.

'Do you want me to help you look?' Annie wondered if she should come back later.

'No, no,' Blackie said. 'It'll turn up. I can get a replacement at the shop. Carry on.' He downed the last of the brandy, packed up his camera, and let himself out of the office.

Once Blackie left, Annie got busy. She worked for a good thirty minutes, dusting the wooden surfaces before she added a bit of lemon oil and polished until they gleamed. She was down on her knees, dusting the base of a side table when she found the tiny screw. She tucked it in her pocket, and moved on with her work. It wasn't until she got to the sideboard behind Mr Carlisle's desk that she noticed one of the drawers was left open. She pushed it shut and didn't think any more about it.

Pleased with a job well done, Annie returned the box of cleaning supplies to the cellar and removed the apron that now smelled of lemon oil. She made her way upstairs, moving through the house with a deliberate soft-footed silence. She met Marie on the upstairs landing.

'I've put a treat on your bed, Annie. You've been working so hard,' Marie said. 'You can take a few hours for yourself. I'll call when we need to get started in the kitchen.'

'Thank you, ma'am.'

Annie hurried to her room. On her bed lay a sketchpad and a box of pencils. She delighted in it, and spent the afternoon curled up on her tiny bed, sketching the trees outside, secure in the knowledge that things would be okay.

Chapter Three

Cat wandered aimlessly after her attack. Her eye throbbed. Her ego was bruised. She wanted to be angry – her usual response to life's injustices – but the only emotion she experienced was a burning fear that took away her ability to think in a rational manner. She thought about going to the police, but soon realised that reporting the assault would be a mistake. Reginald hadn't explained why he needed Catherine to do the jobs he gave her, but he had been very clear about the secrecy required. She wondered what he would have to say about Cat's attacker. He would have to say something, for the woman hadn't been after Cat's wallet. She had reached for the envelope.

Cat thought of Thomas Charles. He had said, 'She won't be back.' How had he known that the attacker was a woman? He hadn't been close enough to see her features clearly. How had he known that she wouldn't come back? The time had come for Reginald to be honest with her. If he wouldn't trust her, she would have to make other arrangements. *What other arrangements?* Cat nearly laughed out loud at the absurdity of that statement. She had no power in her relationship with Reginald. Until today she assumed she was doing menial courier work, a job thrown to her out of pity. Working for Reginald gave her the promise of independence. She wanted to cry out with frustration.

Cat started walking with no particular destination in mind. She couldn't bear the thought of explaining her swollen face to Isobel, who would be quick with questions and even hastier with judgement. Rather than head towards the Carlisle house, she turned the opposite direction, grabbed a taxi, and gave her aunt's address in Bloomsbury.

Aunt Lydia's flat – one of four in a neat row, all brick, with a black front door and a half-moon window above – was two streets away from Bedford Square, a wooded park with ample benches to while away a summer day.

This neighbourhood wasn't as posh as Kensington, but Cat preferred its utter lack of pretence. The front stoops weren't scrubbed every day, nor were the pedestrians dressed in finery and jewels, but Cat had been happy here. She considered Bloomsbury her home. She walked up the steps to the front and rang the bell. When no one answered, she went down the steps to what used to be the service entrance to the below-street-level kitchen. She lifted a loose piece of flagstone and took the key that lay hidden there. She let herself into the kitchen.

She stood for a moment, taking in the familiarity of the house, letting the comfortable surroundings soothe her. Oh, how she wished she could escape back to this house, with its happy memories of her young adult life, to the time before she so naively married Benton Carlisle. Aunt Lydia had taken Cat under her protective wing after the motor-vehicle crash that killed her parents. Cat's father was on leave for a week from some secret location where he served as a cryptographer. Her mother had gone to meet his train, and they planned to spend the week at home, together. Cat stayed behind to finish her schoolwork, so she could spend as much time with her father as possible. Until the knock on the door, the policeman with the sad eyes, and the news that changed Cat for ever.

Aunt Lydia had swept in, like an angel, and took Cat under her strong and capable wing. She had stayed with Cat just long enough to arrange the funeral and to see to the handling of the house. There was a small allowance that Cat would receive each quarter, enough money to live on if she stayed in Rivenby, the small northern village where she had lived so happily with her parents. But Lydia had other plans for Cat.

'You need to figure out what you want to do with your life, darling. There's no future for you here. Come to London and get yourself sorted out. You need to be around young people, darling. Rivenby will always be here, but you need to see a bit of the world before you settle.'

Cat, too shocked to make any decision on her own, capitulated without question and moved to London with her aunt. Now she stood in the foyer of their home, letting the familiarity sink in. It had been twenty years since her parents died. Once again Cat marvelled at the passage of time. She placed her palm flat on the wall, as if touching it like this would allow her to commit the comfort of the place to memory, as if the memory in turn would become a tangible thing she could keep with her.

She put the key back in its hiding place and went upstairs to the living room that overlooked the street. Now an old sofa covered with a sheet rested against the far wall. The big window flooded the room with light so vivid that its brightness jumped out from both of Aunt Lydia's works in progress. One of the canvases portrayed Hector the Horse, the beloved character of the children's books

Aunt Lydia illustrated. The other was a still life depicting a large bouquet of flowers arranged haphazardly in an old milk jug that had at one time belonged to Cat's mother.

The bunch of foxgloves, sunflowers, a stray imperfect rose, along with a handful of desiccated stems and twigs, didn't appeal in their natural state. The flowers were on their last legs and the design of the arrangement was flawed. But Aunt Lydia used these flaws as the theme of her painting. Cat saw it right away. It gave the work an emotional pull that had successfully marvelled critics and enticed collectors for decades.

A large piece of wood positioned across two sawhorses served as her aunt's work table. A cup of unfinished tea sat near a jar full of brushes and a box of paints. An open sketchpad lay on the table, revealing a pencil rendering of Hector the Horse arguing with a milkman. Next to it, a mock-up of the book was covered with Lydia's unique angular scrawl.

An unbidden tear, hot and wet, spilled onto Cat's cheek. Surprised, she wiped it away. She moved to the window and looked up and down the street before she went to the upstairs bathroom for a cool cloth.

Upstairs, Cat moved down the corridor to the room that used to be her own until her marriage to Benton. It was a dear room, situated in the back corner of the house, with a cosy bed, a dresser, and a case full of books. She and Aunt Lydia had painted the walls sky blue. On a whim, Lydia had painted the sun, with puffy white clouds floating by. She shook her head to clear the nostalgia. The motion caused her eye to throb.

In the bathroom, she splashed cold water on her face before she stared at herself in the mirror. The glass was old and warped, but Cat was accustomed to the waves and distortions. When she moved in, she asked Lydia to replace the mirror with a newer one that portrayed an accurate reflection. Her aunt had refused. She explained that looking in the mirror was a stupid way to spend time. Cat remembered laughing at that. The memories didn't do a thing to lift her mood.

Her eye was nearly swollen shut now and had turned a vivid red. Cat rifled through drawers for something with which to cover it, but Aunt Lydia didn't wear cosmetics. Cat sighed. Nothing to be done except go home and lie down with a cool cloth on her eye. She would try to disguise the bruising with make-up before dinner.

Aunt Lydia arrived home just as Cat went down the stairs. She carried a large basket of groceries, a bottle of champagne sticking out the top.

'Cat? What are you doing here? My God, what's happened to your eye?'

'Hello, Aunt Lydia,' Cat said.

'Catherine, tell me that Benton didn't do that to you. I swear, if he so much as laid a finger on you, I'll throttle him myself.'

Lydia Paxton's hair was once as thick and curly as Cat's. Now, at sixty-nine years old, the vivid locks had turned a burnished ginger spun with silver threads. She was shorter than Cat, and paid no attention to fashion. Today she wore baggy trousers – probably purchased at the men's stall at some jumble sale – which were too long. Lydia rolled them up just enough to reveal the bright purple socks and the pink ballet slippers that adorned her feet. She wore a long-sleeved button-up shirt, another reject from some jumble sale, which was now splattered with paint. A network of fine lines sprayed out from the corners of her eyes, the result of a thousand smiles.

'He did not,' Cat said. 'Promise.'

'Come keep me company while I put away this lot.' Aunt Lydia held up the grocery bags.

'Let me help you,' Cat said. She took one of the bags out of Lydia's hand.

Cat followed her aunt into the kitchen, trying to concoct a story as she walked, knowing full well that if she told Lydia the truth about being attacked, Lydia would know that Cat was holding something back. She always knew. Cat learned at a young age there was no keeping secrets from Aunt Lydia. Neither spoke while Cat took the items from the wicker grocery bags and put them away. Lydia tended to the kettle. While she waited for it to boil, she turned her attention to Cat and studied her face, letting her gaze linger on Cat's eye and cheek, which throbbed with pain.

'What's happened, Cat? You're in some sort of trouble. I can see it all over your face.' The look of concern in Aunt Lydia's eyes broke Cat's heart. She girded herself to lie to her aunt, something she had never done.

'I was attacked in Kensington. A woman grabbed my purse. We scuffled. I didn't let go. She hit me.' Cat laughed it off. 'It was rather ridiculous, actually, and would have been funny if she hadn't hit me. Now I'm left with a black eye and swollen cheek.' Cat waited while Lydia digested her words. 'God knows how I'll explain this to Benton.'

'Did you report it to the police?' Aunt Lydia took a clean linen cloth out of a basket on the worktop and drenched it with cold water. She wrung it out and handed it to Cat. 'Hold that against it. The cold will help.'

'I don't think it would do much good. She didn't actually steal anything, so I figured there was no sense in bothering the police for nothing.' Cat took the cold cloth from Lydia and dabbed it on her eye. She winced when the rough cloth touched the tender skin.

'You've gained some weight back, and your cheeks aren't as pale,' Lydia said.

'I'm fully recovered from my influenza, Lyd.'

Aunt Lydia stuck a cigarette in her mouth and left it dangling out the corner. She didn't light it. She never did. She gazed at Cat through squinted eyes, staring at her with that inscrutable glance that was her trademark.

'Why are you looking at me like that? It's just a black eye. People get attacked in London every day.'

'Maybe. But they rarely get attacked in Kensington. It just isn't done. And something's different. You've lost that haunted love-is-lost look.'

'*Haunted love-is-lost look*? I don't know what you mean.'

The kettle whistled. Lydia poured steaming water into the pot, grabbed two cups, and set the lot down on the table.

'I know that things haven't been good between you and Benton for a long time, Cat. And don't bother to deny it. You're a horrible poker player. You wear your feelings on your face for all to see. It broke my heart when you lost your baby, and the two that came after.' Lydia grabbed Cat's hand and squeezed it tight, as if she knew she was treading into dangerous territory.

Cat resisted the urge to pull away. That familiar knot of grief, the anguish that she made it her life's work to hide, shimmied to the surface. It pushed on her heart, contracted her lungs, and threatened to take her breath away. She had loved Benton. He had been her first. She believed he would be her only. They lost three children

55

together, each tragedy adding another brick in the wall that grew between them. After the third miscarriage, Benton had forsaken Cat and turned his love to another. Devastated, Cat waited for him to return to her, return to the love they shared when they first married. That would have been enough for Cat. It was not enough for Benton.

When she was hospitalised with influenza, Benton hadn't even come to see her. He sent a bouquet of yellow and white roses to her with a trite get-well note written in his secretary's hand. Why had she ever thought they could rekindle the spark that burnt itself out so long ago? Yet here she was now, desperate for any scrap of affection he might throw her way. She swallowed the lump in her throat.

'Why do you stay, love? Just answer me that. I don't know how you handle it in that house. Your husband's never home. Your sister-in-law is an ogre.'

Cat smiled at the apt description of Isobel.

'Thank for not saying I told you so. Never once,' Cat said.

'He swept you off your feet, love. That's what men like Benton Carlisle do. Then you marry them, and the prince on the white horse turns into a spoiled child who doesn't want to get his shoes dirty. I call it a fairy tale in reverse.' Lydia sipped her tea. 'How do you share a roof with Isobel and her trained lapdog? I truly believe that house made you ill.'

'You're right about Benton,' Cat said. She met Lydia's eyes, surprised at her words. The honesty was a revelation. Giving voice to this truth galvanised it into reality. 'He doesn't love me. I doubt he'd even notice if I left.'

'Isobel would notice, though. Let's be clear about that. And once you leave, she'll do everything in her power to keep you from returning.' Aunt Lydia took the cigarette out of her mouth and set it on the table. 'I've never understood the relationship between Isobel and Benton. And that secretary of hers, Marie. Why does she stay? How long has she been with Isobel – twenty years? Remember when you first married, how Marie was so kind and pretty. Now she looks like a startled fawn, facing down a wolf.' Lydia pushed a lock of Cat's hair behind her ear. 'It might do you good to step away and get some perspective.'

The gesture touched Cat's heart. Aunt Lydia – who was famous for wielding her honesty like a blunt instrument and not caring who she offended in the process – hadn't spoken to Cat in that tone of voice since her parents' deaths twenty years ago. They had been sitting at this same table, when Lydia said, 'You've a home here, my love. Get yourself sorted and decide what you want to do with your life. You're a clever girl. There's money for university, if that's what you want.'

Cat had been seventeen at the time. She tried to find a calling, something she was passionate about. Then she met Benton, and realised all she wanted was a family. She had the house; she wanted to fill the rooms with Benton's children. When the children didn't come, Cat wanted him. And he had rejected her.

'Are you listening to me, love?'

Cat pulled herself out of her daydream.

'I was saying that you could just come here for a few days.' Lydia was rummaging through a drawer. 'Here it is.' She walked back to the table and plunked a key along with a whistle on a heavy chain on the table. 'I had the locks changed when I replaced the front door. This is for you.'

It was made of heavy brass, attached to a thick chain. The words 'MET' where etched across the top.

'A blast from this beauty will surprise any assailant and effectively summon any policeman who happens to be nearby. Put it on and keep it handy. Why don't you come and stay here for a few days or a week, as long as you want – no, let me finish before you say no.

'I'll set up the guest room for you. You can come and go as you wish and I promise not to bother you. I've Hector drawings due next week, so I'll be working.' She pushed the key towards Cat. 'You can get away from those people, have a rest. You can take the car if you want, and go to the sea.'

'Thank you, Aunt Lydia. I'll think about it.' Cat reached across the table and took the proffered key. 'I don't know what I'd do without you.'

'You'd figure something out.'

Cat stood.

Lydia stood too. She placed her hands on Cat's shoulders and looked her straight in the eye. 'You're still keeping something from me, love. Don't think I can't see it.'

Cat remained silent.

'Ah, well. I'm here when you're ready. Now I'm going to ask you a question. Don't answer me. I just want you to think about it. You've told me that Benton doesn't love you. Do you love him? Is that why you stay? I don't think you love him. Not any more.'

Cat splurged on a taxi, using some of the money from Reginald to pay the fare. The driver took one look at her torn suit and swollen eye and jumped out of the car to help her into the back seat. He didn't speak during the ride, but when the car slowed at the traffic lights the driver looked back at Cat, concern etched into the lines on his forehead. She ignored him, leaned back, and closed her eyes.

She thought about her aunt's offer. What would happen if she just left? Would they even miss her?

By some stroke of grace, the house was quiet when Cat let herself in the front door. She noticed the empty chairs, still arranged in a half circle from the morning's meeting with Alicia Montrose. Clean cups and saucers remained on the table, next to a stack of neatly folded linens. The silver tea service was polished and ready to be put away, the coffee pot suspended over a small flame, which had gone out ages ago.

Cat heard movement down the hall, so she crept up the stairs, hoping not to see anyone. Once in her room, she reached behind the armoire and pulled out her purse. She added the money Reginald had given her that morning to the growing pile of notes and slipped it back.

She was about to head into the bathroom for a flannel doused in cool water when she noticed that the top drawer of her bureau was opened ever so slightly. Cat went over to it and pulled it open all the way. Her undergarments, which she folded and arranged in perfect rows, were stuffed into the drawer without method, as though someone had taken them out and tossed them back in again. Isobel. Snooping. Again. Cat sighed and made a mental note to find a new place to hide the purse where she kept her money.

She lay down on the bed, the flannel over her throbbing eye. She forced herself to think of something positive, of freedom, of a life that didn't include the Carlisle house or any of the people who lived in it. This thought brought Cat peace and gave her the smallest glimmer of hope. She whispered, *I'm going to leave Benton,* as if saying the words out loud gave them weight and meaning. The utterance was a commitment to herself and her future, whatever it may hold. She sighed and slipped into sleep.

Chapter Four

Annie navigated the stairs as she carried a tray for Mrs Carlisle. She filled the pot to the rim because she paid attention. She knew that Mrs Carlisle had gone straight up to her room for a rest before dinner. She also knew Mrs Carlisle would awaken in need of some refreshment, and that not only would she drink every drop of tea, but she would eat all the toast and marmalade as well. Mrs Carlisle ate like a man twice her size. Despite all the food she consumed, she had the tiniest waist Annie had ever seen. Annie rested the tray on her hip, freeing up a hand, so she could knock on Mrs Carlisle's door.

'Come in,' a muffled voice said.

Annie stepped into the room, took one look at Mrs Carlisle's battered face, and would have dropped her tray if Mrs Carlisle hadn't hurried over to help her.

'Oh, Annie, thank you. I'm famished.'

'You're welcome, Mrs Carlisle,' Annie said. She tried to avoid looking at the older woman's eye, which was red and swollen, as though she had been in a fight. She put the tray down on the writing table.

'Please, call me Cat. Mrs Carlisle makes me feel old.'

'I can't. Miss Isobel –'

'Isobel wouldn't like that, would she? How about you call me Miss Catherine? That's a little less formal.' She touched a damp cloth to her face and winced. 'In case you're wondering, I was attacked today while I was shopping.' Annie stepped into the corner out of Miss Catherine's way, just like Miss Marie trained her to do – while Miss Catherine poured herself a large cup of tea. She added milk and sugar, took two pieces of toast and a large dollop of marmalade before she sat down at the vanity and stared at her reflection in the mirror. 'What am I going to do? Isobel will have kittens if I come down to dinner looking like this.'

Annie started to giggle, but stopped herself.

'May I get you a fresh cold cloth?' Annie moved away from the window and stood with her hands in front of her.

'Thank you, Annie,' Miss Catherine said.

Miss Catherine's bathroom was tiled in white, with a large tub with what Miss Marie referred to as a mahogany surround. A basket full of flannels sat on a table near the tub. Annie dampened one and came back into the bedroom just as Miss Catherine unpinned her hair and let it fall around her shoulders. It took all of Annie's effort not to stare at the red curls, which shimmered with a life all their own. Annie thought it was the most beautiful hair she had ever seen.

'Will there be anything else, ma'am?' Annie asked.

'I suppose Isobel has you running all over the place.' She turned around on the vanity stool and faced Annie.

'Yes, ma'am. Tonight I'm to serve at table. It's my first time. Mr Carlisle and Mr Sykes are eating tonight, all formal like. And I'm to change into a proper black uniform with a white apron to serve. Miss Isobel bought it for me special.'

'Thank you, Annie. You've been very helpful and I'm sure you'll do a smashing job at dinner tonight.'

By half past three, Annie had finished setting the table for dinner, the last of her chores. Under Miss Marie's watchful eye, she aligned the knives and forks to the plates, and arranged the flowers. A roast lamb had gone in the cooker hours ago. Miss Marie hurried around the kitchen, slaving over the gravy, a precise recipe, which consisted of the drippings taken from the roaster seasoned with a concoction of nutmeg, claret, and the juice of an orange. Miss Marie had opened a bottle of claret to make the sauce and sipped on it as she cooked. She poured Annie a small glass and said, 'Taste this. It'll put the roses in your cheeks.'

Annie sipped, thought it disgusting, but didn't let on.

'I don't have anything else for you to do at the moment, Annie.' Marie glanced at the clock. 'Back down at half past seven?'

'Yes, ma'am,' Annie said. She hurried from the kitchen before Miss Isobel showed up and found something for her to do.

At a quarter past seven, Annie stood before the small mirror in her room and studied her appearance. The black dress fit her properly, giving a sleek profile. Annie double-checked the chignon to make sure it would stay in place for the evening before she put the white cap on. After the hat was secured with pins and she double-checked that her uniform would meet Isobel's discerning scrutiny, Annie headed downstairs.

She found Miss Marie in the kitchen scraping the drippings out of the roaster, through a strainer and into a saucepan.

'Annie, would you take the drinks tray to the men? They're in the drawing room. And when Mr Sykes comes, you could take his coat and show him through.'

Annie took the tray that held a dish of olives, fresh ice, and the soda syphon to the drawing room. Blackie was at the sideboard, filling a glass with brandy while Mr Carlisle sat in one of the club chairs reading a newspaper.

'Ah, the lady with the ice. Let me help you with that,' Mr Carlisle said. He jumped up and took the tray from Annie.

'Thank you, sir.'

'No trouble,' Mr Carlisle said. Annie felt her cheeks go hot. Mr Carlisle looked like a cinema hero. He had lovely blond curls and navy blue eyes. It was all she could do to not stare at him.

When the bell rang, Mr Carlisle said, 'That'll be Freddy.'

'I'll go, sir,' Annie said. She scurried out of the room before Mr Carlisle saw her blush.

Freddy Sykes was a short stout man, with thick yellow hair as straight as straw. A lock of it hung over his forehead, giving him a boyish look. His tortoiseshell glasses had lenses thick as the bottom of a milk bottle. When Annie opened the door, he bowed. 'Freddy Sykes, at your service.'

Annie stood aside and let him come in.

'May I take your hat, sir?'

'Of course,' Freddy said. He handed Annie his hat. 'You're new aren't you?'

'Yes, sir,' Annie said.

'I mean new to service,' Freddy said. 'Pardon me for saying so, young lady, but you don't seem like the type of girl to be a servant. There's a certain poise about you that one doesn't often see in a serving girl.'

'Thank you, sir,' Annie said.

'Forgive me,' he said. 'I didn't mean to make you feel uncomfortable.'

'Mr Benton and Mr Blackwell are in the drawing room, sir,' Annie said.

'I actually require a private word with Isobel.'

'Oh, I'm not sure –'

'Never fear.' He moved towards the staircase. 'I'll just go and announce myself.'

Helpless to do anything else, Annie stood by as he took the stairs two at a time.

'Don't worry, young lady. I'll make sure that Isobel knows you did your best to stop me.'

***

Cat found everyone in the drawing room, the murmur of voices and the sound of ice in crystal glasses letting her know that cocktail hour was underway. By virtue of the dim candlelight that Isobel preferred of an evening and the careful application of make-up, Cat would be able to downplay her black eye.

She paused for a moment before she entered the room, listening as Blackie, Freddy, and Benton argued about politics. Cat stood in the doorway, girding herself to face them all. She stepped into the room. All conversation stopped. Cat didn't move, as if awaiting judgement. Isobel sat off by herself on the settee in the corner of the room, nursing a sherry and staring out the window. Freddy was the first to break the silence.

'What the devil's happened to your eye, Catherine?'

When she explained that someone had tried to steal her purse and in the process had punched her, everyone was mortified, but after Cat's assurances that she was not really hurt, the conversation moved back to politics, and no one seemed to care. Freddy Sykes was the only one to take Cat aside. He gave her that direct gaze that was uniquely his and said, 'I say, old thing, you're not really hurt are you?' She tried to convince him that she was fine, but he pushed. 'You can tell me, darling. I'm your friend, you know. And for my part, I think Benton is a brute to you.'

A friend. The words touched Cat. She stared into Freddy's face, the boyish lock of hair in direct contrast to the myriad of fine lines at the corners of Freddy's eyes. It was nice to know that someone cared about her, even if it was only poor Freddy, who couldn't keep a job and depended on the charity of his wealthy relatives to pay off his gambling debts.

'Your words are very noble, Freddy.' She offered him her arm. 'Now escort me to dinner, if you will.'

Isobel, with her predictable penchant for tradition, insisted on using the Carlisle china, the good silver, and fine crystal goblets – used by the Carlisles since Victoria was queen – for every dinner. The dining room had no windows. The dark green wallpaper, along with the glow of the two candelabras, cast the room in a depressing gloom. Cat used to think the dining room was warm and inviting. Now she found everything about it detestable.

Annie, with the help of Marie, carried the tureen of soup and a succession of serving dishes into the room and placed them on the mahogany sideboard. Benton enjoyed his role as man of the house. He presided over the head of the table and carved the meat, putting each slice on a plate, which Annie distributed.

'What a treasure that young lady is,' Freddy said after Annie left the room.

'She's taken on a lot of responsibility,' Isobel said. 'The agency wasn't able to send someone with any training.

There's simply no one to be had. We don't need a full staff any more, thank goodness. If Benton was still entertaining like he used to, I don't know what I'd have done. Annie's a good worker, especially given her age.'

'Give her a rise, Isobel,' Freddy said. 'She deserves it. I know women who would pay dearly for a decent girl to work in their houses.'

'Enough domestic nonsense,' Benton said. 'Let's raise our glass and drink a toast …'

Cat got through dinner by drinking too much claret. It went down easily. The food was sublime. Cat ate in silence and let the others carry the conversation.

Benton talked of Winston Churchill, who believed that war with Germany was imminent, a direct contradiction to the beliefs held by other members of his party. Benton scoffed at appeasement. Blackie agreed with him, while Freddy didn't believe for a minute there would be war.

When Blackie spoke, everyone stopped what they were doing and turned their attention to him. He had never spoken of his life in Germany. 'Hitler's building planes and conscripting an army. Why would he do that if he wasn't going to war? He's of the opinion that Germany should get back what she lost. He makes no bones about it. They took my wife, you know. And her brother.

'It was those damn pamphlets. I don't know what Leni was thinking, or if she was thinking at all. It was in March, before the Olympics. They – she – had a box of flyers in the flat, stuffed in the back of her wardrobe. One of them was called, "Learn About Beautiful Germany." Inside, they raged about Hitler, provided a map of the location of all the camps, and the conditions under the Nazi regime.'

He gulped his wine. Time seemed to stop. All eyes were on Blackie, who didn't seem so nervous and fragile now.

He looked around, seeing nothing. His gaze lingered on Cat. 'Women aren't allowed to attend university any more. Hitler believes a true German woman's place is in the home, producing children and caring for family. There's no individuality at all. Everything belongs to the Reich. Women are to give children to the Reich; the people are to make sacrifices for the Reich. The Nazis control what Germans read, what they eat – and there wasn't much in the way of food when I left. All extra resources are going to the war machine.

'People don't meet their neighbours' eyes any more. The slightest indiscretion could attract the attention of the Gestapo.' With a shaking hand he poured more claret into his glass. 'I was coming home from work, expecting dinner and a stein of beer. I stood in the rain and watched as my wife and her brother were hauled to the car, thrown in the back and driven away.'

'Couldn't you hire a solicitor and get them released?' Cat couldn't believe – didn't want to believe – there was nothing to be done.

Blackie laughed, scoffed really, and looked at Cat. 'You don't question the Gestapo. You hope that your loved one is done away with quickly, but given my wife's offence, I am certain she suffered. The penalty for disseminating anti-Nazi literature is death. They always torture first. If the offender has any secrets, he won't hold them for long.' Blackie's hand started to tremble. He set his glass down. The claret sloshed up the sides and dripped onto the white linen tablecloth, like drops of blood.

Cat swallowed the lump that formed in her throat.

'My wife stared at me out the back window as the car drove away. I'll never forget the look on her face. One of the men stayed to search our house. I asked where they

67

were taking them. The man beat me with his stick and told me to mind own business or they would take me, too, never mind that I was English. The next day, I tried to find out where they were taken and was told they were at the Gestapo prison centre. I went there, thinking I could get them released, offer money – I didn't know what else to do. When I walked by I heard the terrible screaming.' A sob broke from Blackie's throat. He tried to disguise it with a cough. 'I'm sorry. Excuse me.'

He pushed away from the table and hurried out of the room.

No one spoke. Cat blinked back her tears. Benton took out his handkerchief and dabbed at his eyes.

'I had no idea,' Freddy said.

Cat didn't know how long they sat in the candlelit stillness after Blackie fled. No one spoke. The treachery hung in the room, a sour note to a barely tolerable evening.

Isobel broke the silence. 'He's with us now. We'll see that he's taken care of.'

'Let's talk of something else,' Benton said.

'It's charity ball season. Freddy, let me tell you all about my latest project,' Isobel said.

'Best just to promise her some money now, Freddy,' Benton said. 'She'll get it out of you anyway.'

'Short on funds, I'm afraid, Isobel.' Freddy swallowed and dabbed the corner of his mouth with the white napkin. 'But we'll figure something out, won't we?'

Isobel's cheeks flushed scarlet. Was that fear that flickered through her eyes?

Cat bit back a sigh when Isobel droned on about the orphanage that she would build. The wine flowed. The noise level rose as alcohol loosened tongues. Cat tuned them all out and concentrated on the food, thoughts of Blackie's story running through her mind. Her heart broke for him. The men had resumed their discussion of politics. Isobel had gone quiet. Cat caught her staring at Freddy Sykes with a strange look on her face. Was Isobel angry with Freddy? Cat refilled her glass, knowing that she would have a pounding headache tomorrow.

After dinner there was discussion about a quick game of bridge before Benton and Freddy went out for the evening, but Cat begged off claiming a headache. She hurried up to her room, kicked off her shoes, and climbed on top of her bed still dressed, like a very drunk bird in a gilded cage. The room started to spin. She took deep breaths and wished she were someplace else.

Cat woke shivering. She left her window cracked and cold but sobering gusts of air flowed into the room. Her eye, which had finished swelling all the way shut while she slept, pounded. She reached up to touch it, wincing when her fingers made contact. Her mouth was dry as the Sahara. A claret-induced headache pounded in her head. She needed an aspirin and a glass of water and would have to go down to the kitchen to fetch them. She flicked on her bedside lamp, surprised that it was only a quarter past ten. Safe in the knowledge that Benton and Freddy were either drinking in Benton's study or out for the evening, Cat decided to slip downstairs.

***

Annie enjoyed the time of night when the work was done and she had the kitchen to herself. The men were in Mr Carlisle's study, smoking cigars and drinking brandy. Marie told her that she could clear the drawing room tomorrow morning. Isobel had congratulated her on a job well done and had promised to discuss another small rise in salary. 'We don't want you thinking you're not appreciated.'

Annie stood and stretched her back. She was tired. Her feet were sore and she was certain she could sleep for a week. She hung her apron on the hook, double-checked that the kitchen was just as Miss Isobel expected it to be, and headed upstairs to her tiny yet welcoming bed. She stopped on the landing nearing Miss Catherine's bedroom. She felt the hair on her arms rise. Her breath caught. She wasn't alone.

As her eyes adjusted to the light, she could just make out the shape of a man lurking in the shadows. She reached for the switch, flipped it, and in the dim light she saw Freddy Sykes, leaning against the wall.

'Hello, sweetheart.'

'What are you doing up here?' Annie knew the question was impertinent the moment it left her lips. 'Did you need something? Your coat's downstairs –'

'I was looking for you, actually.' Freddy Sykes moved towards Annie. She recognised that look. She had seen that same expression on her stepfather's face when they were alone together. Heart pounding in her chest, Annie tried to sidle past Freddy. If she could just make it to the stairs that led to the third floor and her room, which thank goodness had a lock, she might be safe. Surely a gentleman wouldn't chase a simple maid such as herself. Would he?

Freddy was inches away now. Cold sweat broke out between Annie's shoulder blades. She didn't know what to do, how to act. Freddy stepped close to her, blocking the stairs that led to freedom.

'I'm very fast at running up stairs.' Freddy smiled. He spoke in a lazy manner, like a tiger stalking its unsuspecting prey.

Annie's heart pounded. She thought she had run away from this. In one fell swoop, Freddy scooped her into his arms and pressed her against the wall.

'How old are you, Annie?' he whispered into her ear. He wrapped his arms around her, rendering her helpless as he pushed his body against her, grinding his hips into hers.

She filled her lungs and screamed with all the force she could muster.

Freddy clamped his hand over her mouth. Annie couldn't breathe. Panic caused the adrenaline to pulse through her veins. She kicked and thrashed, but Freddy held her fast.

She wanted to die. Maybe she would die. People did sometimes, when men did this.

'What the hell is going on here?' Miss Catherine's voice cut through Annie's fears. 'Freddy, let her go. Right now.'

'Who's going to stop me?' Freddy smirked. 'This little lady and I were just talking, weren't we, sweetheart.'

Annie started to shake. She couldn't move. She couldn't speak.

Miss Catherine moved towards Freddy. 'I'm not afraid of you, Freddy Sykes. Let her go. Right now.'

Freddy let Annie go. He clenched his hands into fists. 'You know, Benton should have beaten you into submission long ago. You forget your place.'

'Spoken like a true friend,' Miss Catherine said.

Annie watched, horrified, as Freddy cocked his fist and stepped back, ready to swing at Miss Catherine.

Miss Catherine was quicker. She kicked Freddy in the groin, hard. He groaned as he sunk to the floor. Annie just heard him utter the word, 'Bitch.'

Miss Catherine took a key out of the small purse she carried under her arm and handed it to Annie. 'Go to my room, lock the door, and wait for me there.'

Annie hesitated.

'I'm the mistress of this house; do as I say. Go. Now. You'll be safe in my room.' Miss Catherine's voice was firm, but her face was kind. Annie Havers was a good girl. She would rather leave this home with no reference than lose her virtue to a man like Freddy Sykes.

'Yes, ma'am.' She ran.

Chapter Five

Cat stared at Freddy Sykes, who now lay in a heap on the floor. She resisted the urge to kick him. 'Get up, Freddy,' Cat said. 'Show a little bit of manly pride.'

Freddy grunted. He struggled to his feet and faced Catherine, eyes blazing, snorting like a wounded beast.

'You'll regret that.'

Cat stepped close and whispered just loud enough for Freddy to hear. 'Don't you ever step foot in this house again.'

'Ready, old man? I'm feeling lucky tonight,' Benton said as he came out of his room. He didn't even look at Catherine. 'Are you all right, Freddy?'

'I'm fine,' Freddy snapped.

'Then we're off. Goodnight, Catherine.' He put his arm around Freddy's shoulders, and they headed out the front door. Benton full of laughter, oblivious to Freddy, who limped along beside him.

'Good riddance,' Cat said under her breath. She jumped when Isobel stepped around the corner.

Anger rose up in Cat. She was tired of Isobel's spying. 'I imagine you witnessed that?'

Isobel's face softened. 'I saw what Freddy was doing to that child. I would have intervened.'

'Oh, really?' Cat couldn't keep the sarcasm from her voice. She didn't believe for one minute that Isobel would do any such thing.

'A little more tactfully, perhaps, but yes. I would have stopped it.' Isobel gave Cat a condescending smile. 'Men like Freddy have been having their way with servants since time immemorial. It's just the way things are.'

'You think that defiling a fourteen-year-old girl is *just the way things are*?' Cat took a breath, forcing herself to speak rationally. 'I've let you run this house for all these years because I didn't want to cause a strain in our relationship. You don't like me, Isobel. That's fine. I couldn't care less. Annie is now my maid. She doesn't answer to you, and she won't be doing anything else for you that will put her in the kind of jeopardy she was in tonight.' Cat played her trump card. 'We can go to Benton with this, but you know how he hates dealing with domestic problems. I'm afraid I'm asserting my role as mistress of the house on this issue. Find yourself another maid.'

Isobel sighed. 'I don't know what to make of you, Catherine. This is all your fault, you know. You bring about this trouble with Ben. If you acted like a proper wife, you wouldn't have these problems with him. And you'd do well to get that temper of yours under control. I saw what you did to Freddy. One of these days you'll assault the wrong person.'

'Stop it, Isobel. Just stop. I'm in no mood.' Cat turned towards her room.

Cat didn't have to knock on her bedroom door. Annie opened it, ashen-faced and trembling.

'Are you all right, Annie?' Cat said.

'Is he gone?'

'He's gone. You're safe now. We're going to change the arrangements as far as your duties and responsibilities go. I'll not have you upstairs in a servant's room by yourself. How about if you stay here?' Cat walked over to an alcove near the window and opened a door there to reveal a small room with a bed covered in a brightly coloured quilt. An eiderdown was folded at the end of the bed, at the ready for the cold London nights. Four bronze hooks with white ceramic balls painted with flowers hung on the wall. Next to the bed, a table held a candle and an old Bible. A round window saved the room from being pitch-dark. Another small narrow door led out into the hallway. There was a key in this lock. Catherine took it out and handed it to Annie.

'What's this room?' Annie asked.

'It used to be the maid's quarters, back in the day when the Carlisles had a full staff. This is your room now. You have the only key. You'll be safe here. I'll go upstairs and fetch your things. You don't need to be roaming the dark corridors of this house alone.'

'Thank you, ma'am.'

'Annie, you need to be careful. I can't be here all the time.'

Annie's eyes darted to the door at the gentle knock.

'It's Marie. I want to see Annie. Isobel told me what happened. Is she all right?'

Cat opened the door and let Marie in.

'Annie, you poor thing.' Marie went over to Annie and put an arm around her.

Annie said, 'Miss Catherine got him to stop. She kicked him.'

Marie gave Cat a worried glance. Both women knew there would be repercussions for Cat's actions tonight. Marie put her arm around Annie's shoulder. 'We'll see you stay safe, Annie.'

'You stay with Marie, Annie. I'll go and get your things.'

Cat scurried up the tiny staircase that led to the long-deserted servants' quarters. She found Annie's room, and her heart broke at the young girl's meagre possessions. She found the cloth valise under the bed and packed Annie's things. Back in her room, Cat found Annie and Marie sitting on Cat's bed.

'I think she'll be all right,' Marie said. 'I'll see that she's not left alone.'

'If she gets scared, I've instructed her to come up here and lock herself in. I can't be here all the time, but she'll have a safe place to go. That's the least we can do.'

Marie nodded. 'I'll speak to Isobel.'

Cat was surprised at the conviction in Marie's tone.

'She'll listen to me,' Marie said. 'I let her push me around when it comes to matters of society, but this is a non-negotiable issue.' She stood. 'Annie, do you want to stay here? Do you feel safe? If you want to leave, I'll see that you're compensated and that you get a proper reference.'

'I want to stay,' Annie said. She looked at Marie and Catherine. 'I'll be fine. I want to work.'

But her voice had a tremble to it, which only made Cat angry with Freddy Sykes all over again.

After Marie left, Annie went into the tiny maid's quarters. Cat followed, and lit the candle on the dresser. Together they tucked a sheet around the feather mattress on the little bed. The flames flicked against the wall, causing their shadows to dance. A locket on a heavy silver chain came untucked from Annie's dress. It swung in a circle as Annie bent over the bed.

'What a pretty locket.'

'Thank you. My gran gave it to me. She died, but she left it to me in her will.'

'What's inside?' Cat sat on Annie's bed. She patted the spot next to her. Annie sat down.

'A picture of my parents.' Annie removed the locket from around her neck. She pushed a small button on the side and the locket sprang open. She handed it to Cat. 'That's my mum, and that's my dad.'

'Both of your parents are dead?'

'I – um –' Annie stammered. 'No, ma'am. I told Miss Carlisle a lie. I'm not an orphan. My mum is still alive. My dad died six months ago. He said I could go to art school when I'm old enough, but after he died, there wasn't enough money. My mum is a seamstress, but she doesn't earn much. We had a house, but Mum couldn't pay the rent. We tried, but we just couldn't make a go of it. Never enough money. She married Harold. We left our home and moved to the rooms over his shop. I ran away, ma'am. I ran away and lied to Miss Isobel.' Annie sat down on the bed and bowed her head.

Cat sat down next to Annie. She wanted to take the child in her arms, and assure her all would be well. Finally Annie looked at Cat, meeting her gaze with a stubborn determination that broke Cat's heart. 'Am I going to lose my place here? I'll not go back to my mum, miss. I promise you that. I'll run away first.'

'Oh, Annie,' Cat said. 'That'll be our secret, all right?' Cat wondered what this Harold had done to frighten Annie so, but something in the girl's eyes begged Cat not to ask. Not now.

Annie sighed. Relief washed over her in a wave. 'Thank you.' Annie wiped her eyes with her sleeve.

'Now, what should we tell Isobel tomorrow? Do you want to continue with your duties?'

'Yes, ma'am,' Annie said.

Cat thought for a moment. 'How about if I tell Isobel that you will continue with the same duties you had before, at least for the time being. We'll see where we are in a few days. Does that suit?'

'Yes, ma'am,' Annie said.

'Are you comfortable being here with Marie? I can't be here all the time, Annie. I want you to feel safe.'

'Yes, Miss Catherine. It's not the family's fault what Freddy did.'

'Very well. I'll see to it first thing in the morning.'

'I can never repay you for what you did for me tonight, Miss Catherine. I'm grateful,' Annie said.

'There's nothing to repay, Annie. I just did what I felt was right. I'd like to think you would do the same thing if someone needed your help,' Cat said.

The two of them sat for a few minutes in the flickering candlelight, side by side on Annie's tiny bed, each suffering in her own way. Annie yawned. Cat stood.

'Goodnight, Annie.'

'Goodnight.'

Cat undressed, washed, and crawled into bed. She expected sleep to come immediately, but it didn't. The look on Annie's face as Freddy Sykes pinned her against the wall ran round and round in Cat's mind.

Chapter Six

The next day dawned overcast and dreary, a perfect reflection of Cat's mood. She was angry with Reginald. If he had given Cat documents that were worth stealing, why didn't he tell her? She wondered if yesterday's attack was some sort of test, but dismissed that thought. Surely Reginald wouldn't be so cruel as to put Cat in jeopardy like that. Would he?

Cat realised that her relationship with Reginald could all be a lie. Maybe he hadn't known her father at all. She wondered if yesterday's events were nothing more than a horrible nightmare, but her reflection in the mirror told her otherwise. Her eye had swollen into a mottled orb overnight and was now a fetching shade of blue. Her head pounded from the claret. Her stomach gurgled from the rich food.

She drank a glass of water and dressed for the day. The effort caused her head to throb with renewed vigour. She tried to cover her eye with make-up, but gave that up. She would eat some breakfast – and hopefully calm her queasy stomach – and check the newspaper. She must talk to Reginald, demand an explanation.

A scintilla of fear warned her to stay home where she would be safe, but she pushed it away. If Reginald had further work for her, she would take it, but she would demand that he tell her specifically what she was doing for him. She knew the errands she ran were not so innocent, but she would need the money if she were going to leave Benton and made a new life for herself. She stopped, realising that she had made up her mind. She was going to leave her husband, leave this house. She'd have to take Annie with her, but that didn't matter. They would go to Aunt Lydia's and see where things stood.

Downstairs, Isobel was seated at the dining table, while Blackie filled a plate with kippers and eggs from the chafing dishes on the sideboard. The smell of them made Cat's stomach roil. She took two pieces of dry toast, filled a cup with tea, and sat down at the table.

'Good morning,' Blackie said. He set the newspaper down, revealing an article about the pageantry of the recent coronation of King George. 'How's the eye this morning?'

'Swollen, but not as painful,' Cat said. 'I imagine it will get worse before it gets better.'

'Probably,' Blackie said. 'They usually go from blue, to purple, to green, then yellow.'

'Blackie, dear, how do you know about these things?' Isobel asked. She didn't even acknowledge Cat.

'Used to box a bit as a teenager, Izzy. I've had my share of black eyes.'

'Did you really?' Isobel put the newspaper she was reading down. 'I had no idea. I'm surprised your parents approved.'

'They didn't know,' Blackie said. 'My mother would have been furious with me.'

Isobel shook her head. 'I remember you hated fighting when we were little. You used to cry –'

'That was a long time ago, Isobel,' Blackie said. He refilled Isobel's tea before he poured for himself. 'What's everyone doing today?'

80

Isobel dabbed her mouth with the linen napkin and added sugar and milk to her cup. 'Meetings all week. So busy. Small committee meeting today, then our big meeting tomorrow, here at the house. We're going to be over-run with women, Blackie. You may want to take your midday meal out. We've got plans to host a luncheon and jumble sale and a dinner-dance in addition to the charity ball. Three separate fundraisers. And a man from *The London Times* has taken pictures and interviewed me. The exposure will be wonderful. There are a lot of other events competing with ours, especially given the coronation. Too much exposure on the social aspect of the charity balls, I'm afraid. I'm hopeful the *Times* article will convince people how necessary an orphanage is. Maybe he'll do a feature article, and more people will come forward with their support. There is much to do, but if our projections are correct, we should have enough money to start construction on the new orphanage next year.'

'That's commendable, Isobel,' Blackie said. 'You're remarkable.'

'It's important to make a contribution,' Isobel said. She cast a disapproving glance at Cat, who ignored her altogether.

'What about you, Catherine? Big day planned?'

'Yes,' Cat lied easily. 'I have a few errands to run.' Annie came in, carrying a small silver tray that held the morning post. She carried the tray towards Cat, but Isobel grabbed the letters before Annie could stop her.

'Thank you, Annie. You may go and eat your own breakfast now,' Isobel said.

'Thank you, ma'am,' Annie said. She flashed a shy smile at Cat and Blackie and hurried from the room.

81

Isobel rifled through the letters, inspecting each one. 'Here's one from Alicia Montrose.' Isobel started to open it, until Cat caught her name scrawled across the front.

'That's addressed to me, Isobel.' Cat extended her hand.

Isobel checked the front of the envelope. 'Oh, of course. Sorry. Usually Alicia writes directly to me. Shall I open it for you? I'm sure it's to do with our charity function –'

'No, thank you,' Cat said. She snatched the envelope from Isobel.

Cat felt Isobel's eyes on her as she opened the letter, and read Alicia Montrose's perfect handwriting. 'Cat, Please come to the country with me this weekend. The air will do you good! You can become acquainted with my boys, and we can catch up. I don't want to pressure you, but ring if you're so inclined. In fond friendship, Alicia.'

Cat thought about chucking it all, taking Annie, and heading to Bournemouth to Alicia's rambling estate. There were empty cottages scattered about the property. If she wanted to, Cat and Annie could stay there as long as they wanted. She smiled.

'What does Alicia want?' Isobel asked.

'Really, Isobel, can I not have a modicum of privacy?'

'We need to discuss a few things before you leave today,' Isobel said. 'Such as Annie's duties. Will she still help Marie with the cooking?'

'She can continue with her duties as long as one of you is within reach of her at all times. I won't leave her alone in this house at the whim of Benton's friends. However, I'm going to Lydia's for a few days, and I'm taking Annie with me.'

'When are you going?' Isobel demanded. 'I've got my committee meeting today and my tea tomorrow. I can't do it without Annie's help.'

'I'm not sure, maybe tomorrow or the next day.'

'I hope you'll let Annie stay and help with the meetings that I have planned.'

'Of course,' Cat said. 'As long as Annie is amenable.'

'We'll need to assure her that she'll be safe. She won't want to stay here without Catherine otherwise,' Marie said. 'I can't say that I blame her.'

'Don't you think that you and Catherine are taking things too far?' Isobel said. Before Cat could say anything further, Isobel spoke. 'Very well. When you're not here, Marie will be responsible for Annie's safety.'

Isobel picked up the crystal bell that sat by her teacup. Soon Annie appeared.

'Yes, Miss Isobel?'

'Annie, Cat is going to stay with her aunt at some point. She wants you to go with her. Do you mind staying until after my meeting tomorrow? I assure you that Freddy Sykes will be nowhere near, and if for some strange reason he comes to the house, I promise to keep him away from you. The choice is yours.'

Annie looked at Cat.

'I'll keep you safe, Annie,' Marie said.

'If you don't feel comfortable, you are under no obligation to stay. You're free to do as you wish. You're not in trouble. The choice is yours,' Cat said.

Isobel rolled her eyes. 'Really,' she muttered just loud enough for everyone to hear her.

'Do stop it, Izzy. The child has every right to be mistrustful.' Marie's cheeks flamed with indignation.

'It's up to you, Annie,' Cat said.

'When are you leaving?' Annie asked.

'I'm not sure. Maybe tomorrow or the next day. You don't have to stay here alone if you don't want to.'

'I can stay until after the meeting,' Annie said.

'We'll keep you safe, Annie,' Marie said. 'I give you my word on that.'

'I know. I trust you, Marie.' Annie took the empty teapot without being asked and went to the kitchen to fill it.

'How is Lydia?' Marie asked.

Cat took the last piece of toast. 'Aunt Lydia is fine, thank you for asking.'

'Please tell her I said hello. Now, if you'll excuse me, I'll get us more toast.' Marie picked up the toast rack as she left the room.

'Does Benton know that you're leaving us?' Isobel asked.

Cat ignored her and spread a thick layer of butter onto her toast.

'Are you going to ignore me? I asked if my brother knows you're leaving,' Isobel said.

'I'm not ignoring you, Isobel. I'm just not going to discuss this private matter with you.'

'The matter is not private when it concerns my brother. He needs a wife by his side. Have you ever given a moment's thought to anyone other than yourself?'

'Apparently not,' Cat said.

Isobel shook her head and focused on her mail. She always got stacks of it and spent a good part of her day locked in her office with Marie, answering and writing letters, most of it to do with the charity work that consumed her life.

'Cat? Are you listening?' Blackie said. 'I said, do you want the paper? I've finished with it.'

'Oh, yes,' Cat said. She took the paper and pretended to read the front page. It wouldn't do for her to go right to the

84

personals in search of a message from Reginald. Cat wanted to see him today, and hoped she would find a message there. She had to be careful, though. Despite his bumbling ways, Cat suspected Blackie saw more than he let on.

She took her time perusing the tedious articles on fashion and housekeeping and Lady Shelton's at-home, before she turned to the personals. She skimmed the ads until she found the message from Sir Reginald. 'Sir Edmund's pippin in the garden today.' *Thank God.* Cat felt Blackie's eyes on her. She didn't look up, rather she smiled, as though entertained by what she read.

'Listen to this one,' she said, 'will the lady with the green eyes and the hair like mink please come back to the bench under the rowan tree Tuesday at four. I think we are meant to marry and I must know your name.'

Blackie laughed. 'Read another –'

Isobel yelped and dropped the letter she was holding. A photograph slipped out of the envelope and landed next to it, face down on the table. She snatched it up, tore it into pieces and put the pieces in her pocket. Her breath came in short gasps. She put her hand on her heart, as though she were having a heart attack.

'What is it?' Blackie rose and hurried over to her.

Like a flash, Isobel grabbed the letter, pushed away from the table, and ran out of the room.

'What just happened?' Cat asked. She had never seen Isobel lose her composure.

'I've no idea,' Blackie said. 'What should we do?'

'I'm not going to do anything.' Cat stood up. 'I'm the last person she'd turn to for help. Isobel isn't one for unsolicited comfort, Blackie. I'd leave her be.'

Blackie ignored Cat's warning and hurried after Isobel, leaving Cat free to slip out of the house.

Reginald was already at their bench. Cat stopped and watched him as he took seeds from the packet and tossed them at the birds that scurried around his feet. Something was different today. Cat thought it might have to do with the clouds that blocked the sun, but when she got close to the bench where he sat waiting, she noticed the worry in Reginald's eyes.

'Don't get up,' Cat said. She sat down next to him. 'The black eye isn't from Benton, if that's what you're thinking. When I was making my delivery yesterday, I was attacked. I'm quite certain the woman who attacked me wanted the documents I was carrying.' Cat glanced at Reginald, looking for some remorse. She saw none. 'I'm asking you to trust me, Reginald, and tell me the truth. Who are you? Who do you work for? What, pray tell, have you got me into?'

Reginald didn't speak for a long time. He and Cat sat side by side on the bench, in the grey day. A passer-by would think that the young woman was sharing a quiet moment of contemplation with her grandfather or aged uncle. Cat and Reginald had shared this garden square bench for years. As Cat reflected on her relationship with him, she realised she had never met anyone like him before. He taught without being pedantic. He was a well-travelled sophisticate, yet he never condescended. He always had a kind word. Because of knowing him, Cat learned to enjoy the space between words, the comfortable silence that good friends can share. Now she wanted some answers; she wanted some assurances from this man whom she so blindly trusted.

'Things are escalating now.' He spoke in a tired voice as he rubbed his hand over his face.

'You don't seem too surprised by this.' Cat pointed to her bruised eye. 'What's going on, Reginald? What have you gotten me into? Did you expect me to be attacked? Who was it? Why did she –'

Reginald didn't answer. He just waited while the questions spewed from her like a veritable fountain, and watched her with that immovable patience, as though he were deciding just how much to tell her. Cat let her final unfinished question hover between them. She tasted the acrid tang of her own fear. She felt like running, but something held her pinned to the bench.

'Did your father ever mention MI5 to you?'

Everything stopped. It seemed as though the very blood that flowed through Cat's veins stilled as the magnitude of Reginald's words sunk in. *Oh, dear God. What have I gotten myself into?* Cat took a deep breath. She turned to face Reginald, so she could gauge his reaction to her words.

'My father never uttered one word about MI5. My mother told me that he worked for them. Very hush-hush, she said. She painted him as a hero, told stories of my father singlehandedly fighting the Hun. She romanticised it.'

The corners of Reginald's mouth turned up in a slight smile for a brief second before he became serious. 'I need you to listen to me now. I need you to not react until I've finished. You'll have questions. I'll tell you as much as I can. Agreed?'

Cat swallowed. She willed herself to form words, but they wouldn't come. She nodded, cold all of a sudden despite the sunshine.

'The Germans are building up their military. Hitler is an incendiary idiot, reckless – war is brewing. Hitler's building an army. He has an air force that's every bit as strong as England's and makes no secret of it. The bombing in Guernica in April is a sample of what the next war will look like. Bombs falling from the sky, cities and towns levelled. Terror among civilians. Mark my words, the next war will be fought in the air. It will be horrific, like nothing we've ever seen. Hitler won't stop at the Sudetenland. He will turn to France, and then his eyes will light on England.

'Your husband's company has a contract with the Air Ministry for several inventions that revolutionise early detection of planes and ships. This technology is crucial. The Germans are developing their own system as well. It's a bit of a race, with potentially catastrophic results for the loser. England is making great progress. Unfortunately, the Germans are now aware of it. We've received intelligence that some of the original concepts have fallen into the wrong hands. We've been investigating Benton's company for months and have recently discovered that someone in your household has been taking documents from your husband's safe and sharing them with a team of local German agents.'

'What? How do you know all this?'

Reginald shook his head. 'I can't tell you. You're going to have to trust me.'

'Are you with MI5?'

'Was, not so much any more. On my way out, actually. I'm ready to spend my days in the country, painting and reading. I've got shelves of unread books and an old shabby chair to sit in. I'm tired, Cat. MI5 is peripherally involved in this operation, along with a group of industrialists who are preparing for the inevitable.'

Cat wanted to trust this man. Not only had he been close to her father, he had also thrown her a lifeline at a time when she was drowning. She needed to trust him. 'Surely you don't think Benton would betray his country, do you? My husband has many flaws, but I assure you he is loyal to King and country. If I'm to trust you, you need to trust me. Tell me who you work for.'

'I cannot do that,' Reginald said. 'I will tell you we've exonerated your husband. He works on the design schematics at his office, but refuses to leave them unattended. Given his talent and dedication, he's been allowed to take documents home after he has a session with them and lock them in his safe. The documents are then transferred by a ministry driver under secure conditions to the man who works on them next. This scenario has worked fine until the past six months or so.'

'Blackie,' Cat whispered the words.

'Michael Blackwell? He's the logical candidate. All this started happening at about the time he arrived on the Carlisle doorstep. His story about escaping surely rings true, and it checks out. We've double-checked and discovered that a Michael Blackwell fled Nazi Germany after his wife and his brother-in-law were arrested for possession of anti-Nazi propaganda. He's not lying about that.'

'This all sounds so cloak-and-dagger. Surely things aren't as bad as that. And war? I've been hearing talk about war a lot lately. It seems to be a common topic among Benton and his colleagues. But why isn't anyone else speaking about it? Why isn't anyone writing about war with Germany in the newspapers?'

'That, my dear, is a long conversation for another day,' Reginald said.

'It all sounds so farfetched. You're telling me we are preparing for another war with Germany, even though we've barely recovered from the last one, and someone is stealing my husband's work and feeding it to the Germans.' She looked askance at Reginald. 'This sounds like the makings of an espionage novel.'

'This isn't fiction, Catherine, as evidenced by your black eye.'

'Who attacked me yesterday?'

Reginald hesitated. Cat stood.

'I want to know what I'm getting myself into. Trust works both ways. If you can't tell me who I'm up against –'

'Very well.' Reginald beckoned her to the empty spot on the bench. Cat sat.

He didn't meet her eyes as he spoke. Instead he looked at two women who pushed prams past them, laughing and happy. 'Before I tell you what I can, I need you to understand the utter discretion and secrecy involved here. Knowledge of what I'm to tell you has gotten people killed. You're going to have questions, and I am not going to be able to answer them. You need to decide if you can trust me. You need to decide if you want to take this job you've been doing for me any further. If you do not, I understand. If you do, things will change for you. I'm giving you a choice, Catherine.'

Cat let Reginald's words sink in. *I should have known this wasn't simple courier work.* Everything was just too easy. How convenient to run into her father's friend on a park bench in Kensington Gardens. How convenient that he offered her a job when she was searching for some sort of meaning in her life. Cat shivered. The hairs on the back of her neck stood up.

'What is it?' Reginald asked.

'I feel like we're being watched,' Cat said. She looked around the park. As far as she could tell, they were alone.

Reginald reached into his pocket and handed Cat an envelope. When she recognised her father's familiar scrawl, she reached for it.

'He wrote it to me shortly before he died. Read it,' Reginald said.

The envelope was worn thin, the paper soft and creased.

March, 1917

Reg,

I'm off for much-needed leave. I've not seen my wife and daughter for over a year and am desperate to lay eyes upon them. I expect my daughter, Catherine, will have blossomed into a young woman. Things are difficult here. We try to keep our spirits up, but the men are tired, war-weary. It seems that each mission becomes more dangerous, the conditions more treacherous. God only knows what they're suffering in the trenches. Many of them should have been sent home months ago. I worry about the cost of this war, not in pounds spent but on the emotional toll it takes from our soldiers in the line of fire and from the nation itself. My only hope is that this brutal fight will be the last war we will see in our lifetime.

I think of my daughter, Catherine, remembering how I so wanted a son. But as I've watched her grow and develop, I realise that this young lady that Victoria and I brought into the world has the courage and fearlessness of any man. I love her so much it aches. I look around and know that everyone in this conflict – even the enemy – has families at home that they love. But I've been asking myself of late why men resolve their differences in battle, in killing. I have been questioning that. I've told myself that we kill each other so our offspring do not have to, a feeble consolation.

I have a request for you, old friend. If anything happens to me, please have a care for Victoria and Catherine. They will not want for anything, I've seen to their financial security. I'm asking you to look after them, from afar if that suits you. See that they are well …

The page was cut short. There was more, but it had been cut away.

'Where's the rest?' Cat asked.

'Classified.' Reginald held out his hand. 'And I need that back. I'm sorry. I can arrange for a copy for you, if you'd like.'

'Thank you.'

'The woman who attacked you is known to our agents as Marlena X. She's English by birth, but spent her formative years in Germany, thus the loyalty to Hitler. She's a skilled typist and has a knack for insinuating herself in with people who have something she needs. She managed to get clearance for a job in naval intelligence. You can imagine the damage she could have done, had we not found her out. We've had agents try to follow her, to find out where she is staying, but she manages to lose them. As you can imagine, we are very concerned that she is near your house, your husband, and the work that he is doing. Someone in your house passed a set of blueprints to her. Luckily, the designs were incomplete. I can't help but be suspicious of Mr Blackwell.'

'Blackie's yet to recover from his escape,' Cat said. 'He drinks constantly. He jumps at his own shadow. I just don't see him involved in this.'

'Catherine, I am asking you to put yourself in danger. I'm giving you a chance to do something for your country, but I'll not deceive you about the potential risks. You need to be aware of that.'

'No, I want to help,' Cat said. She thought of Blackie's trembling hands and the fear in his eyes. 'What do you want me to do?'

'Your husband has a packet of documents that he is going to bring home this evening. You're to switch them with falsified documents, which I will provide. After you do that, you'll meet me or one of my operatives to hand off the documents that you've taken. That way, we can be sure the proper documents are safely out of harm's way.'

'But what about when Benton goes to retrieve them? Won't he know that the documents have been falsified?'

'He doesn't look at them once he's finished with his work. He works on them at his office, brings them home, and locks them away in a safe until they are handed on to a courier. We expect him to bring documents home tonight, but tomorrow he has a meeting that will last a good part of the day. The exchange with the courier has been delayed. Everything's been arranged. All you have to do is make the switch. If you're careful, no one will be the wiser, at least not for a week or two. Eventually the Germans will realise they've been given faulty information, but that may take a while. We will give them authentic drawings, but the schematics will be skewed. With any luck, they'll think what we're working on isn't ready yet.'

Cat sat, silent, letting Reginald's words sink in.

'You see how important this could be.'

For the briefest second Cat realised that Reginald could be working for the Germans, convincing her to commit treason. But he wasn't. Cat knew that with a conviction that surprised her. She prided herself on her intuition. She trusted it now. 'How long until they discover that I've been switching documents?'

Reginald shook his head. 'There's no way of knowing that.'

Cat turned away from Reginald, so he couldn't see the fear in her eyes. 'What should I tell Benton if he catches me in his office? I need an explanation of some sort.'

'You can't get caught, Catherine. We can watch the house, but we would be hard pressed to offer assistance should you run into trouble.' Reginald took a packet of seeds out and threw them to the birds that gathered around them. Across the green, a robin pulled a fat worm out of the grass and flew away with it. 'We figure we can switch documents twice – if we're lucky – before we're discovered. I will prepare you and give you detailed instructions, give you a back-up plan, if you will. There are things you can do to protect yourself –'

Reginald told her to double-check everyone's activities, with an eye towards going through the safe when Isobel and Marie were engaged in their meeting, which would take place across the house, far away from Benton's study. Reginald suggested that Cat give Annie something to occupy herself as well. He told her to sit in her room and mentally plan what she was going to do, and figure out to the second how long it should take. He was frighteningly thorough and went through every scenario that could make things difficult, telling Cat that it was best to have a back-up plan for every eventuality.

'The documents are tucked in here,' Reginald said. He handed Cat a dog-eared copy of *Britannia Magazine, The Special Coronation Number*, its glossy blue cover graced with the crown, the orb and sceptre, its pages full of the pageantry of the coronation that took place in April.

'The switch should take no more than five minutes, so if you're smart and careful it will be easy. Be accountable for every second. If ten minutes go by and you still haven't been able to switch the documents, abort the mission. Report back to me and we will reassess our approach. I suggest you pack a small carryall with essential items, in case you need to make a hasty getaway – not that you will. This is a simple switch.' He handed her an envelope full of notes. 'Here's some money, just in case you do indeed need to run.'

'If I need to leave, how will I get in touch with you?'

'Call me at this number from a call-box. Mention the code word. Memorise the number, please.' He handed her a small sheet of folded paper. Cat memorised the exchange and handed the paper back to Reginald. He put it back into his wallet.

'What about Marlena X?'

'We don't know where she is, but I've got people looking for her. You should assume you're being watched all the time. Be careful. Try not to find yourself in dark alleys alone. Just use your common sense. Your diligence could save your life.'

Cat took the money and tucked it in her handbag. 'Is it normal for me to be exhilarated and frightened at the same time? I'm absolutely terrified.'

'The brave soldier faces his fears and carries on. You've got fire in you, Cat, and you're extremely intuitive. You're being given an opportunity to serve your country. Just open the safe and switch the documents. When you've successfully completed the mission, open your bedroom curtains halfway. I'll meet you here tomorrow afternoon at half past four.'

They said their goodbyes. As Cat watched Reginald lumber away, she realised how she had underestimated him. She wondered what other secrets he carried and hoped she hadn't been reckless in placing her trust in this man who claimed to have been close to her father.

Chapter Seven

Annie sat alone at the tiny table, looking at the Carlisles' overgrown garden and the dilapidated shed that rested in the far corner near the fence. Hawthorn grew bushy, intermingled with tall weeds. Foxglove sprouted in thick clumps in the shady corners. The effect was wild and reckless – Mother Nature left to her own devices. An old fountain of a woman holding an urn stood dry and forlorn amid the mess. Annie found she rather liked it and longed to paint it. She liked paintings with character. Annie was surprised at this state of affairs. Isobel was so organised and fastidious, it amazed Annie that she let things get so out of hand.

'Our gardener, Davis, is cook's husband. He's the man who suffered the heart attack,' Marie said.

Annie started. This wasn't the first time Marie had sidled into the room, unnoticed. Because of this unnerving habit, Annie was always on her best behaviour, lest Marie was watching her, skulking in some corner.

'They'll be back eventually. Benton thought we should get another man in to replace him, but Isobel wouldn't hear of it. She's loyal that way. Says that Davis, his father, and grandfather before him, have been with the family so long that it would be a breach to find someone else to do his job. She also insisted on continuing to pay the man's wages. Loyalty is important to Isobel. So is honesty.'

Annie tried to push her fears back as she bit into a biscuit, but the buttery sweetness turned to sawdust in her mouth.

'Your mum is here,' Marie said. The look of disappointment in her eyes broke Annie's heart. 'We trusted you, Annie. Why did you lie?'

Annie wondered what would happen if she ran out the door, through the garden, and out onto the street. She would just run and run until she collapsed. No. That wouldn't do. Annie Havers might be a liar, but she was not a quitter. She would never go back to her mother's home. Her mother couldn't force her to go live with Harold Green. If she tried, Annie would run away. She knew that she would have to face her mum at some point. She had run away in the middle of the night, after all. But she didn't think her mother would ever find her here in Kensington.

She stood up, ready to do battle. If Isobel fired her, she'd get another job. This time, she'd be honest. She was a good worker – no one could deny that. She had to trust that she would not starve on the streets.

'You'll have to take my word that I have a good reason for my falsehood, Miss Marie. My father is dead. That part wasn't a lie.' She met Marie's scrutiny head on. 'I'd best go and speak to my mum.' She pushed away from the table. It seemed the time for reckoning was upon her.

Annie walked down the hall towards the drawing room, where she could hear her mother's hushed tone and Miss Isobel's clear, ringing voice.

'Honestly, Mrs Green, we had no idea that Annie had any family at all. She told us she was an orphan.'

Annie paused outside the doorway just in time to hear her mother gasp. She threw her shoulders back and stepped into the room.

'Hello, Mum.' Annie didn't expect the rush of emotion at seeing her mum. It washed over her in waves, knocking her off balance. Tears threatened, but Annie bit them back. Her mum had faded since Annie had last seen her. Violet Havers Green had started her new life with a glow in her cheeks and the promise of a better future, for her and her daughter. She had been a beauty as a young girl, and age had only refined her features. Her clean complexion, pink cheeks, and dark luxuriant hair turned heads, even now. That beauty hadn't diminished when Annie's father had died. The youthful glow had gone – Annie knew that tragedy could do that – but Violet Havers' beauty just took on a new dimension, one of depth and character.

Annie noticed the silver threads laced through her mum's hair, and the pinched look on the mouth that used to smile all the time. The sky blue dress and matching hat did little to flatter her already wan complexion.

'Oh, Annie,' Mrs Green said. She stood up and opened her arms. Without thinking Annie ran to them.

Miss Isobel didn't move. When she had shown Mrs Green into the room, she had taken the middle of the big sofa, forcing her visitor to sit in one of the spindly chairs opposite. Annie peeked over her mum's shoulder and caught Miss Isobel watching them, a look of calculated judgement on her face. Annie realised what was at stake. She needed to convince her mother and Miss Isobel that she was better off here in the Carlisle home. She realised that she would have to tell the truth and that the telling of it could change her life in ways that she might not like.

After an eternity, her mother pushed Annie away, holding her shoulders in a vice grip while she stared in her eyes. 'Why did you run away? Harold and I have been looking everywhere for you. We only got lucky because

Harold knows someone who knows someone – oh, never mind. That's not important. I've found you. That's all that matters. You can explain yourself on the way home.'

'No,' Annie said. She disentangled from her mother's embrace and stepped out of her reach. She lined herself up with the door on purpose. She'd run if need be.

'Annie Green, you listen to me right now –' Her mother's voice threatened to grow shrill with indignation.

'Stop it. I'm not Annie Green. I'm Annie Havers. I'm not taking his name. I'm not going home with you.' Annie cast a glance at Miss Isobel.

'Mrs Green, perhaps we should let Annie explain. Although I agree that Annie is a child, and should do what you ask, perhaps if we let her share her side of the story –'

'I'm not explaining anything –' Annie started to back away from her mother and Isobel.

A key turned in the lock. The door opened and shut, followed by the unmistakable cadence of Miss Catherine's footsteps in the hall. 'Where is everyone?' Miss Catherine called out. Annie could have sobbed with relief.

Before Miss Isobel could commandeer the situation, Annie called out, 'We're in here, Miss Catherine.'

'What's going on?' Miss Catherine stood in the doorway, beautifully dressed, a magazine tucked under her arm. Stray curls had escaped her hat. Her eyes – even the swollen one – were alive with energy, her cheeks flushed. She took off her gloves, and tucked them in the handbag she held, while she surveyed Annie, Isobel, and Violet Havers Green. 'Annie? What's happened?'

Annie nodded towards her mother. 'This is my mum. She wants me to come home.'

'Mrs Green, I'd like you to meet my sister-in-law, Catherine Carlisle.'

'Please forgive my unseemly black eye.' Miss Catherine smiled widely. Only Annie could tell the smile was forced. Only Annie noticed the wild look in Miss Catherine's eyes. While Miss Catherine set her handbag and the magazine down on the coffee table and extended her hand to Annie's mum, Annie moved a little closer to the door.

'Annie hasn't been quite truthful with us,' Miss Isobel said.

'Really? Please explain.' Miss Catherine said.

'She's not an orphan,' Mrs Havers said. 'She's got a mother and a father who want her home with them. Annie, I'll not have you work in service.'

Annie resisted the urge to run. 'I'll not go home with you, Mum. Harold Green is not my father. My father's dead.'

'Let's discuss this like rational adults, shall we?' Mrs Carlisle sat down on the other vacant chair. A small matching stool sat next to her chair. 'Annie, come in the room, please. No one is going to force you to do anything you don't want to do. Come sit beside me.' Miss Catherine pointed to the stool. She smiled and faced Annie's mum.

'I'm the wife of Mr Benton Carlisle, Mrs Green. Annie was originally retained as a maid to work in the house. But I was thinking we'd have a little renegotiation of Annie's duties. I was thinking that rather than working as a maid – in service, as you say – we could get creative and think of something else.'

'This is the first I've heard of this,' Isobel said. Her cheeks flushed crimson. Annie couldn't tell whether from anger at being usurped by Miss Catherine before a witness or from sheer embarrassment.

'I think we should discuss any arrangements privately, Catherine, don't you?' Miss Isobel's desperation to resume control over-rode her sense of social decorum.

'No, I don't. Especially since Mrs Green is here. She should have a say in the matter, I think. She is Annie's mother, after all, and I'm sure she'd like to leave today knowing that Annie is in good hands,' Miss Catherine said.

'My daughter was not raised to be in service,' Mrs Green said. 'Had her father not died, she would be getting an education, finding a husband.'

'I understand that, Mrs Green. Lucky for us, your daughter is an excellent worker. She is charming, poised, and a joy to be around. She is a credit to you.'

Mrs Green blushed. Annie sensed her soften towards Catherine. 'Thank you.'

Miss Catherine leaned back and crossed her legs. 'I think I've come up with a solution that will work for all of us.'

Annie sized up the women in the room, Miss Isobel and her mum against Miss Catherine and Marie, who slipped into the room unnoticed and now stood in the corner, watching the drama unfold. Marie caught Annie's eye and gave a slight smile.

'I am proposing that Annie work for me as what, I believe, is known as a paid companion. She will do some light chores for all of us. We don't have much staff, and Annie has been helping Marie in the kitchen.'

'I like cooking,' Annie piped up. 'And Miss Marie is teaching me.'

'Annie's a smart girl, a fast learner,' Marie said. 'She's been a great help to me.'

Miss Isobel stood up. She reached for the magazine that her sister-in-law had placed on the table next to her handbag, but Miss Catherine put her hand on top of it. 'If you don't mind, Isobel. I haven't read that yet.'

Miss Isobel sniffed. 'Mrs Green, it was nice to meet you. I'll leave you and your daughter in Mrs Carlisle's capable hands. Marie, come.' Miss Isobel walked out of the room, Marie following behind her like a well-trained dog, desperate for approval and eager to please.

After they had gone, Cat continued. 'Annie has told me a little bit about why she left home. I think you should hear her out before you force her to return. I would very much like her to stay with me. I've grown fond of her. She has a nice place to stay here, and you can visit her any time you like.' Mrs Carlisle turned to Annie. 'Do you want to stay with me, Annie?'

'Yes, ma'am,' Annie said.

'Why did you run away, Annie?' Mrs Green said.

Annie cast a desperate glance at Miss Catherine.

'Tell the truth, Annie. She's your mother.'

Annie knew that her very future hung on the words she spoke at this moment. She also knew the devastation her revelation about her stepfather would cause. She swallowed, and tried to figure out how to explain, knowing her words would ruin her mother's life.

'Do you remember the night after the wedding, when I had a nightmare?'

Mrs Green nodded. 'Of course I do. You hadn't cried out like that since you were a wee thing.'

Annie moved over to her mother. She knelt down in front of her and took her hand. 'I'm sorry to tell you this, Mum. I know you're going to be mad. Harold came into my room. I woke up and found him standing over my bed,

Mum. He puts his arm around me, and pulls me onto his lap when you're not home –'

'Enough,' Mrs Green said. She turned on Miss Catherine. 'Have you been putting these ideas in my daughter's head?'

'She hasn't. She wouldn't!' Annie cried out. 'Mum. It's true.'

Miss Catherine sat on her chair, still as a statue, somehow withdrawn into herself, as though she wanted to give Annie and her mother this moment alone. Mrs Green had let go of Annie's hand. The tears that welled up in her eyes spilled over now. The black that she used to darken her eyelashes loosened and ran like inky rivers down her cheeks.

'I'll keep her safe, Mrs Green. I promise you that. She'll be well looked after.' Miss Catherine opened her handbag and pulled a handkerchief out, a fine linen thing with lace as thin as a spider's web. She handed it to Annie's mum.

Mrs Green did what she could to clean her face, while Annie and Miss Catherine sat by watching. After a minute, Mrs Green composed herself.

'I won't force you, Annie. You're a good girl, and I love you, but I don't believe you. Not one word.' She stood, so did Miss Catherine. Mrs Green stared at her daughter. 'I don't even know you any more. Good day, Mrs Carlisle. I'll see myself out.' Annie watched as Miss Catherine extended her hand, but her mum ignored it. She walked out of the room, down the hall, and out the front door.

'I'm sorry, Annie. Sometimes women don't want to see what's right in front of them.' Miss Catherine studied Annie's face.

'I'm glad the truth is out, ma'am. And thank you.'

'It's been an emotional afternoon. Why don't you go take a walk in the fresh air?'

'Thank you, ma'am. I'll bring up a tray before I go. There's fresh biscuits.'

'Thank you, Annie.'

Annie headed out into the square and walked with purpose on the path that circled it. With each step, the tension slipped away. Miss Catherine had come to her rescue, and now she was free. But the victory was a painful one. Annie would never forget the look on her mother's face when Annie told her about Harold's attempt to visit her room in the night. Her mum hadn't believed her.

Annie understood the desperation that drove her mum. After her dad died, there wasn't enough money for Annie and her mother to live on. Mrs Havers always said they'd make do, but they hadn't. They'd started to sell things. Annie used to see her mum sitting at the kitchen table, staring at the pile of bills that needed to be paid. Harold Green offered the promise of security, a home, the knowledge there would be meat for the pot. Mrs Green was now financially secure, but it seemed she'd traded one problem for another. At least Annie wouldn't have to go back to Harold's house. She was safe from his unwanted attentions. Thanks to Miss Catherine.

Annie avoided Miss Isobel, who spent the rest of the day in her room, complaining of a headache. Dinner was uneventful. Blackie was out. Miss Isobel and Miss Marie ate in Miss Isobel's suite on a tray. Mrs Carlisle and Annie ate in the kitchen, together. By nine o'clock sharp, Annie had cleared and washed the dinner dishes, laid the trays for the morning, and put away the linens that were delivered earlier by the laundress. She was just about to head upstairs when someone banged on the door.

It's Mum and Harold come for me. Annie's heart thudded as she undid her apron, hung it on the hook, and hurried to the door.

'Who is it?' Miss Isobel stood on the second-floor landing.

'I don't know, Isobel. I cannot see through doors.' Miss Catherine hurried down the stairs ahead of her. By the time she opened the door, the banging had become a loud relentless staccato.

'Blackie? What on earth –'

'So sorry. Forgot my key.' Mr Blackwell stumbled into the room. He lost his balance but righted himself at the last minute. He stood swaying, smiling at everyone, alcohol fumes emanating from him in waves.

'Annie, you can go on up to bed,' Miss Catherine said.

'Make some coffee first, Annie,' Miss Isobel said.

Annie turned to the kitchen.

'I don't want her seeing this, Isobel. She doesn't need to contend with a drunk.'

'Don't be ridiculous, Catherine. She's a sensible girl. She's seen Blackie drunk before. You and Marie are acting foolish over this girl. You know nothing of housekeeping, what's appropriate for someone of Annie's status to tend to,' Miss Isobel said.

Miss Catherine acted as though she hadn't heard Miss Isobel. 'Annie, go on up. I'll make Mr Blackwell some coffee.'

Annie didn't have to be told twice.

Chapter Eight

The next morning, Cat lay awake in her bed as the sun crept up. The windows sparkled and the wood furniture gleamed from Annie's polishing, but Cat didn't notice it. She spent the entire night reviewing her plan to switch her husband's documents, looking at it from every angle for problems and unforeseen scenarios. She imagined what she'd say if Isobel caught her in Benton's study, going through the safe. She would simply explain she was looking for her birth certificate or some other document. She had as much of a right to be in Benton's office as Isobel did. When Annie entered carrying a tray laden with food, Cat nodded, hoping that the girl would drop the tray and leave her alone.

'Thank you, Annie. I know you're busy this morning.'

They were interrupted by a knock on the door, before Marie pushed it open and entered the room, a sheepish look on her face.

'Annie, are you ready to help me today?'

'Of course,' Cat said. 'And since you're both here, there's something we need to discuss. I thought I'd leave for Lydia's this evening. I'll leave Annie with cab fare, and she can join me after the meeting tomorrow.'

'Very well,' Marie said.

'You can change your mind, Annie,' Cat said. 'Do you want to come with me this evening? Isobel can get help from the agency.'

'No, ma'am. I'll stay.'

'See that she gets her wages, will you?'

'Of course.' Marie put her arm around Annie. 'Now be a good girl and set up the tea service. I'll be right behind you.'

Once they were alone, Marie turned to Cat. 'You're not coming back, are you?'

Cat shook her head. 'No. And I'd appreciate it if you wouldn't tell Isobel. I'd like to speak to her and to Benton myself, when the time is right.'

'I hate to see you go, Catherine. I know Benton and Isobel have been difficult to live with, but I've always enjoyed your company.'

Dear Marie, the sweet underdog, the kind soul among the sour faces. 'I'll stay in touch, Marie. Isobel won't mind if you visit me. And if she does, we won't tell her.'

Marie gave Cat a wistful smile.

'I'm actually not feeling very well, so I think I'll spend the day resting. Don't anyone make a fuss. I'll be fine. I just need a good rest.'

'You do look exhausted, but nothing that a good lie-in won't cure. Very well. I'll leave you be. The meeting starts at a quarter to eleven, with Alicia speaking at precisely a quarter past. I hope we won't be too loud.' Marie looked at her watch.

'I'm not going to be sleeping, Marie. Just reading. Don't worry about me.'

'When do you want lunch? I'll see to a tray.'

'Please don't bother. If I want something, I'll simply fetch it myself.'

'I'll miss you, Catherine,' Marie said.

She and Marie hugged. Cat could feel the bones in Marie's back and was surprised at how frail she had become.

Cat shut the door and locked it behind her. She stood off to the side of her bedroom window, her eyes scanning

107

the garden square for Marlena X. Taxis rolled to a stop. Smartly dressed women came in groups and alone, up the path towards the Carlisle house. A photographer – Cat assumed it was the reporter from the *Times* – snapped photos of the guests as they headed up the walkway, like brides walking up the aisle.

At precisely seventeen minutes past eleven, Cat tucked the *Britannia* magazine under her arm and headed down the stairs, mindful of the sound of clinking teacups and the low murmur of women's voices. She let herself into Benton's office. Once inside, she closed the door, locked it, and listened for two minutes exactly. All she needed was Alicia to come searching for her. She felt the usual pang of guilt at the way she had treated her friend, but shook it off. More important things were in play now.

When no one interrupted her, she moved over to Benton's desk and squatted down to face the safe behind it. She used the combination that her husband had shared with her fifteen years earlier – their wedding anniversary – hoping that it still worked. She turned the dial to the final number, and with a click the safe popped open. There, on the top was an exact replica of the envelope that Reginald had given Cat yesterday. She was about to switch it and hurry away, when curiosity got the best of her.

Careful to keep things exactly as she found them, Cat pulled a stack of documents out of the safe. Many had been in there for decades and carried a musty smell that caused Cat to sneeze. Keeping them in order, she went through the pile of deeds, letters written to Benton by his grandfather, and Benton's childhood stamp collection.

At the very bottom of the pile was a thick envelope, a milky rectangle of fine paper. Cat recognised Freddy Sykes's childish handwriting scrawled across the front.

The message made her blood boil. *Benton, Allow this to serve as a gentleman's IOU – Two thousand pounds on my word. Cheers, F.* Freddy Sykes owed her husband quite a bit of money. Interesting, especially considering how stingy Benton was with her. After she placed everything back in the safe, she tucked the documents she switched back into the magazine, closed the safe, and moved over to the door, where she stood listening, not daring to breathe.

She heard Alicia, as she addressed the women passionately about the need for an orphanage devoted to educating the children, so they could have a means to support themselves when they came of age and ventured out into the world. Before her bout of influenza, Cat would have been the woman doing the speaking to the group.

Cat opened the door and peeked out into the hallway. Once sure that no one was about, she crept up the stairs and shut the bedroom door behind her. When she was safely inside her room, she exhaled, as an uncontrollable shudder of relief ran through her body. She sank down, her back sliding against the door as her knees buckled. In the back of her mind a frisson of hope bloomed. She had done something useful for the first time in her life, and taken one small step towards freedom. The risk had been immeasurable, but she had triumphed.

She was going to leave Benton. She knew that once she left the house, there would be no chance of a reconciliation. Benton would never take her back, even if he wouldn't divorce her. That was a risk she was willing to take. She stood up, brushed off her skirt, and moved across the room where she opened the curtains halfway. She put the *Britannia* magazine with the switched documents in her big handbag, thought better of it, and wedged the envelope up under her writing desk. No one would ever find it there.

She had followed instructions. Everything had gone according to plan. Now all she had to do was wait.

***

Thomas sat next to Sir Reginald on the fine leather seats as they slowly drove the streets of Kensington. At a nod from Sir Reginald, the driver turned onto the quiet block of houses. Neither man spoke until they drove past the Carlisle house, and saw the curtains in the upstairs window opened.

'She's made the switch,' Thomas said.

'I knew she'd succeed,' Reginald said. 'She's got her father's blood pumping through her veins.'

'Took a chance asking her,' Thomas said.

'I felt a duty to her father. She's married to a man who has nothing to do with her and she's tiring of the fundraising work she does. She's an intelligent woman, with no children, and no purpose in life,' Reginald said. 'I do believe everyone should know their purpose. Don't you?'

'So she's like a low-lying fruit?' Thomas didn't bother to hide the sarcasm in his voice.

'Something like that,' Reginald said. 'She's intuitive and reckless, but she's brave. We'll tame the recklessness out of her and make good use of the intuition. Her social contacts will be useful.'

'How will her social contacts be useful? If she divorces her husband, his friends won't touch her. I know these society types. They stick together.'

'Not divorcing. He won't give her a divorce. They are splitting up, living apart.' Sir Reginald kept his eyes forward. His hands clasped his cane, as if he were ready to swing it. 'I don't understand young people today, Tom. Don't understand them a bit. In any event, Alicia and Jeremy

110

Montrose have a large circle of friends, some of whom have become very passionate about Hitler this past few months.'

'And Mrs Carlisle can help you with this how?'

'Not sure,' Reginald said. 'She can start by simply observing, telling me what these people are up to.'

'Chloe?'

Sir Reginald glanced at Thomas. 'Chloe thinks that Mrs Carlisle is singularly unqualified for this sort of work.'

'Maybe she's right.'

'I don't think so,' Sir Reginald said. 'Chloe takes her orders from me.'

'But Chloe's handling Mrs Carlisle. If she doesn't have faith in her –'

The car slowed and pulled to the kerb near the entrance to the square near Cat's house.

'Not your problem, old boy. Make sure the switch goes according to plan. Leave Chloe alone. Report when necessary.'

Thomas got out of the car and headed into the park. He liked to walk among trees. It cleared his head and helped him sleep at night. He walked the perimeter of the square – which took him about forty minutes – watching for any sign of Marlena X. As if she would show herself. Thomas knew better.

Mrs Carlisle didn't know that she wouldn't be dealing with Reginald any more. Chloe St James would be running Cat's operations now. He was worried about the entire situation. He didn't know why. It seemed as though they were missing something important, something in play at the Carlisle house. And he didn't like the idea of Marlena X. For all he knew, she could be watching him right now. He found the bench where Mrs Carlisle and Reginald had been meeting for the past five years, and planted himself behind the thick trunk of a very old oak tree. He wanted to smoke, but he didn't. He waited, still and solid, ever watchful.

**

Cat knew something was wrong the minute she turned into the garden square. Reginald wasn't at their bench. Instead, a young woman with silky brown hair sat where Reginald should have been. She wore a linen suit and a smart hat, with the sheerest of veils over her eyes. Her shoes were of a fine suede, with a delicate strap across the top. Cat nodded at her, ready to walk past, when the young woman addressed her.

'Mrs Carlisle?' Her voice was low and sultry.

Cat stopped. 'Do I know you?'

'Reginald sent me.'

Cat panicked. Her mouth went dry. 'I don't know any Reginald.'

'Reginald had to go to France. And I've been out shopping for my family today. We needed apples. We seem to go through St Edmund's pippins. My husband loves them, and so do my children.' The woman waited for Cat to register the code word. 'Won't you sit, please, Mrs Carlisle?'

Cat sat down, reluctant and all of a sudden nervous.

'How did things go today? Any problems?' The woman smiled and acted as though she were discussing the weather.

'Rather well, actually,' Cat said. When she was sure that no one watched, she took the magazine out of her bag and handed it to the woman. The woman skimmed through the magazine, took the envelope from between its pages, and tucked it in her own bag.

'We have a problem.' The woman spoke in a light tone. Anyone who passed by would think that she and

Cat were discussing the mundane topics favoured by housewives all across England. She opened a fashion magazine and scooted close to Cat. As she spoke, she smiled and nodded, while pointing at an advertisement for rayon frocks. 'Your husband is going to bring home an extremely important document tonight. You need to do another switch for us.'

'Switch it when he's home?'

'Smile and act natural, Mrs Carlisle. Always assume you're being watched. This is important.'

Cat slowed her breath. She sat back on the bench and crossed her legs. 'May I?' She pointed to the fashion magazine. When the woman handed it to Cat, she flipped through the pages and held the magazine open at a full-page colour ad for women's shoes. 'I rather like these shoes,' she said. 'But yours are much finer. Where did you get them?'

She met the woman's eyes and didn't look away. The two women sized each other up. Reginald's minion, with her fine clothes and independent confidence, and Cat, a sophisticated socialite, who had the means to open doors this woman would never have access to, no matter how fine her clothes.

'Do you have a husband?' Cat asked.

The question caught the woman off guard. She hesitated and stumbled over her words.

'I didn't think so,' Cat said. 'I'm well aware of how important this is. I'm the one taking the risks here. I'm assuming you have a plan for me to switch the documents when everyone is home. If you'd be so kind as to tell me what that plan is, I'll be on my way.'

'Very well. Tonight after dinner you are to put some powder in your husband's drink. It's tasteless and odourless, so don't worry about that. After twenty minutes, he will be sound asleep. I will send you away with a document to replace the one that your husband brings home. Switch the document. That's all you need to do. Your husband won't know what you've done. The powder will make him sleep for the night. It won't be the first time he's spent the night passed out in his study. Tomorrow morning, you will come here at nine o'clock, as per usual. Sit on this bench. Feed the birds. An agent will take the document from you. That's it.'

'How will I know who the agent is?'

'He will say that it's good to see you and ask if you've recovered from your skiing accident in Switzerland. You'll respond that you haven't been to Switzerland in ages. Now repeat back what I just told you.'

Cat repeated what the woman had said to her, verbatim.

'Very good.' The woman put a straw shopping bag on the bench between them. It was stuffed with bread, leeks, and a worn-looking apple. 'The envelope that you'll switch and the sleeping powder are in the bottom of the bag. I cannot impress upon you how important this mission is. We rarely have someone without proper training do this type of work, Mrs Carlisle. Drug your husband and leave him be. Wait until everyone is out of the house and safely out of your way. Switch the documents. Keep your wits about you and you'll be fine.'

'Benton will know I've drugged him,' Cat said.

'Not likely.' The woman shook her head. 'He's been drinking since noon. He and his cronies went to the London Club after their meeting. They're still there. Tomorrow morning he'll wake up with a hangover and assume he just drank too much.'

'What about Isobel and Marie? Isobel hovers over Benton like a fussy mother,' Cat said.

'Isobel and her secretary will be gone this evening,' the woman said. 'We've arranged a dinner engagement, after

114

which she will be given a very generous donation to that orphanage she is so passionate about. Mr Blackwell will be working late at his shop, and the child who is your paid companion will be at the cinema with the neighbours' cook and maid.'

'How did you make all these arrangements?'

'With great care, Mrs Carlisle. That is how we get things done without getting caught. You are to carry out this mission according to the exact instructions I have given you. Have I made myself clear?' The woman smiled that fake smile. Cat wanted to slap her pretty face. An uncontrollable bubble of laughter laced with the tiniest amount of hysteria came unbidden out of Cat's mouth.

'Are you all right?' The woman looked at Cat with genuine concern. Cat ignored her.

'My husband and I haven't spoken in days. He's going to think it strange when I bring him something to eat and drink, as though all is well between us.'

'Apologise. Tell him you are sorry. Throw yourself on the sword, if you will.'

'He won't believe me,' Cat said. 'He'll laugh in my face and tell me to go to hell.'

'You look like someone who is rather adept at manipulation. I suggest you use those skills now. Bring your husband his milk or wine – it doesn't matter which. Convince him to drink it, Mrs Carlisle.' She gave Cat a penetrating look. 'Are you able to do this? I need to know now. If this is beyond your ability, we can make other arrangements.'

'Good day.' Cat stood up and grabbed the shopping bag. Energy crackled through her, like electricity arcing on a wire. Her senses hummed. She craved activity. She left the garden square and started walking. She had no destination in mind. She just walked, clipping along the pavement, her breath fast and hard as she stepped in time with it. She passed through the residential district and soon came to the shops. She ignored the throngs of people, who stepped out of her way like the parting of the sea.

Her senses were acute, receptive, buzzing with a pulsating, combustible heat. She smelled cooking meat from the café on the corner. She heard the leaves rustle in the afternoon breeze. The greens were lush, the sounds distinct, even the grey of the sky seemed rich and vibrant. Cat walked, clutching the shopping bag the woman left for her in a white-knuckled death grip.

At six o'clock, she found herself in front of a tea shop, her energy spent. She stepped in and found a quiet table in the back. She sat with her back to the wall, so she could scan the whole shop and watch the front door. She assumed she was being watched. She didn't care. She set the shopping bag between her feet, wrapping one of the handles around her ankle, just in case someone decided to grab it.

Cat was a professional now. She had a job to do and, for the first time since this madness with Reginald started, she felt confident in her ability to carry out these missions. She found them exhilarating. She would talk to Benton about their marriage – a conversation well overdue. She would make him think she loved him and wanted to make things right between them. Then she would leave him. She knew her heart would ache, but she would rather be free and broken-hearted than be reminded every day of what had gone wrong in her marriage and her life.

**

Annie sat at the table in the kitchen, a cup of tea steaming in front of her. She was exhausted from the day's labours.

116

Miss Isobel nearly swooned when Annie whipped up a perfect pound cake. Things were going well for her, too well. And now Catherine was leaving and Annie was going with her. Would they come back? What would Annie be expected to do while they were away? She wanted to ask Miss Catherine why they were leaving, but she didn't think it was her place to ask questions, especially of Mrs Carlisle. She found she rather liked the idea of leaving the Carlisle house. If she were lucky – and she believed she was – she would never lay eyes on Freddy Sykes again.

Be grateful, Annie. She stretched her legs, wriggling her toes in the new shoes that Miss Isobel had bought her. Alicia Montrose's speech dragged on. If she peeked her head around, Annie could see all the well-dressed ladies, in their angular hats of various colours and shapes, as they listened to Alicia Montrose's speech about the need for a Christian-based orphanage where 'the children could safely grow into productive citizens. We want them to leave our care with the ability and training to earn their way in the world. I know what you're thinking, but even the girls.'

They all sat utterly still, enraptured by the woman's words. Annie didn't understand them at all. She thought that if she had the money to support such a noble cause, she would simply give it over and be done with it. *Why all this show?* Adults were strange, indeed.

Her thoughts turned to Mrs Carlisle, as they had throughout the morning. Annie knew the role that Mrs Carlisle played in allowing her to stay. If it weren't for Mrs Carlisle, Annie in all likelihood would have returned to Harold Green's with her mother. Of course she would have run away, and heaven knew where she'd be now. She had visions of sleeping under a hawthorn bush in one of the many garden squares, trying to stay safe from the vagrants and criminals that her mother warned her about.

Annie was afraid of the night, but she was more afraid of her stepfather. She bit into a sandwich and tried to push away the continual niggling worry about Mrs Carlisle. Something wasn't right. Mrs Carlisle was – as Annie's grandmother used to say – wound tight as a spring.

Marie came in carrying a tray of empty cups and saucers. In the drawing room, Alicia Montrose's voice stopped, and polite applause followed.

'I'll get those, ma'am,' Annie said.

'We've conjured up a treat for you, Annie. How would you like to go to the cinema with Mrs Fieldings' cook and the kitchen maid, Claris?'

Annie and her mum had been to the cinema once. Annie loved the theatre, with its plush velvet seats. She loved people-watching almost as much as she enjoyed the movie.

'Miss Isobel and I are going out this evening. We may not be here when you return. We'll give you a key to the front door. You're to lock the door when you come in and leave the key on the hallway table.'

'Yes, ma'am. Thank you, ma'am,' Annie said. She filled the sink with water and added the dish soap and the drop of orange oil that Miss Isobel preferred.

'I'll fetch the rest of the dishes for you then,' Marie said.

Annie busied herself with the washing up, wishing she could shake this feeling of unease.

Chapter Nine

Cat let herself in the front door just as the clock chimed seven. She stopped outside Benton's study, listening for any sign of life. The only sound she heard was the clicking of the grandfather clock. She knew he was in there. She sensed his heartbeat. She tiptoed past the study and slipped upstairs, carrying the full shopping bag with her.

Once in her room, she locked the door behind her. After that, she listened, not daring to breathe, in case Benton followed her up. Silence. She unloaded the groceries, setting the food and vegetables on the counterpane. She put the envelope that she was to switch under the writing table and stuffed the packet of the powder she would use to drug Benton in her skirt pocket. She repacked the groceries and took the bag downstairs to the kitchen.

Someone – Annie probably – had left a generous portion of ham, potatoes in their jackets, carrots and green beans in a warming dish on the stove. There were two plates, which meant that one of them was for Benton. Without thinking, Cat prepared a plate for him. She hadn't been married for all these years without knowing some of Benton's habits. When he drank in quantity – which he made a habit of doing more often lately – he liked his food. She also opened a good bottle of Bordeaux, put three glasses on the tray, and carried the tray to his office.

'Come,' he said in response to her knock. She opened the door and let herself in.

'What do you want?' He sat at his desk with a book open in front of him, reading spectacles slipping down his nose, an empty snifter on the desk. The envelope she needed to switch was on the corner in plain sight. Cat took that as a courage-bolstering omen.

'I thought you might want something to eat,' she said. She tried to keep her voice light.

'Why so solicitous?' Benton narrowed his eyes and stared at Cat. 'Are you in some sort of trouble?'

'Ben.' Cat hadn't called her husband by his pet name in years. She set the tray down and took the chair opposite him. 'I want to talk to you.'

He lit a cigarette, leaned back in his chair, and crossed his legs. 'So talk.'

'I wanted to say I am sorry for my part about the way things are between us. We're both miserable. We don't have to be.'

'If you're going to tell me you want a divorce, you know my answer. No Carlisle has ever divorced. I will not be the first.'

'Wait,' Cat said. 'I'd like it if you would just listen to me, please. Don't get angry and don't react. Because, Ben, if we're going to stay married, I'd like to try and fix things between us. Things would be a lot simpler and easier for everyone if we were civil to each other. I know I'm difficult to live with. I'm stubborn, and am one of those women who are better off unmarried. But here we are. I can live in a loveless marriage, but I don't think I can live in a cruel one. I always thought we were better than that. I know you don't love me any more, but maybe we could find our way back to each other as friends.' She

120

couched her words as a question, and let them hang in the air between them.

'I know you won't divorce me, and I don't care. I'm going to go live with Lydia. I can't bear this house any longer. You can have your freedom. You'll be happier without me here – you know that. We used to love each other, Ben. I'm asking for your understanding on this one issue. I'll be the dutiful wife when you need me by your side. But there's no need to live in the same house. You've got Isobel to run things for you. You don't need me any more.'

The fact Benton didn't belt out an immediate and vociferous no encouraged Cat. He stared at her, as if scrutinising her request for any underlying deceit. Providence chose this minute to smile on Cat. A wave of nostalgia washed over her; she thought back to the time so long ago when they loved each other, when they looked forward to the future. She hoped that Benton would see that.

'Have you taken a lover?' he asked.

'Of course not,' Cat said. She didn't mention Benton's well-known affair with Trudy Ashworth. It seemed there were two very different sets of rules for men and women in British society. Men were allowed to take a mistress, and if a man had enough money and influence, he could even be seen in public with her. A woman could take a lover, but discretion was mandatory.

'Will you stay with Lydia permanently?' Benton asked.

'For now at least. After a while I'll rent a flat somewhere, away from your circle of friends.'

Benton didn't say anything for a long time. He smoked his cigarette and stared at her. Cat got up, and with her back to him, she poured out two glasses of Bordeaux.

With sleight of hand, she dumped the packet of powder into one of the glasses. It disappeared into the thick red wine. She turned and handed Benton the glass. He took it from her, held it up to the light, and studied it.

Cat's heart pounded. *My God, he's going to notice that something is wrong with the colour of the wine.*

'My favourite Bordeaux,' he said, lowering the glass again. 'Our marriage wouldn't have failed if you hadn't been so stubborn. But I married you. And I will stay married to you.'

'I know.' Her words came out as a whisper. This wasn't the time to communicate how she felt, to pick a fight. Cat reminded herself that her little speech was simply for the benefit of getting close enough to slip Benton the sleeping powder.

She thought of the years she'd spent waiting for Benton to come to her, waiting for him to realise that he still loved her, and that their shared grief could make them stronger. In her fantasy, he would apologise and say what a fool he had been to let their love slip away. She had continued to love him, despite the pain of his indifference towards her. Even though she boxed the emotion away and tucked the box deep in her psyche, she could have pulled it out. With a word from him, the love could have been rekindled. She would have forgiven Benton his trespasses and resumed their relationship as man and wife. The box lay open before her now, but it was empty. And much to Cat's surprise, the love she felt for her husband was no more.

'Go and stay with Lydia. I'll have my banker arrange a sufficient allowance for you first thing tomorrow. You're obviously miserable here. At least Isobel will be pleased.'

'Thank you,' Cat said.

'Civility.' Benton held up his glass.

'Civility,' Cat said. They'd struck a bargain and drank to it.

They were discussing the financial arrangements when Benton's speech started to slur.

'What's the matter?' she asked.

'Need to get some fresh air.' Benton stood up on wobbly legs. When his knees buckled, Cat eased him back down into the chair behind his desk. When he slipped into unconsciousness, she gently arranged his head so it rested on his arm, a position she and Isobel had found him in on more than one occasion of late.

After she saw her unconscious husband situated, she poured wine into the third glass and set it and the open bottle of Bordeaux on the desk near Benton, leaving the tray of food near the door. She took the two other glasses into the kitchen, washed them, and put them away. Cat hurried up the stairs, grabbed the envelope, and carried it back to Benton's office. She switched it, careful to leave Benton's desk exactly how it was.

If Benton remembered their conversation tomorrow, it wouldn't matter. Cat would be gone. She hoped he would conclude he had passed out while they were talking, and she'd just left him, as she had done so many times before. Tomorrow she would meet Reginald's agent, collect her money, and make plans for a new life without Benton.

She stared at him before she left the room. She spoke her truth, even though she knew he wouldn't hear. 'I don't love you any more, Ben. I stopped long ago. And I could care less whether or not we remain friends.'

Back up in her room, Cat tucked the switched documents in her large handbag. She took the suitcase out from under her bed and enough clothing to last for a few days. She didn't know how long she would stay at her aunt's, but she knew she wasn't coming back to the Carlisle house – not to live. She'd arrange to get the rest of her things when she got herself sorted. She took a sheet of paper out of her writing desk and left Annie a note with Aunt Lydia's address. She stuck some notes in an envelope, sealed it, and put it under Annie's pillow.

Cat watched from her bedroom window as the blue taxi pulled to kerb.

Cat grabbed her suitcase and carried it down the stairs. She left Benton's door open. He was still asleep at his desk, his head resting on his arm, dead to the world. Isobel would find him that way and think nothing of it. She pulled the study door shut.

'Good evening, ma'am. Let me carry your case, if you please.' The driver smelled of cigarettes and cheap pomade, but he had kind eyes and whistled a cheerful tune as he carried Cat's suitcase to the waiting taxi.

'Where to, miss?' The man held the back door open for Cat.

She could have gone to Lydia's, where she knew a room awaited her. But she felt vulnerable given the documents she was carrying. What if Marlena X was following her? What if Marlena X was watching her now? Cat would never expose her aunt to any danger. Never mind that Aunt Lydia would take one look at her and see that something wasn't right. She would start questioning Cat the moment she set eyes on her. She felt like a ship cast out to sea, and she knew that she needed to navigate this ocean on her own. She reached in her handbag and found the police whistle on the heavy chain. She hung it around her neck, tucking it out of sight underneath the silk blouse she wore.

'The Milestone,' she said.

124

Benton and Cat had been married at the Milestone. The irony of staying there on the night she left her husband wasn't lost on Cat. The cab driver acted as though he wanted to chat, so Cat leaned back in the seat and closed her eyes.

After she had signed the register, Cat allowed herself to be swept up to one of the suites. She explained that she wished to not be disturbed and turned down the offer of a maid who would tend to her clothes and shoes. Finally she lay on top of the bed, knowing that the competent, discreet staff would respect her wishes. She was safe here. At least for the moment. She tried to sleep, but couldn't still her pounding heart.

If she was going to continue in this line of work, she would have to learn to disassociate herself from the potential for danger. She wouldn't be any good to anyone if she were too exhausted to function. She ran herself a bath, adding the lavender salts provided to all the guests. She soaked until the water turned cold.

Sleepy now, she crawled naked between the fine linen sheets, savouring the weight of the thick eiderdown. She thought of Benton and their lost love and of the children they were denied. She remembered the pain, etched the feel of it into her brain, knowing that it was time to move away from that, time to embrace whatever was to happen next. A quiet tear dripped onto the pillow as Cat drifted off to sleep.

**

Thomas didn't tell Sir Reginald that he intended on keeping Cat under surveillance until she delivered the documents safely into Chloe St James's hands. Sir

Reginald would have ordered him to stay away, and Thomas would have defied him. It wouldn't be the first time that Thomas and Sir Reginald didn't agree on procedural matters, but Thomas refused to put Catherine Carlisle in jeopardy simply because Chloe St James didn't realise the gravity of Marlena X's involvement.

Soon Thomas would be finished with Sir Reginald, Chloe, and the influential men who funded this operation. He found he was actually looking forward to going back to work for Maxwell Knight. He thought of Catherine Carlisle, by his side for future operations. M would like Mrs Carlisle. He had a soft spot for a pretty face and a sharp albeit irreverent mind.

Those thoughts ran through Thomas's head as he walked from his flat to the Carlisle home and tucked himself behind the trunk of a large tree in the garden square across the street. He had stood there for three hours, watching the house and keeping an eye peeled for Marlena X. He watched as Catherine came home from her meeting with Chloe, carrying the shopping bag. He saw the light go on in the room that he knew to be Catherine's, and guessed at what went on in the house, while he stood across the street, helpless to do anything.

When a taxi cruised to a stop in front of the house and Mrs Carlisle met it, suitcase in hand, Thomas had panicked. Luckily, an available taxi drove by just as Mrs Carlisle sped off into the night.

'Follow that taxi,' he instructed the driver. He knew Mrs Carlisle had an aunt in Bloomsbury and was surprised when they followed the cab to the Milestone. The hotel overlooked Kensington Gardens, and had a somewhat illustrious past. Thomas knew a fellow writer who was absolutely obsessed with the place and swore it was haunted from its use as an asylum in the nineteenth century. Thomas had the good grace not to scoff at his friend's belief in the supernatural, but he had tuned out the subsequent ghost stories that grew more outlandish the more alcohol was consumed.

'You can pull over here, please.' Thomas watched as the hotel staff swarmed around Mrs Carlisle, one man taking her bag, another holding the front door open for her. The Milestone prided itself on discretion and security. Mrs Carlisle would be safer there than anywhere else in London. It would have been remiss – and potentially dangerous – for her to go to her aunt's while the documents were in her possession. He gave her credit for her foresight.

He paid the driver and decided to walk back to his flat on Kensington high street. He would sleep for a few hours and be outside the Milestone, refreshed and ready to resume his vigil in the morning. Thomas passed candlelit restaurants with white linen tablecloths, where men in dinner suits and women decked out in jewels drank champagne and ate decadently before dancing the night away at one of the many clubs. A man carrying a saxophone on his shoulder got out of a taxi and nearly collided with Thomas. Jazz was in the air. On the surface, England flourished, impervious to the disaster that was percolating in Germany.

Thomas had taken a hiatus from MI5 and had spent the last seven years working for Sir Reginald, the leader of a coterie of men who foresaw the troubles with the Treaty of Versailles, men who had known all along that another war would come. After spending two years in Germany on a reconnaissance mission, Thomas knew first-hand what Hitler was capable of. He was amazed that English newspapers hadn't been reporting on it in more detail. Adolf Hitler was a menace. The Englishmen who were openly in support of appeasement frightened Thomas. By agreement, this was Thomas's last assignment for Reginald and his group. Max Knight had welcomed him back to MI5 with open arms. He services were needed now.

His mind strayed to Mrs Carlisle. He thought of her straight back, her long slender frame, and the gentle curve of her calves where they tapered into her well-shaped ankles. He decided that she was indeed lovely to look at. She had attracted Benton Carlisle, a renowned bachelor, who had sworn to never marry. According to the gossip columns, Benton Carlisle had taken one look at Catherine and had proposed marriage after only two months.

Benton Carlisle was a lucky man. Thomas stopped himself cold when he recognised the emotion that Catherine Carlisle invoked in him. Desire. He marvelled at it, an alien emotion that he hadn't experienced in years. During the war, he'd met a woman in France, Nina, a nurse who also drove an ambulance. Her courage and grace under fire amazed him to this day. They had been lovers for five months. Thomas thought they might marry after the war, until he got word that Nina had been shot in the head while transporting injured soldiers from the battlefield. Now he felt the stir of desire again, knowing while he acknowledged it, that it would be unrequited. Mrs Carlisle was off limits. That was the rule.

As he approached his flat, a fresh-faced young couple stepped out of a café. The man put his arm around the woman and pulled her close to him.

'We're going to have a fine life, Hen. Let's tell our parents tomorrow and get married soon,' he said.

128

'Oh, William,' was all the girl said. They stopped, and William pulled the woman into his arms. They kissed with the passion reserved for the young.

Thomas smiled in spite of himself. The vision of the young man going off to war played in his mind, but he pushed those thoughts away. Thomas was an expert at pushing thoughts away. He unlocked the door and stepped into the lobby of his building. Sofas and chairs were arranged in the common area, with the latest newspapers fanned out on the tables. He had never encountered any of his neighbours in this area. He wondered if they were friendly to each other, if they shared a cup of tea and discussed world events during the day when he wasn't around. He laughed. Maybe one day he would find out.

He headed up to his room, kicked off his shoes, and sat down on the top of the bed. A large knot formed at the base of his neck. He massaged it.

Tomorrow he would make sure Mrs Carlisle's drop went as planned. Then – as instructed by Sir Reginald – he would turn his attention to Michael Blackwell. Reginald's intelligence suggested someone in the Carlisle house was in contact with Marlena X. Thomas intended to find out who that person was. He took a deep breath and lay back on his pillow. He closed his eyes, a pantomime of the sleep that he craved but that he knew wouldn't come.

Chapter Ten

Annie loved spy films best. The bravery of those who risked their lives to serve their country filled her with pride, especially the women spies. Annie believed that women could do anything men could. She told that to her father once and he agreed with her. After seeing *Dark Journey*, Annie was captivated by dark-haired beauty Vivien Leigh. Miss Leigh played a French spy during the war. She was so brave, and she put her country before the man she loved. Annie thought of Miss Catherine, and how she stood up to Freddy Sykes. She thought if there was another war, Miss Catherine would make a wonderful spy.

She thought about these things as she let herself into the Carlisle house. She stood silent for a moment, listening for any signs of life in the house. As she stood in the quiet dark, she wondered if she would make a good spy. Would she be brave enough? These thoughts ran through her head as she took off her coat and carried it upstairs.

After she washed her face and cleaned her teeth, she reached under her pillow for her nightgown and found the envelope with her name written across the top. She tore it open and read Miss Catherine's note. Tomorrow morning she would pack her things, and use the money Miss Catherine left to take a taxi to Bloomsbury. Annie decided to do her morning chores, ask Miss Isobel for her wages, and leave the Carlisle house at noon. She felt very grown up and in charge of her life.

She dreamt she was in her old house. She was in her room painting, secure in the knowledge that downstairs her dad was in his chair with the newspaper and her mum was in the kitchen making an apple pie. Someone rapped on the door. She waited, to see if her father would open it. But the knocking grew louder.

Annie awoke with a start. She wasn't in her childhood room. She was in her room at the Carlisles', and someone was indeed pounding on the front door. She sat up, wondering if she should get it. *What if it's Freddy Sykes?* She decided to stay right where she was, thank you very much. She was alone in the house. It wasn't her place to answer the door.

She sat up, alert, listening. Soon Isobel's bedroom door slammed and her heavy footsteps pounded across the landing and down the stairs, followed by Marie's lighter ones. Annie got up and stepped out in the corridor, where she could peer around the corner and see into the entryway below.

'Who in the world is at the door at this hour?' Marie asked. She followed Isobel down the stairs.

'And why isn't Benton answering?' Isobel said. 'Really this is too much.'

'It's Blackie,' Marie said. 'He's probably forgotten his key.'

'He's probably inebriated,' Isobel said. 'I'm going to discuss this with Benton. Blackie needs medical help. He's been drowning his pain in brandy since he arrived. I'm afraid he's going to drink himself to death.'

'Maybe Benton would let him get some treatment,' Marie said. 'I've heard they have hospitals where you can get a cure. It's a very difficult course of treatment –'

'Blackie, what are you doing?' Isobel's voice was kind.

'Forgot my key.' Hiccup. Hidden in the shadows, Annie peered around the corner at the scene downstairs. Blackie stepped into the hallway. He could barely stand. 'Cousin Isobel, sorry to awake – woke – you.' He fell sideways and hit the wall. 'Had a bit of whisky with the chaps from the shop.'

'Oh, for heaven's sake.' Isobel grabbed Blackie's arm and helped him to stand. 'Marie, take him to the sofa in the drawing room. I'll make him some coffee.'

'– thank you and Cousin Ben for taking me in. So grateful.' Blackie was so drunk he could barely form a sentence. 'So lucky to have family. So. Lucky.'

Isobel knocked on Benton's door. 'Ben?' She knocked again, louder this time. 'Benton? Are you in there?'

Annie heard a loud groan and a cry. 'Help!' Her heart stopped and she couldn't move her feet. She watched, still as a statue, as Miss Isobel hurried away, only to come back seconds later with a key. She unlocked the door to Mr Carlisle's study and hurried in. Annie could just make out Benton's voice. 'That bitch put something in my wine.'

Annie ran back up to her tiny room and locked herself in. She lay down and pretended to be asleep. Minutes later she heard Miss Isobel's voice again. Annie got out of her bed and padded barefoot on the cold floor into Miss Catherine's room. She switched on the light.

'I demand you unlock this door immediately!' Miss Isobel pounded on the door so hard the picture hanging on the wall near it fell to the ground, the glass shattering into a million splinters.

Annie stood still for a moment, unable to move, fondling the locket that hung around her neck. She opened the door. Miss Isobel pushed Annie aside and stepped across the threshold, nearly knocking her down. She stood in the middle of the room, fists clenched, eyes wild with fury. Annie's heart pounded. Miss Isobel moved in a slow circle, studying the room like a hawk ready to swoop on the unsuspecting mouse in the field. Marie arrived in the doorway, her face pale, her eyes frightened.

'Izzy, what's happened?' She spoke in a gentle voice.

'She's tried to murder my brother.' Miss Isobel went to the writing desk and opened the drawers, rifling through them.

Marie cast her eyes on Annie, who all of a sudden wished she could slip back into her own room, under the summer quilt with its bright colours, and sleep until this nightmare passed.

'I don't believe that for one minute, and neither do you.' Marie stepped into the room and put a gentle hand on Isobel's arm. 'Come on. We must see to Benton.'

'Benton is passed out in his office. He can barely stand. It seems his wife brought him a bottle of wine and put something in it,' Isobel said. Something about the calm of her voice frightened Annie. She didn't know what to do. If she moved, Isobel might notice her. She might accuse her of something. She waited, quiet and still, with a forced poise that she didn't feel. She watched as Isobel walked over to the perfectly made bed. She pointed to it. 'She hasn't been to bed.'

'But it's early yet,' Miss Marie said. 'Maybe she's gone to a cinema. Her handbag is gone.'

'She's tried to kill him. I know it.' Miss Isobel moved over to the armoire that held Mrs Carlisle's clothes. She opened both drawers and rummaged through the neat rows of dresses and suits. She pulled the hats off their shelves one by one, looking into each one as though searching for a clue. 'She's packed a bag.'

When Miss Isobel started to rummage through the drawers that contained Miss Catherine's underthings, Miss Marie put a hand on her arm and spoke in a soft voice, as though she were speaking to a child. 'She was going to Lydia's, remember? Izzy, you'll drive yourself mad with this. You know Benton's been at his club drinking all day. It's the day of his monthly meeting. Remember? This isn't the first time he's slept in his office. It won't be his last –'

'No.' Miss Isobel pushed Miss Marie's arm away. 'She's drugged him. Benton said as much. I believe my brother.' She took one last survey of the room.

Isobel's eyes lit on Annie. 'You there, get dressed. Go downstairs and make a pot of strong tea.' She turned on Marie. 'Go to my medicine cabinet and get the ipecac. Benton must be the priority now. I'll deal with Catherine later.'

Annie washed her face, dressed in a hurry, and rushed downstairs. She passed the drawing room, where Blackie was sprawled out, snoring in a rhythmic crescendo. Annie boiled the water and made the tea. It seemed to take for ever to steep. When it was ready, she added milk and sugar. She didn't bother with a tray, just took the cup and a plate with a thick slice of bread and some butter. Her mum always said that sweet tea with bread and butter would cure anything.

The door to Mr Carlisle's study was open. Annie stepped inside and set the cup and plate on a tray that rested atop a bookcase. She moved over to the corner near the window, out of everyone's way, and settled in to wait. Mr Carlisle looked as though he were dead. He rested his

134

head on the desk, cradling it in his bent arm. Annie saw the wine bottle, the empty glass. She wondered what it all meant.

Miss Isobel stood behind the desk, one hand on her brother's shoulder. She rubbed his back with the other and made cooing noises. Miss Marie fiddled with a bottle of ipecac. She put a measure of it in a glass of water and handed it to Miss Isobel.

'Ben, wake up. You need to drink this.'

Mr Carlisle barely managed to lift his head up, but Isobel forced him into a sitting position and poured the water down his throat. He swallowed some. Most of it ran down the front of his shirt.

'Smelling salts,' Isobel barked. Marie handed them over, the nurse to Isobel's doctor. Isobel waved them under Benton's nose. They revived him. He opened bleary eyes and stared at his sister. 'Try and drink this, Ben. If she's drugged you, you need to bring it up.' She held the glass to his lips and this time he was able to drink half of the glass without spilling it.

'No more,' he said.

'Finish it,' Miss Isobel said. 'Trust me.' She held the glass to her brother's lips, but Mr Carlisle took it from her and, with a shaking hand, tipped the glass back and drank until it was empty. 'Now we wait. It takes fifteen minutes or so.' She took a flannel cloth from Miss Marie and dabbed her brother's forehead.

'You can go to bed now, Annie,' Miss Marie said. Miss Isobel nodded.

Annie fled to the safety of her room. She crawled back under the quilt, but try as she might, she couldn't go back to sleep. When the grandfather clock in the hallway struck midnight, Annie decided to go downstairs and get herself a cup of hot milk. She put on her dressing gown, and tiptoed into the hall. The house was quiet now. She headed down the stairs, until she heard voices coming from Mr Carlisle's room. Annie tucked herself into one of the alcoves and eavesdropped. She knew that listening in to other's conversations was wrong, but she couldn't stop herself.

'I need your help, Ben,' Miss Isobel pleaded. 'If this gets out, I'll be ruined. Alicia Montrose will shun me. My life as I know it will be over.'

Mr Carlisle spoke in a softer voice. Annie strained to hear what he said.

'Alicia Montrose is the least of your worries. She doesn't care who you sleep with, Isobel. You should know that.'

'I'm begging you, as a sister. It's not too much. Let's pay and end this once and for all.'

Mr Carlisle spoke. His words flew hard and sharp, like arrows. 'That's just the problem, Isobel. Blackmailers don't stop. You'll pay now, and they'll come back for more and continue on this way until there's nothing left. Why are you protecting this person? Tell me who's doing this to you, and I'll take care of it.'

'And ruin me in the process,' Isobel said.

'You should have been more discreet. Now if you don't mind I feel as though I'm going to be sick –'

'It's not polite to eavesdrop.' A voice whispered in her ear. Annie jumped. Miss Marie. How long had she been there?

'I'm sorry. I didn't mean to – I couldn't sleep. I wanted milk, and I heard shouting –' Annie wanted to die with shame.

'It's all right, child. I heard the shouting, too. Now go back to bed. All will be well in the morning.'

136

'Yes, ma'am.' She hurried back to her room and crawled into bed. But sleep didn't come. She was still awake when the sun crept into the sky, and for the first time since she'd been working at the Carlisle house, she did not look forward to the new day.

Annie found Miss Isobel and Miss Marie in the kitchen. Miss Isobel was drinking tea and reading the newspaper while Miss Marie cracked eggs into a skillet. Annie watched them for a moment, taking in the cosy domesticity, before she stepped into the room.

'Miss Isobel?'

She peered at Annie over the top of her paper. 'Yes?'

'I'll be going to Miss Carlisle's aunt's today. I thought I'd do my chores this morning before I leave,' Annie said. She stood with her hands clasped in front of her and waited for Miss Isobel's certain condemnation.

'Very well. Thank you for staying the morning and for your help last night. I'll get your wages before you leave.' She buried herself in the paper. Annie did her best to disguise the relief that washed over her.

'If you'll start in Mr Carlisle's study, I'll have breakfast for you when you've finished,' Marie said.

'Thank you.' Annie grabbed her box of supplies and hurried to the study.

She knocked twice before she opened the door to Mr Carlisle's office. It was dark and still. Usually Marie opened the curtains and the windows in this room first thing, to let fresh air in. She must have forgotten this morning. Annie wouldn't blame her for that. Last night's events had thrown the entire household off the regular routine.

Annie walked across the room and threw the curtains open in one fell swoop, flooding the room with morning

137

light. She looked at the street below her, and wondered – not for the first time – how different the streets in Kensington were compared to the grit and grime in Bermondsey. Here the streets glistened. Every single house as far as Annie could see had a front stoop that had been scrubbed in the early morning hours. The front doors shone; the kick plates on them, mostly brass, shimmered.

She turned and saw the room in the light for the first time. Her eyes registered the sight before her, but her brain couldn't quite take it in. She saw Mr Carlisle sprawled on the floor in front of his desk. She saw the gash over his eye and the blood, so much blood. He stared at her with a blank, lifeless gaze. The room undulated in dizzying waves.

Annie heard a scream. It took a second for her to realise that it had come from her. She backed out of the room, her breath coming in hard, jagging sobs. She turned, tripped on her skirt, and fell to her knees. She scrambled to her feet and took off running. She didn't even think about it. She just ran without looking where she was going. Mr Blackwell was coming down the hall towards the ruckus.

He grabbed Annie's shoulders before she collided with him. She looked at him, her eyes wide with terror.

'What is it?'

'Dead.' Annie heaved. 'He's dead. In the room.'

'What's going on?' Miss Isobel stood in the hallway. 'What's wrong with Annie?'

'He's dead.'

'What did you say?' Miss Isobel moved close to Annie. She bent down and looked in her eyes. 'Who's dead?'

'Mr Carlisle,' Annie said. Her voice so quiet. Her stomach cramped. She prayed she wouldn't be sick all over Miss Isobel's carpet.

They all moved back to the study, Annie herded by Mr Blackwell, who placed an arm around Annie's shoulders. Miss Isobel went into the study first. Annie didn't want to go any closer, but Mr Blackwell seemed to pull her along. They stood in the doorway and watched as Miss Isobel hurried over to her brother, Marie at her heels. She squatted next to her brother.

'No, Benton? No,' she said. She lifted his head and positioned his body so she could cradle him next to her heart, like a baby. Miss Isobel's grief mesmerised Annie. Try as she might, she couldn't look away. Miss Isobel made crooning sounds and started to rock back and forth, clinging to her brother, keening, not caring that her blouse, her cheek, and her lips were now covered in his blood.

'Marie, do something. She can't carry on like that,' Mr Blackwell said.

Miss Marie gave Blackie a helpless look before she took a tentative step towards Miss Isobel. She put a hand on her shoulder and spoke in a gentle voice. 'Izzy, come dear. We need to leave Benton now. You need to get cleaned up before we call the police.'

Blackie's arm tightened around Annie at the mention of the police. Annie glanced up at him just in time to see the look of sheer panic that passed through his eyes. And just like that it was gone. Blackie walked over to Miss Isobel. He squatted down, so they were at eye level.

'Isobel, come on, love.'

Miss Isobel gently placed Benton's corpse on the floor. She took Blackie's outstretched hand and allowed him to help her up. Once on her feet she looked at Annie, Mr Blackwell, and Miss Marie, a pitiful, childlike look of expectance on her face. She threw her head back and let out a primordial wail that caused the hair on the back of Annie's neck to stand up.

'Come with me, Annie. You've seen enough. Just lean on me, child.' They walked together, Mr Blackwell holding Annie fast, keeping her on her feet, until they reached the drawing room. After Annie was situated on the couch, Mr Blackwell took two glasses. He poured a small bit of brandy in one glass, and a large dollop in the other. He brought both glasses to the loveseat where Annie sat. She had started to tremble. Blackie handed her one of the glasses.

'Drink this.'

Annie drank a tentative sip. It seared a trail of fire in her throat and left a spreading warmth in her belly.

'That's awful,' she said.

Mr Blackwell finished his brandy in one go. He took Annie's glass and set it on the marble-topped table. A knitted shawl that belonged to Miss Isobel was tossed in the corner. Blackie took it now and draped it across Annie's shoulders. Annie thought that Miss Isobel wouldn't like anyone using her shawl, but she couldn't form the words to express this. She found she didn't care about Miss Isobel any more. Annie sat in a state of suspension, as though she were outside herself and had no control over her body. She heard footsteps and the sounds of Miss Isobel's sobs, as she allowed Marie to lead her upstairs. She shut her eyes tight, thinking that if she opened them, this would all go away, before she immediately chastised herself for acting like a child. This was real. Mr Carlisle was dead.

Annie sat still and quiet until Marie came back downstairs. 'Is Annie all right?'

'She's had a shock, poor thing. How's Isobel?'

'Better. She's upset, but that's understandable. I am going to call the police,' Miss Marie said.

Mr Blackwell's face turned white as a winter snow.

'Blackie?' Marie's voice questioned.

He didn't respond. He stared into the empty glass at the table.

'Are you all right, Mr Blackwell?' Annie asked.

Startled, he looked up. He stared at Annie as though he didn't know who she was.

'Yes, Annie,' he said. 'Just a bit shaken. Will you excuse me? There are some things I should see to.' He stood up and, without waiting for Annie's response, headed towards the door.

Annie shivered, cold again from the deep chill that encircled her heart. She couldn't stop thinking of the blank look in Mr Carlisle's lifeless eyes. She wondered why Mr Blackwell was frightened of the police.

'Where do you think you're going, Blackie?' Miss Isobel stood in the doorway. She stared at Blackie with red-rimmed eyes. Annie didn't like the colour of her skin, but she had changed her clothes and pinned up her hair. She had applied lipstick, which looked like a red slash against her white skin.

'I was just –'

'You'll stay here with us. We need to stand united when the police get here. That woman murdered my brother, and I intend to see her prosecuted. The police have a tendency to make a fuss where one isn't necessary. I need everyone here, standing behind me, showing support. And Blackie, you're the man of the house now.'

'Of course, Isobel,' Blackie said. 'Whatever you need. I am at your disposal, but I hardly think Catherine –'

'I'm going to be with my brother. I don't want him left alone.' Miss Isobel saw Annie, as if for the first time. 'You poor child. This must be so difficult for you. I know you think highly of Catherine.'

Annie didn't know what Miss Carlisle meant.

'Catherine did this,' Miss Isobel said. She let her gaze travel around the group, Marie, Blackie, and Annie. She let it linger for a second on each of them, as if making eye contact would assure their opinion on the issue. No one dared disagree with Isobel Carlisle.

'I don't know what you mean,' Annie said.

'Annie, you know as well as I do that Catherine was going to leave my brother. She didn't have the courage to come right out and say, but she was leaving us. I can only imagine they had some sort of a row –'

'Izzy, stop,' Marie said. 'We don't know that.' She stepped towards Isobel and once again placed a gentle hand on her arm, the same gesture she used when Isobel was huddled over Benton's body. Isobel hadn't minded the physical contact then. Now she pushed Marie's hand away.

'No, Marie. Do not try to protect her. She murdered my brother. I intend to see justice done. Now, if you'll wait here, I'll call the police. After that, I'm going to be with my brother's body. I don't want him to be alone.' She turned around at the last minute and addressed them. 'And just so we're clear on this issue, my family has taken each and every one of you into this house, given you financial help, shelter, and comfort. I expect your support on this.' She walked away from them, sure in the knowledge that they would do her bidding.

'Excuse me,' Marie said. She hurried after Isobel, white-faced and frantic, gently closing the door behind her.

Fifteen minutes later, Miss Marie and Annie sat in the drawing room, untouched cups of tea between them, unsure what to do without Miss Isobel to bark out orders. Annie numb and in shock, sat in silence, while Miss Marie sobbed gently into her handkerchief. Every now and then she would shake her head and mutter incomplete sentences, 'I just don't know … I can't imagine … What will Izzy …'

Mr Blackwell excused himself to use the telephone in Miss Isobel's suite and make arrangements to be away from his shop for a few days.

Miss Isobel came into the room, startling Marie and Annie out of their silence. 'The police have come,' she said. 'Annie, please put a tray together. Tea and biscuits. We'll see them in here. Marie, fetch Blackie. He's still making his telephone calls.' Miss Isobel put her hand on Miss Marie's shoulder. 'Come with me. We'll face them together. I won't have them tramping through this house and disrupting us. They'll have to be managed carefully.'

Annie poured milk in a pitcher and put out the rest of yesterday's biscuits. She carried the tray to the drawing room, where she was met by Isobel's imperious voice.

'Of course, I'll make myself available for a statement. We all will. The house will be in mourning, and I've preparations to see to. Perhaps you can come back tomorrow? Or we can come to you, if that's more convenient –'

'Madam, if you please.' The voice was well modulated and not the least bit agitated at Miss Isobel's tone. 'Take a seat.'

Three policemen were in the drawing room. One of them wore a uniform. He stood near the door. Another man, this one in a suit, took the winged chair near the fireplace. He took a small leather notebook out of his pocket, and held a pencil, ready to take notes. Miss Isobel and Miss Marie sat on the couch. Miss Isobel sat with her arms across her chest, a surly look on her face. Marie fidgeted. Mr Blackwell sat on the other winged chair. He lit a cigarette. Annie noticed his hand trembled as he did so. The third policeman, the man who was doing the talking, remained standing. He wasn't a tall man, but there was an inexplicable strength about him. He addressed the group.

'I'm Detective Chief Inspector Bellerose.' He met Annie and helped her set the tray on the sideboard. 'Miss Havers?'

'Yes, sir,' Annie said.

'Have a seat, please. Next to Mr Blackwell, if you would.' He pointed to the footstool next to Blackie's chair.

Annie looked at Miss Isobel, not quite sure if she should do as the man requested, but Miss Isobel wouldn't meet Annie's gaze. She stared at Chief Inspector Bellerose, her cheeks blazing. Annie sat.

'I'll be leading the investigation into Mr Carlisle's murder.' Chief Inspector Bellerose clasped his hands behind his back. 'Given the nature of Mr Carlisle's work, we are going to try to find out what happened to him, and see justice done – of course, with the least amount of fuss. I am familiar with Mr Carlisle's work and realise the last thing we want is the attention of the newspapers. I would request that you all stay in this room until I am ready to take your statements. I would ask that you not discuss what happened until you've spoken to me. With your cooperation, we should get through the preliminaries rather quickly. You'll need to stay out of Mr Carlisle's office for the time being.'

'Stay out of his office? I cannot promise you that,' Miss Isobel said.

'I'm not asking, Miss Carlisle. My men are securing the room. They will be standing guard. Mr Carlisle's study is off limits. As of now.'

Miss Isobel's eyes flashed. Chief Inspector Bellerose ignored her.

'Of course we'll cooperate,' Miss Marie said. She gave Miss Isobel an imploring look.

'I'm sorry,' Miss Isobel said. Marie attempted to hold Miss Isobel's hand, but Miss Isobel pushed it away. Chief Inspector Bellerose saw the exchange. Annie watched him as he watched Miss Isobel and Miss Marie. *He's smart. Doesn't miss a thing,* she thought.

'None of this is necessary, you know. I can tell you who murdered my brother. His wife. She drugged him last night and left him to die. She treated my brother horribly. He gave her a beautiful home, fine clothes, plenty of money – all she could ever want. She was going to leave him. She *did* leave him. At least that's what she told us, made a big fuss about going to her aunt's house. We were all out last night. I'm certain she sneaked back and murdered him. In cold blood. *After* she drugged his wine.' Isobel worked herself into a fury. Spittle flew as she raged against Miss Catherine. An ugly blue vein thrummed across her forehead.

'Where is Mrs Carlisle?' Chief Inspector Bellerose asked.

'At her aunt's in Bloomsbury,' Miss Marie said. 'I'll get you the number.'

Annie wondered why the room had become so hot all of sudden. If she could just get some fresh air … She heard Chief Inspector Bellerose's voice come at her like fog, thick and soupy.

'She's going to faint,' someone said.

Chapter Eleven

At seven o'clock Cat woke up from a deep and dreamless sleep. *In two hours, my task will be completed.* She wanted nothing more than to deliver the documents she had stolen from Benton. If she was caught with them … She took a deep breath. Best not think of that. Her stomach growled. Under normal circumstances she would have heeded the call and ordered eggs and bacon, toast, tea, and some fresh fruit from room service. But these weren't normal circumstances. She had drugged her husband and stolen classified documents. She bit back the panic that threatened to take over.

Cat thought about her actions this past week and admitted that the intrigue captivated her. She finally found something that she was good at, a purpose to life. Cat washed and dressed, ignoring the hunger in her belly.

Once dressed, she stepped over to the window and surveyed the street below her, with the sweeping view of Kensington Gardens. A series of wrought-iron benches lay near the pathway that led into the park, strategically arranged around the groomed hedges and wild patches of growth for privacy and shade.

From her vantage point Cat could see all the benches. Two old ladies with little dogs sat on one, dressed in similar outfits – bright coats and straw hats with an abundance of fruit attached to the sides. They talked and laughed, one of them gesticulating with her hands, while the other listened attentively. One of them pulled a small canister out of her purse. As if on cue, the dogs both sat up on their haunches. When the women threw them treats, the dogs jumped up in tandem and snatched them out of the air.

Cat almost missed the man who was sitting on one of the benches. He was tucked away in a corner, holding a paperback book on his lap. She watched him for a good five minutes, and he never turned a page. He looked familiar. Who was he? He set his book aside and scanned the walkway in front of him, giving Cat a clear look at his face. It was the historian, the man who'd helped her after she was attacked.

She went to her handbag and rummaged around until she found the card. *Thomas Charles. Historian.* She walked back over to the window and looked at Mr Charles. She reasoned he'd been following her since yesterday. How else would he know that she had come to the hotel? Maybe he lived in the area. Maybe his appearance at that particular bench was simply a coincidence. She dismissed that from her mind. Cat didn't believe in coincidence.

***

Thomas had finally dozed off to sleep, only to be plagued by the usual nightmares, dreams of gristle and gore, the trenches, dead men and dead horses, the smell of death. And the mud. Good God, the mud. He woke at dawn, gasping for air. He waited for his eyes to adjust to the dim light and focused on his surroundings: the leather-winged chair, the familiar stack of books, last night's teacup. He wiped his damp cheeks, surprised to find tears there.

He washed and dressed, made himself a cup of strong coffee, and was parked at Mrs Carlisle's hotel by eight a.m. He sat in the car for a while, but found he was restless, so he grabbed a paperback – one of the many in the back seat of his car – and found a bench across the street from the hotel. From his vantage point he had a clear view of the hotel lobby. If Mrs Carlisle left, he would see her.

At half past eight Catherine Carlisle stepped out onto the pavement. Once again, Thomas was struck by her beauty and amazed at his response to it. A blue taxi pulled up to the kerb. Mrs Carlisle's eyes roved, as if making sure no one followed her. Thomas tried to duck out of sight. Too late. Mrs Carlisle looked right at him. Their eyes met. She recognised him. He could feel it.

Damn. Mrs Carlisle got into the car. It sped away, heading east on Kensington Road. Thomas hurried into his own car and followed. By the time the taxi merged onto Knightsbridge, Thomas had the cab in sight. He kept a few cars back, expertly driving between the traffic. He followed the taxi onto Park Lane, past Hyde Park and the Dorchester.

He was sitting at a traffic signal, his eyes riveted on the taxi, when Mrs Carlisle got out of the back seat and stepped into the line of stopped cars. She wove through traffic just as the light changed and she crossed the street. Traffic started moving just as she flagged another taxi going the other direction, leaving Thomas penned in with no chance of following.

'Damn!' He slammed his hands against the steering wheel.

The light turned green and traffic inched ahead. Thomas thought about driving back to the Carlisle house, parking his car, and walking to the drop site. He came to another stoplight and a gaggle of pedestrians crossed in front of him. The passenger door opened. Chloe St James got in the car. Her expensive perfume did little to disguise her anger. It emanated from her. Thomas found it amusing. Anger – or any emotion, for that matter – simply did not serve in this line of work. The traffic light changed.

'Just drive.' Her voice cut sharp as a rapier.

Thomas stared at her, ignoring the traffic that was backed up behind him. Someone tooted a horn.

'I said drive,' she snapped. She clutched a thick brown envelope to her chest.

Thomas put his vehicle in gear. He drove on, not caring where he went. The sooner he got rid of Chloe the better. He turned away from the high street and drove.

'What are you playing at, Thomas? You're not Mrs Carlisle's contact. I am. She spotted you and she's spooked. You do realise what's at stake here? You do realise what a disaster it would be if the documents Mrs Carlisle is carrying fell into the wrong hands?'

Thomas turned down a side road and parked his car in front of a cobbler's shop.

'What are you doing?'

'Miss St James, I am under no obligation to explain myself to you. I don't think it was prudent to send Mrs Carlisle alone to a drop –'

'What makes you think she was alone? The taxi driver happens to be one of ours. I've got operatives surrounding the bench where she is to make the drop.' Chloe shook her head. 'No. I'm under no obligation to explain myself to you. How dare you question me! This is my operation,

Mr Charles. Just because I'm a woman doesn't mean I'm incapable of handling Marlena X. You've just jeopardised my mission. I'm wondering if your attitude towards Mrs Carlisle is something other than professional. She is rather beautiful. What are you playing at? Do you see her as some damsel in distress? Do you envision yourself as the hero come to rescue her?'

Thomas felt the pulse behind his right eye, the portent of the migraine to come. He'd never liked Chloe St James. He'd heard that she could handle a gun and was not half bad in a fight, but he didn't appreciate her manipulations. She was a career woman, a climber of the ladder. He had known women – and men for that matter – like her. They would step on anyone to get where they were going. Thomas didn't trust her for a minute, but she was right. Catherine Carlisle was not his responsibility. Sir Reginald had seen fit to give that job to Chloe St James. He reminded himself that he and Chloe were on the same side of a conflict that could potentially grow to biblical proportions if it wasn't handled properly.

Thomas turned to face Chloe. 'Miss St James, I've been at this a long time. I've developed an instinct, if you will. Something's not right here. We're missing something. It has to do with the Carlisles. I can feel it in my bones.'

'I don't deal with instinct, Mr Charles. I deal with facts, with professionally gathered intelligence. I suggest you do the same. Stay away from Mrs Carlisle. Stay out of my way. I'm warning you. Don't make me go to Reginald with this.' She tossed the sealed envelope that she was carrying onto Thomas's lap. 'Here's the Blackwell dossier. Reginald will expect you this evening to report your findings. I suggest you follow orders and turn your attention to Michael Blackwell.' She hopped out of the car. Thomas watched in the mirror as she walked across the street and got into the back of a waiting saloon.

Thomas's eyes lit on the plain brown packet. He took it and broke the seal. Inside was another envelope, this one marked 'Confidential' in red letters. He opened this second envelope. Inside was a folder, surprisingly thick, which held the deep background dossier he'd requested on Michael Blackwell. This wasn't the quick check done by the secret service when Michael repatriated back to England with the Gestapo on his heels. This was Michael Blackwell's life in its entirety, starting with his birth certificate, tracking his medical history, his education, where he shopped, and with whom he consorted. Everything that Michael Blackwell had ever done that resulted in writing of any sort was contained in this file.

Thomas scanned the street to make sure he wasn't being watched. He locked the doors to his motorcar, just in case Chloe St James decided to join him again, and settled down to read.

***

Cat left the taxi and walked the few remaining blocks to her hotel. She ducked into a glove shop and took her time looking at the beautiful handmade gloves. She chose a pair for herself, in the sea-green shade she favoured, all the while watching the mirror behind the counter, which provided a perfect view of the pavement outside.

Thomas Charles may be a historian, as his card proclaimed, but Cat was sure he was involved in this scheme in some way. He'd been following her the day she was mugged, just as he was following her this morning. Maybe he used his job as a cover for clandestine activities, whatever they were. On a whim, she purchased another pair of gloves for Annie. These were a soft grey, with pearl buttons. Annie would be delighted with them. She paused before she stepped onto the pavement, scanning the street until she was sure no one followed her, and walked the rest of the way to the hotel.

She wondered what Mr Charles's game was. Was his concern for her after Marlena X attacked her just an act? She remembered those kind grey eyes and the worry she'd seen in them and decided his concern was real. *Never mind that. Stay focused.* She walked among the crowds, weaving in and out between the people, her senses alert.

Harry Hinton had been the porter at the Milestone since 1922 when it changed from a private residence into an exclusive hotel. He loved his job and took pride in giving the same consideration to every soul that passed through its doors. From lords and ladies to businessmen to spinsters on holiday, Harry Hinton had a genuine smile for each and every person who crossed his path. And he never forgot a face. When Cat had arrived yesterday, he'd remembered her name and greeted her accordingly.

'I remember you and your husband stayed here when your home was being renovated: 1927, if memory serves?'

Now Harry was standing at attention in front of the door, his white-gloved hands clasped in front of him.

'Good day, Mrs Carlisle,' Harry said. 'Going to rain, I believe.'

Cat stood in the June sunshine, under a blue English sky with white puffy clouds floating by.

'It's my knee, Mrs Carlisle. It calls for rain, and it hasn't been wrong yet.' Harry leaned close. 'Your friend is waiting for you in the lobby.'

152

'Friend?' Cat forced a smile.

'Yes, ma'am,' Harry said. 'Pretty lady, sleek hair. She said that you were expecting her.'

Cat's heart pounded. Had Marlena X found her?

'Thank you, Harry,' Cat said. She headed into the hotel, like a mouse walking into a well-laid trap. Once inside, she paused behind one of the columns near the clerk's desk, where she could peek into the lobby unseen. Comfortable chairs had been arranged in groups for conversation. Newspapers were fanned out on tables scattered around the room. The lobby was empty.

Cat approached the clerk and asked for her key. When he turned around to fetch it, Cat snatched a knife-like brass letter opener from his desk and tucked it in her handbag. Rather than take the lift, she scurried to the staircase at the back of the lobby and walked up the three flights of stairs to her room.

Cat approached her room holding the letter opener like a weapon. The hairs on the back of her neck prickled like a porcupine's. The corridor that led to her room was empty at this time of day. Cat took advantage of the solitude and stood still for a moment. She forced herself to remain calm and pushed away the fear that tightened the muscles in her shoulders and neck. She listened, straining for any indication that someone watched her in the corridor. She took the envelope with the stolen documents out of her purse and tucked it under the waistband of her skirt. She took a deep breath, put the key in the lock, and let herself into her room.

The velvet curtains had been pulled to, leaving the room as dark as night. Cat stood still, her senses on high alert, as she listened through the silence. She heard it, the whisper of another breath, the beating of another heart. Cat wasn't alone. She set her handbag down and sidled to the light switch. She flipped it on. The wall sconces bathed the room in a dim glow.

'You can put that letter opener away, Mrs Carlisle,' the woman from the park said. 'I'm not going to attack you.'

'What are you doing here?' Cat stormed across the room and whipped open the curtains. 'You've no business breaking into my room.'

She was sitting in the only chair, so Cat was forced to stand. She noticed the wardrobe door was open. She pushed it shut.

'We can't speak in public, Catherine. I needed to be sure you weren't followed, so I came up here and watched your approach. You weren't by the way.'

'I know I wasn't followed back here, but I was followed to the park. That's why I didn't go to the designated place.' Cat reached in her bag and took out Thomas Charles's card. She handed it to Chloe. 'This man helped me after I was attacked. He's been following me. I didn't know if he was working with Marlena X or not.'

Chloe grimaced and tucked the card into her purse. 'I'll just take the documents, if you don't mind, Mrs Carlisle.'

Cat turned her back on Chloe and pulled the envelope out from under her waistband, while Chloe watched, her eyebrows raised.

'I didn't know what I was walking into, and my handbag was the obvious place.' Cat handed the envelope to the woman.

'Well done, Mrs Carlisle,' Chloe said.

'I'm glad to get rid of those,' Cat said. 'What's your name? If I am going to be working with you, I'd at least like to know your name.'

'For me, Mrs Carlisle. Not with me. And it's Chloe. You'd better sit down. You need to be debriefed, after which I'll tell you exactly what's going to happen next.' She nodded at the bed. Cat sat down.

'We've a bit of a situation,' Chloe said. 'Unfortunately, I can't tell you what it is. Something's happened, Mrs Carlisle, and things are going to be a bit difficult.'

'What?' Cat asked, her mouth suddenly dry.

Chloe ignored her. 'Tell me exactly what happened last night. Leave nothing out.'

Cat started at the beginning and told her everything she had done, down to the most mundane detail. She told her about the tray of food and how she put the powder in Benton's Bordeaux. 'We decided to be civil to each other. We agreed to live apart; he just wouldn't divorce me. He's going to arrange an allowance, so I can get a small flat. I am certain he was pleased with our arrangement. It was the first civil conversation we've had in years.'

'You didn't fight?'

'No,' Cat said. 'When he passed out I switched the documents – the envelope was in plain sight – and arranged his head on his arm, a position he had been in many times before, let me assure you. This wouldn't have been the first time my husband passed out at his desk.'

'If it should come up, you can discuss that. Tell the truth about the dinner tray and your conversation. Do you understand?'

'Does Benton know the documents were switched?' A surge of adrenaline washed over Cat. She stood up and started to pace. 'Does he know I drugged him?'

'Take a breath, Mrs Carlisle. Worrying is not helpful, especially in this business. I need you calm. I need you rational. Mostly, I need your reactions to certain events

155

to be genuine. It's best that you do as I say and carry on as though you haven't a care in the world. You've done a good job so far. Can I count on you?'

Cat took a deep breath and sat back down on the bed.

'That's the spirit. Now this is what I need you to do. Stay here at the hotel until after noon or so. Have a meal; take your time with it. After half past one or so, take a taxi to your aunt's house. On the way, stop for flowers for your aunt. When you are asked to explain where you've been, tell them about your separation from Mr Carlisle. Explain you needed some time alone, so you left home and came here.'

Cat nodded.

'This is for the best, Mrs Carlisle. You're going to have to trust me.' Chloe stood. 'I will contact you when I am able. I don't need to remind you that the things you've done for us these past few days must be kept secret at all costs. You understand that?'

'Of course,' Cat said.

'Very well. Goodbye, Mrs Carlisle, and good luck.'

Chapter Twelve

Annie Havers didn't faint. She kept her eyes riveted on Miss Isobel's shawl – which was now draped over her lap – and the tiny stitches of cream thread that ran through it. If she focused on following the way the threads tucked in and around each other to form the herringbone pattern, the room stopped spinning. She took a deep breath, concentrated, and by sheer willpower, she didn't topple.

As she watched Miss Isobel rave about Miss Catherine, a seed of anger flamed in the back of Annie's mind, its heat low and blue and pulsing. She continued to focus on Miss Isobel's shawl as the policeman escorted first Isobel, then Blackie and then Marie into the dining room for a formal statement. She watched them go knowing that soon it would be her turn.

Annie Havers prided herself on her loyalty. Her dad spoke often of the meaning of friendship. His motto was *True friends stick together through thick and thin.* He was especially adamant about loyalty during times of crisis, towards those who helped you and to whom you owed a debt. He reminded her every chance he got that the price of betrayal – though not immediate – would be costly.

Annie remembered when she was just a wee thing on holiday with her parents and their friends at the seashore. One of the children in the group took Annie's favourite chocolate when Annie wasn't looking. Annie ran to her dad, expecting him to take up for her and get her chocolate back. He hadn't. Instead he took her aside and squatted down so his eyes met hers. She could still feel the warmth of his hands on her shoulders.

'Never be a tattletale, Annie. It's disloyal.'

'But she took my chocolate,' Annie replied.

'Then go ask for it back. Resolve your differences directly with your friends. My love, no one likes a tattletale.'

'But what if she doesn't give it back?' Annie said.

'Then keep a better watch on your chocolate.' Her dad tugged on her braids, kissed her forehead, and walked back to the group of adults. She could still picture the back of him as he walked away. She forgot whether or not she'd asked the child for her chocolate, but Annie remembered later that night she found another bar of chocolate under her pillow.

At the time, she didn't really understand what her dad meant. Some farfetched notion of loyalty did not lessen the injustice of thievery, nor did it assuage the anger at losing her precious chocolate. Annie never forgot how important honour was to her dad. At his funeral, his friends – and he had many – spoke of it. She wondered what her dad would think about her now, lying to get away from her mother, only to live in a house where a man had been murdered.

Now it was her turn to give a statement to the police, and in doing so defy Miss Isobel. She now understood what her dad had meant all those years ago.

Annie walked into the dining room. A uniformed policeman – a young man with red cheeks and darting eyes – held the door open for her. She braced herself and stepped through. The door shut behind her. By daylight the room didn't hold the magic that it held during the dinner two nights ago. Without the candlelight's reflection off the silver and crystal glasses, and the shimmer of the sparking golden champagne and blood-red wine, the room looked like any other room in any other musty old house. The only light came from the chandelier overhead, which hadn't been lit during the dinner. Its glaring light drew attention to the aged wallpaper and the threadbare spots on the carpet.

Chief Inspector Bellerose sat at the far end of the long dining table. His sergeant sat next to him, paper in hand, pencil at the ready.

'Miss Havers, good. Come in. Have a seat.'

Annie swallowed the dry lump in the back of her throat.

'No need to be afraid, Miss Havers. I just want to ask you a few questions. Sergeant Perkins here is going to take notes while we talk.'

Chief Inspector Bellerose rose so he could pull out the chair for her. After she was situated, he resumed his seat. A tattered notebook lay before him on the table. He opened it and read. The silence filled the room and took on a life of its own. Annie wanted to squirm, but she sat on her hands and forced herself to stay still. Her mother had always told her she was a patient child. She reminded herself that patience is a virtue.

Finally, Chief Inspector Bellerose closed the notebook and looked up to meet Annie's eyes. He smiled – not a cunning smile, designed to take her off guard, but a real smile. When he spoke his voice was soft.

'I'm going to ask you a few questions, Annie. I know you work for Miss Isobel, and that she has certain opinions about what happened last night. I just want you to tell me what you saw. Nothing more. You won't get in trouble for anything you say, Annie. I aim to get at the truth.' Chief Inspector Bellerose glanced at his notebook. 'You were out of the house last night?'

'Yes, sir. I went to the cinema and got home around half past ten or thereabouts.'

'And Mrs Carlisle was gone at that time?' While Chief Inspector Bellerose asked the questions, Sergeant Perkins wrote furiously.

'Yes, sir,' she said. 'She was gone when I returned.'

Chief Inspector Bellerose paused.

'Tell me how you came to work here, Annie.'

He knew. He knew she'd lied her way into the job. Annie wanted to jump up and run out of the room. She dug her fingernails into her palms, focusing on the pain rather than on the sheer panic at the question.

'I'll tell you everything, but I'll not go back to my mum's,' she said. 'Not while she's married to Harold Green. If you make me go back, I'll run away.' Tears threatened. Annie clenched her fists harder.

'I'm not going to make promises I can't keep, Annie. I give you my word that if you are honest with me, I'll help you. Now why don't you want to go back to your mum's?'

'My stepfather –' Annie hesitated. She felt the emotions spiral inside her head as her control slipped away. The events since her mother's marriage and her arrival at the Carlisle house bubbled deep in her belly like a pot of soup on the stove that came to a boil. The words came spewing out of her mouth. Powerless to stop them, Annie let them come, unedited sentences spoken like a confessor to a priest.

'He came to my room. In the night when my mum was asleep. He stood in the door to my room above his

160

horrible butcher shop and told me that I was his little girl now. He told me there were things I could do that would make him happy. He sat down on my bed. Just as he leaned over me, I screamed. My mum came running. She was ever so mad at me. I knew that if I told the truth, we'd be out on the street. We hadn't any money and no place to live. Things have been difficult since my dad died. She married Harold for security. So I pretended I'd had a nightmare. After Mum and Harold left my room, I locked the door.

'The next day, after Harold left for his shop and Mum went to market, I stole a suitcase, packed my belongings, and ran away. I found an advert in the newspaper for a maid, no experience necessary. I slept in the train station and came straight to Kensington. Miss Isobel hired me, you see.' Salty tears spilled over and sloped down Annie's cheeks. Chief Inspector Bellerose handed her a handkerchief. She used it to dab her eyes, but still the words came.

'And then Freddy Sykes – that's Mr Carlisle's friend – he tried – he tried – he pushed me against the wall. Miss Catherine came just in time. She kicked Freddy hard. And when my mum came to fetch me, Miss Catherine said no. She wouldn't let me go back to Harold, and that I was to be a paid companion.' Spent, Annie stopped talking. Her breath came in rapid gasps. She hiccupped and wiped her eyes. 'And now she's gone to her aunt's. I was to go there after my morning chores. I'll not go back to my mum's.'

Unable to keep up with Annie's rapid-fire monologue, Sergeant Perkins stopped taking shorthand. He sat, pencil poised, until a nod from Chief Inspector Bellerose, so subtle that any casual observer would have missed it, told him to stop writing and pay attention. When Annie stopped speaking, Sergeant Perkins – doing his part in a specifically choreographed dance – got up and poured Annie a cup of tea. He added cream and sugar, stirred it, and put it on the table in front of Chief Inspector Bellerose, who in turn pushed the teacup to Annie.

Annie kept her eyes focused on her hands. They rested on her lap now, red welts in her palms where she'd dug her nails into the soft skin there. What was she thinking, telling Chief Inspector Bellerose about Harold?

'Here, Miss Havers,' the inspector said as he pushed the tea to Annie. 'Have a sip. My gran always said that hot tea with milk and sugar will cure anything that ails you.'

Annie looked up at him, her eyes wide. 'Mine, too.' She reached for the tea and took a sip. 'And bread and butter.' Annie's stomach growled a loud rumbling reminder that she hadn't yet had breakfast. Her confession to Chief Inspector Bellerose had lifted her burden; the release and the freedom it brought were palpable. Her words cleansed her, similar to the times when she had a bad stomach ache. After she got sick, the pain was gone.

'I'd like to ask you a few more questions, Annie. Did you know that Mrs Carlisle was leaving?'

'Yes, sir. We arranged to go to her Aunt Lydia's house. I agreed to stay on and help with the committee meetings, but I was to go this morning. Miss Catherine gave me cab fare.'

'And last night,' the inspector said, 'what time was it that Mr Carlisle claimed to have been drugged and received the ipecac from his sister?'

'I don't know. I was asleep when Mr Blackwell banged on the door. He forgot his key.' Annie didn't tell the police that Blackie was too drunk to stand up.

'Two more questions, Annie. Did you know that Miss Catherine was leaving her husband?'

Annie shook her head. 'No, sir. I knew she was going to her aunt's, but I thought she was just going for a visit.'

'Do you think Miss Catherine could have come back here after she left yesterday?'

'No, sir. Why would she?' Annie realised why after she uttered the words. 'Sir, Miss Catherine didn't kill her husband. I know it.'

'How do you know, Annie? Anything you can tell me would be helpful.'

Annie took her time formulating a response. She thought of her own mum and dad – when her dad had been alive, and the way they were together. They lived each day with care for the other. Annie remembered her mum stirring a pot on the stove and her dad coming up behind her and kissing the back of her neck. She remembered the notes her mum would leave when she went on an errand, loving notes for Annie and her dad.

'Sir, I don't believe that Mr Carlisle and Miss Catherine loved each other. Killing is a passionate thing, isn't it? It takes a certain amount of anger to do a murder. I just don't think Miss Catherine had that much feeling about Mr Carlisle one way or another.' She stopped speaking and let her words hang in the air. Maybe she'd said too much. She didn't care.

'Thank you, Annie,' Chief Inspector Bellerose said. 'You are free to go. If I need to speak further with you, I'll contact Miss Catherine's aunt. If you gather your things, I'll have Sergeant Perkins take you to Mrs Carlisle's aunt's house.'

Annie nodded as she pushed away from the table. She was just about to walk out of the room, when Bellerose called her back. 'Annie?'

'Yes, sir?' She turned around to face him. The look on his face had changed now; he gave her a flinty gaze.

'Would you like me to have a word with Mr Green and Mr. Sykes? I'll see to it that neither one of them bother you again.'

'No, sir. It wouldn't go well for my mum if you did. Harold's all she's got.'

'But Annie –'

'Please, sir. My mum would suffer. I've caused her enough pain.'

'Listen to me. I am a policeman and I don't like to hear when children are mistreated. You go to Mrs Carlisle. If you need any help, come to me, Annie. We have women constables who can help you. Sergeant Perkins will see that you have a means to contact me. I mean what I say, Annie. If Harold Green puts you in danger, do not go back there. I can promise to help you on that count.'

'Thank you, sir.'

Annie once again walked towards the door. This time she felt Chief Inspector Bellerose's gaze on her back. She let herself out of the dining room – there was no young officer to hold the door for her now – and stepped out in the hallway. She took a deep breath, relieved to have shared her various burdens with the inspector.

'Annie,' Miss Isobel said.

Annie turned and faced Isobel. She knew in an instant that Isobel heard everything Annie said to Chief Inspector Bellerose.

'You betrayed me, Annie. You betrayed this family.' Isobel stepped close to Annie. Annie stepped back. Isobel stepped closer.

'Your bags are packed. I want you out of this house. You can keep your new clothes in exchange for your wages. I could ask you to pay me back all the money I've spent on you, but I won't. I want you gone. And don't expect a reference from me. Go. I can hardly stand to look at you.'

'I'm not going to lie to the police, Miss Isobel. Not even for you. Miss Catherine didn't kill Mr Carlisle and you know it.'

Isobel laughed. 'You are a fool, Annie. She came back. Surely you can see that's possible.'

Sergeant Perkins opened the door. 'That's enough, Miss Carlisle. Leave the girl be.'

'I'm going to call your superior right this instant,' Miss Isobel said. 'You and that chief inspector of yours clearly are not capable of handling a situation such as this. My brother is – was – a very important man ...' Her voice trailed off into tears.

'Come on, lass. I'm to go with you.' Sergeant Perkins picked up the valise that Isobel brought down the stairs. Annie followed him out to the kerb, where a police car waited.

Sergeant Perkins saw Annie situated. He climbed into the front of the car and, with a nod to the driver, they were off. She closed her eyes, unable to take in everything that had happened. She'd found Mr Carlisle's dead body, and – in a move that could only be considered reckless – she'd told a policeman about Harold Green. What was she thinking? What had she done?

Annie had last been to Bloomsbury as a ten-year-old. Her dad had conjured a special treat for her mum and her and had surprised them with a trip to the British Museum, followed by a picnic in one of the beautiful garden squares. Annie remembered the lazy buzz of the bees and the vivid flowers as though it were yesterday. Her father had told her about all the different trees, and made up stories about them, imbuing them with personalities of their own. There was the wise old rowan and the whimsical oak.

Today she stared out the window, unseeing, as the taxi passed the Ritz Hotel and the Palace Theatre. Sergeant Perkins and the driver spoke to each other, but Annie tuned out their voices. She couldn't stop seeing Mr Carlisle's lifeless eyes, staring at her in a never-ending plea for help.

The police car pulled to a stop in front of a row of flats made of blood-red brick. Sergeant Perkins got out of the front seat and opened the door for Annie. The policeman who drove handed Annie's valise to Sergeant Perkins.

'I'll come in with you, see that you're all right,' he said. 'I need to have a word with Lydia Paxton.'

Annie smelled cooking meat from a café down the street. Her stomach rumbled. She was ever so hungry. She took a deep breath and followed Sergeant Perkins. He knocked on the door. They didn't look at each other while they waited.

The door was opened by a woman who had the same red corkscrew curls as Miss Catherine, but this woman's hair was streaked with grey threads. It was arranged in a precarious bun, held in place by two crisscrossed paintbrushes. She had the same kind eyes and full lips as Miss Catherine, but where Miss Catherine was tall and willowy, this woman was short and a wee bit stout. Where Miss Catherine wore expensive clothing, handmade by fine dressmakers, this woman was dressed in men's trousers and a baggy button-up shirt, the front of which was covered in paint. 'Can I help you?' She peered at them over the top of her gold-rimmed spectacles.

Annie swallowed, not quite sure what to say.

Sergeant Perkins flashed his identification before the woman's eyes. Before he put it away, she said, 'No so fast. May I see that, please?'

He handed the leather wallet to her. She studied the card. 'You lot should have photographs on your identification. What's happened?' Her eyes lit on Annie and softened. 'And who're you?'

'I'm Annie. Miss Catherine's companion. We were to come here, only Miss Catherine's gone and Mr Carlisle – Mr Carlisle – I found him –' Annie reached the end of her ability to cope. She wanted her mother, but chastised herself for that childish thought. Her mother wasn't available to her any more. Annie Havers was on her own.

'Oh, you poor thing.' Aunt Lydia stepped outside and put her arm around Annie's shoulders. 'I'm Lydia Paxton, Catherine's aunt. Please come in, both of you.' They stepped into a hallway painted in cheery yellow. A red carpet covered the wood floor. Off to the left, a narrow stairwell led to the upstairs rooms. A handbag and a satchel of books sat on the bottom stair.

'If I could have a word, ma'am,' Sergeant Perkins said.

'Of course.' She turned to Annie. 'Why don't you wait in my studio? You can pull the sheet off the sofa and have a seat.' The woman pointed to the room off to the right. She took Annie's valise from Sergeant Perkins and set it at the bottom of the stairs.

Sergeant Perkins and Lydia stepped further into the hallway. The sergeant did most of the talking, but he whispered, so Annie couldn't hear what he said. She headed into the brightly lit room. A large couch had been pushed against the wall and covered with a paint-splattered sheet. Annie didn't bother to sit down.

The walls were filled with paintings, most of them large vivid prints of flowers, painted with such detail they looked real. An old wooden door resting on two sawhorses served as a table. Jars of paintbrushes, tubes of paint, and sketchbooks covered the surface. A soup tureen filled with a large bouquet of flowers sat in the window on an old milk crate. Some of the petals had dried and fallen to the floor. Two easels were set up near the table, both covered with a sheet.

At home among art and the art supplies, Annie relaxed for the first time since she'd discovered Mr Carlisle's body. She loved this room, loved the smell of the paint. She didn't even mind the chaos, which was comforting to her in some strange way. She eyed the large window and imagined the light that would flood in the room – perfect for an artist.

An open sketchbook on the table tempted Annie. She so wanted to look at Lydia's sketches, but didn't dare do so without permission. Instead, she moved around the room and studied the paintings that covered the walls. All of them had the same signature, 'Lydia,' in the bottom right corner. When she came upon a cover of one of her favourite childhood books, *Henry the Horse*, she reached out to touch it. There in the corner was the signature.

Soon Lydia and Sergeant Perkins came back into the room. They found Annie standing before one of Lydia's paintings, studying the masterful brushwork.

'I love your paintings. They are wonderful. You're so lucky to be able to spend your days here.' Annie reached out to touch the painting, but pulled back her hand at the last minute.

'Are you an artist too?' Lydia came into the room. Sergeant Perkins leaned on the doorjamb.

'Not professional, like you. But my dad was going to send me to art school …' She stopped speaking.

Lydia Paxton filled the space created by Annie's silence, as if she sensed the girl's discomfort. 'I am the illustrator for the *Henry the Horse* series. That book pays my bills. I also paint florals, a secret passion of mine, but they don't sell as consistently.' Lydia sat down on the couch.

'Annie, Sergeant Perkins told me what has happened. You're welcome to stay here until Catherine comes. Would you like that?'

Annie didn't bother to hide her relief. 'Yes, please. Thank you.'

'Then I'll just wait in the car,' Sergeant Perkins said. He put his hat back on, smiled at Annie, and let himself out the front door.

'Would you like something to eat?'

Annie's stomach rumbled. 'Yes, ma'am. I've not eaten yet today.'

'Very well. I've got ham and a slice of apple pie for your pudding.'

Annie followed Lydia into the kitchen. Lydia sat with her while she ate hungrily from the plate that was placed before her. She could have eaten second helpings of everything, but didn't want to appear greedy.

'How about I show you to your room and you can lie down for a while? You've had a terrible shock. A proper rest will do you good. And then you can take a hot bath and eat another meal.'

'I can do the cooking, Miss Paxton. I'm rather good at it,' Annie said.

'Not in this house, love. Children don't do the work here.' Lydia stood. 'Come on, I'll show you to your room.'

Lydia had just reached the stairwell to fetch Annie's bag, when they were interrupted by banging on the front door. Annie's heart stopped. Her mouth went dry. *Surely her mum and Harold hadn't heard of the murder yet.* She looked around, plotting an escape route while Lydia opened the door.

'Isobel,' Lydia said. 'What are you doing here?'

'My brother is dead. Catherine murdered him. I demand to see her.'

'She's not here, Isobel.' Lydia's voice was low and calm.

'I don't believe you.' There was a pause in the conversation. 'Her maid is here. Where is she?'

'I think you should leave,' Lydia said.

'You are a disgrace. Look at you, dressed like a man. I blame you for Catherine's reckless ways. You weren't fit to raise a child. I'm surprised –'

'I've work to do, Isobel. If there's nothing else?'

'I demand –'

'Then I'll wish you a good day.' Lydia slammed the door.

Annie stood, mouth agape, impressed at Lydia's bravery.

'I've just poked the hornet's nest, and I don't care,' Lydia said. 'I've always wanted to do that. Poor Annie. I've shocked you haven't I? I'm sorry. Isobel has been a thorn in my side since Catherine married into that family. Now, follow me.'

Lydia showed Annie into a tiny room behind the kitchen with a stained-glass window that cast colours of the rainbow in the dancing light. A trundle bed was in the corner.

'You can have this room. I'll put Catherine upstairs in her old room.' Lydia got a quilt out of a cedar chest and made up the bed. 'You have a nice rest, Annie. I'll come get you in a couple of hours.'

Annie lay down on the bed, surprised that her eyes felt heavy. Try as she might, Annie couldn't stop seeing Benton Carlisle's death stare. She tried thinking about Lydia's paintings and the brushstrokes it took to create them. Thinking about brushstrokes always lulled Annie to sleep. She painted in her mind, heard the whoosh of the brush on the canvas. The imaginary sound rocked her into the deep dreamless sleep of the emotionally exhausted.

Chapter Thirteen

Cat opened the curtains after Chloe left and stood at the window, looking out at Kensington Gardens. The warmth of the sun did little to thaw the chill that cramped in her belly. Something was very wrong. Trouble was brewing. No. Trouble had brewed. It had boiled over and made some sort of mysterious mess. Cat understood Chloe's reasons for keeping her in the dark. She was to carry on, act natural, and know that things would unfold in their own time.

She shivered. She no longer cared what Benton thought or said. She had spent fifteen years married to him. Ten of those years were spent in a desperate cycle of waiting for him to come back to her, while trying to live as though she didn't care that he preferred his mistress to her. If Benton accused her of drugging him, she would lie and tell him that he was being foolish. What possible reason would she have for drugging him? Hadn't they had a civilised conversation, the first one in years? Hadn't Cat capitulated to his refusal to get a divorce?

As these thoughts ran through her head, an undercurrent of joy came through. She didn't care what Benton felt or thought. She didn't need anything from him. She would go to Lydia's for the time being. Once she was sure that the work for Chloe would continue, she would get a small flat. She and Annie would stay together. She would make it work. Without Benton. Without a farthing of Carlisle money.

She picked up the phone and ordered lunch and a pot of tea. While she waited, she packed her small bag and collected her thoughts. After she ate, she would take her suitcase down to Harry for safekeeping while she dashed out for a gift for her Aunt Lydia.

She walked along the high street on the lookout for anyone following her. That man reading the paper? That woman with a shopping bag? Cat paused to browse in a window, studying the display until she was sure all was well. She dashed in Derry and Toms and, using the precious funds that Reginald gave her, bought cashmere socks for Lydia – who had no fashion sense whatsoever, but enjoyed luxury socks – and a new hat for herself to replace the one she had lost when Marlena X attacked her.

On the way back to the hotel, she stopped at a wine shop in Kensington High Street and purchased a bottle of champagne. She wouldn't broadcast that she was celebrating her freedom, although she suspected Lydia would take one look at her face and see the change in her. Lydia always knew what Cat was thinking, sometimes even before Cat did.

Once back at the hotel, she hailed a cab, loaded up her purchases and her suitcase, and set off for Bloomsbury.

Cat sat in the back seat and thought about the conversation she had with Chloe St James. What had gone wrong? She'd followed Chloe's instructions – and Reginald's before that – to the letter. Now, as the cab sped towards her aunt's house, she wondered what disaster awaited her. She shook off the worry, rationalising that if Aunt Lydia or Annie were hurt, Chloe would have told her. They weren't involved in the business with the switched documents, so there would be no reason for Chloe to keep that from Cat. That left Benton or Reginald.

Was Reginald hurt? Dead? Is that why Chloe showed up at the park? *Stop it. Worry will do you no good.*

The taxi turned onto Lydia's narrow street and pulled up to her house. The front window was open, but there was no sign of Lydia. She let the cab driver carry her bag, while she carried her purchases. Cat was just heading up the stoop when a tall man with intelligent brown eyes and a thatch of blond hair approached her, followed by a uniformed constable.

'Mrs Carlisle?'

'Yes,' Cat said.

'Mrs Catherine Carlisle?'

'Yes. What's wrong? What's happened?' Cat dropped her bags on the stoop and made to hurry up the stairs. 'Where's Lydia?'

'Your aunt's fine, Mrs Carlisle. I'm Detective Sergeant Perkins.' The man nodded to the uniformed constable, who picked up the bags that Cat had dropped. 'We'll just step into your aunt's house so we can talk in private.'

Lydia opened the door just as Cat, Sergeant Perkins, and the constable reached the front step. She stared at Cat with red-rimmed, puffy eyes, taking in her clothes, the shopping bag, and the bottle of champagne sticking out the top.

'Oh, Cat. It's so terrible.'

'What's happened?' Cat said.

'Come in, love. Prepare yourself for a shock.' Aunt Lydia nodded at the sergeant. 'You can use my studio. I'll make tea.'

The constable put Cat's suitcase and the shopping bags down in the entry hall. Cat followed him into Lydia's studio. Sergeant Perkins placed a hand on her arm and led her to the sofa. The constable stood near the door. 'Have a seat, Mrs Carlisle.' He didn't sit. He moved over to the window.

'When did you last see your husband, Mrs Carlisle?'

174

'Last night,' Cat said. 'I brought him a tray. We chatted for a while. And I left.'

'He was found dead in his study this morning,' Sergeant Perkins said.

'Dead?' Cat buried her face in her hands. *I've killed him.* She looked up at him, with a question in her eyes. 'What happened? How did he die?'

'Someone attacked him in his study. He suffered a fatal head injury. He may have hit his head on his desk. We don't know yet. Your maid, Annie, found him in his study this morning. She's suffered a hell of a shock.'

'I didn't –' Cat buried her face in her hands once again, a feeble effort to disguise the relief that washed over her. *Benton's dead, but I didn't kill him.* She wished she could cry. But the tears didn't come. Cat felt nothing. She was utterly numb.

Lydia came in with the tea tray. She set it down and handed Cat a handkerchief. Cat took it, but she didn't need it. Her eyes were dry as bones.

'Such a shock. Here, love, have some tea.' Lydia handed Cat a mug.

'I shouldn't have left Annie there. I shouldn't have trusted –' She stopped herself.

'The detective brought Annie here an hour or so ago. He told me what happened. They thought you were here. I didn't know what to tell them.'

'Where is Annie?' Cat asked.

'She's asleep.'

Cat was aware that Sergeant Perkins was watching Cat and Lydia's interaction, gauging Cat's response to the news of her husband's death.

'Where did you go last night, Cat? We didn't know where you were,' Lydia asked.

'Excuse me, Miss Paxton, but I'll ask the questions, if you don't mind,' Sergeant Perkins said. 'You can stay with your niece, but you'll need to keep quiet. If you can't do that, I'll take her down to Scotland Yard and question her there. Mrs Carlisle, please tell me what you and your husband discussed when you saw him last night.'

Cat didn't hesitate. 'We talked about separating.'

Lydia shook her head.

'I'm not going to lie. It's the truth. We didn't love each other. Benton wouldn't give me a divorce, but I couldn't stay in that house any longer. He acknowledged that we were both miserable. We agreed to part. He was going to give me an allowance.'

'So where did you go after your conversation?' Sergeant Perkins asked.

He doesn't believe me. He thinks I've killed my husband.

'I went to a hotel. I wanted to be alone, to think things through.' Cat cast a glance at Lydia.

'Do you know anyone who would want to harm your husband, Mrs Carlisle?'

'You know about his work? His company is working on a classified project for the Air Ministry. It's very hush-hush.' Cat fidgeted, calculating in her mind just how much she should say. 'I found something in his safe when I retrieved my passport and some of my jewellery, an IOU from one of Benton's friends, Freddy Sykes. It was for rather a lot of money: two thousand pounds. Freddy has a gambling problem. His grandmother, who's been paying his debts these past years, has refused to help him further.'

'You and your husband didn't argue? Have words? A disagreement?'

'No.' Cat shook her head. 'Last night was the first civil conversation we've had in years.'

'Thank you, Mrs Carlisle. I don't need to tell you not to leave town.'

'Am I a suspect?' Cat asked. 'My marriage to Benton has been over for a long time. I admit that. But I didn't kill him. I had no reason to.'

'Your husband was a very wealthy man. Do you know who inherits under his will?'

'No, but I imagine he left his money to his sister, Isobel. They were very close.'

'Thank you, Mrs Carlisle,' Sergeant Perkins said.

'I'll see you out,' Lydia said.

She sat for a long time after the police left, waiting for the inevitable waves of grief. All she felt was the emptiness of the dark, yawning chasm that had opened up around her heart. Benton was dead. Murdered. And Cat didn't feel a thing. What would Sergeant Perkins make of that?

She wondered about the goings-on at the Carlisle house. Who was passing documents to the Germans? Blackie? Had poor feeble Blackie killed Benton? What about Freddy Sykes? Cat always thought of Freddy as a rather bumbling idiot, but his altercation with Annie revealed a dark side to his personality that had taken Cat by surprise. He was a rapist. He was a gambler. Was Freddy capable of murder? Would he kill to retrieve the IOU? Had Benton – who had an undeniable cruel streak, despite his outward charm – used his hold over Freddy? The questions went round and round in Cat's head. She had to do something. She just didn't know what. She had to trust someone. She just didn't know who.

'It's hard to believe, isn't it?' Lydia said.

177

'I don't know what to think. I feel nothing. I'm numb.'

'You're in shock, love. What you need is a good rest,' Lydia said.

'Is Annie okay?'

'She's got a belly full of food and now she's sleeping. She's a lovely child. Offered to do the cooking.' Lydia shook her head. 'What are you going to do about her? What are you going to do about you? Of course, you can stay here as long as you want – you know that.'

'Thank you. And I'm going to keep Annie with me. She's had a horrible time of late.'

'So have you,' Lydia said. She put the unlit cigarette back in her mouth.

'I need to make a phone call,' Cat said.

'Of course.' Lydia stood up. 'I'll be down in the kitchen.'

Cat headed into the hallway to the alcove where the telephone was situated. She dialled the phone number that Reginald had her memorise.

'Yes, hello. This is Catherine Carlisle calling for Reginald. I'm coming by with the St Edmunds' pippins and was wondering if he wanted me to make him a pie.'

The woman who answered the phone was silent. Cat could hear breathing, but she didn't speak.

'I'm sorry, ma'am, but I have no idea what you're talking about. There's no one here by the name of Reginald.'

'No, you're mistaken. I was given this number – Hello?' Dry static came through the line. Cat slammed the phone down. Was Reginald turning his back on her now that he had made use of her? What about Chloe St James? *I'll contact you.* Cat took a deep breath. It seemed she would by necessity navigate this ocean on her own.

Cat headed down the stairs for a cup of tea and the familiar surroundings of Lydia's kitchen, with its flagstone floor and the scarred pine table. She could hear Lydia banging pots and pans and reckoned her aunt would start chopping carrots and onions in preparation for her chicken soup, her go-to activity in times of crisis. Lydia claimed the soup was an ancient family recipe with medicinal properties, but Cat knew that the mundane chopping of vegetables and the careful tending to the pot was just as healing as the actual broth.

Her thoughts were on this mundane matter when she stepped off the final step into the kitchen and skidded to a stop. Alicia Montrose stood next to Lydia, pale-faced, her eyes filled with concern.

'Alicia.' The words caught in Cat's throat.

'I came as soon as I heard,' Alicia said. 'Cat, what can I do? What's happened? Are you okay?'

'I'm not sure,' Cat said. 'I really don't know what happened or what I feel –' Of course Alicia would show up at this, Cat's most desperate hour. How could she not? Alicia Montrose was nothing if not loyal, despite the horrible treatment she received at Cat's hand.

'Please let's let bygones be bygones, Cat. You need a friend now. Don't turn me away,' Alicia said.

'How can you be so kind to me, Alicia? I'm not deserving of your charity.'

'I need to tend to something upstairs,' Lydia said. She scurried away, leaving Cat and Alicia alone.

'I've been horrid to you.'

'Cat –'

'I turned my back on you and didn't even have the guts to tell you why,' Cat said. 'I'm ashamed of the way I treated you. You were a good friend and didn't deserve it.'

Alicia looked at Cat with sad eyes. 'I know why, Catherine. It's the boys. I can't imagine what it must have been like for you to watch me keep a child after losing yours. And then when I got pregnant again and again –' Alicia shook her head. 'I admit to being angry at first, but then I realised that every time you saw me and my children, it was a reminder of all that you'd lost. I can't fault you for that.'

'I'm so sorry,' Cat said. 'Can you ever forgive me?'

'There's nothing to forgive, darling. You've had a hellish go of things.'

'We've got some catching up to do,' Cat said, 'but you don't need to involve yourself with this.'

'Don't be ridiculous. You need help.'

They sat down at the table.

'How did you hear?'

'From Jeremy. He has a friend who works with Benton at the Air Ministry. Everything's very hush-hush, thank goodness. Hopefully the newspapers won't track you here.'

The newspapers. Cat hadn't even thought about how the reporters would swarm. 'The police in all likelihood think I've killed him. Isn't the spouse always the suspect? The police will talk to Isobel – I can only image what she'll tell them. If they didn't suspect me, they will after they speak to her.'

'You didn't kill him, Cat. That's all that matters,' Alicia said.

'I left him. I was leaving him.'

'What?' Alicia couldn't keep the surprise from her voice.

'We reached an understanding. We weren't divorcing. Benton would never grant me a divorce. But I couldn't

180

bear that house any longer, so I told him I was moving out. We were simply going to live apart. We've not shared a bed since I lost the last child.'

'You mustn't tell that to the police,' Alicia said. 'No good can come of it.'

'Too late,' Cat said. 'I've already told them.'

'Jeremy's agreed to help you in any way he can. He's offered to hire you a solicitor. He's ready to make the call. He can get you in to see his man this afternoon.'

'Thank you, Alicia. I don't think I'm quite ready for a solicitor yet. Let's wait and see what the police do.'

'Are you saying they came and questioned you here? At least they didn't take you away with them. That must mean something.' She stood. 'I hate to rush off, but I need to get the boys. Should I have Jeremy ask around and find out what's happening? He has connections.'

'Let's just sit tight and see what comes, shall we?'

Alicia cocked her head to the side and studied Cat. For the briefest second, Cat had the impression that her friend knew she carried a secret. The moment passed. Alicia fussed with her hat, kissed Cat's cheeks, and promised to call the next day.

'I don't know how you can remain so calm. You'll call me if you need help? You're not alone, Cat. Promise me you'll call.'

'Promise,' Cat said.

'I've missed you,' Alicia said.

'Me too. I'm glad you came.'

Alicia swept out of the kitchen, leaving a slightest trace of Jean Patou Joy in her wake.

Chapter Fourteen

Thomas ate a late lunch: ham and potatoes, followed by nuts and cheese and a pot of coffee, brought in by Mrs Billows, an oversolicitous woman who had lost her husband and sons in the war. In an attempt to ameliorate her all-consuming grief, she'd spent her life savings on lavish memorials for all of them. In order to earn a living, she'd converted the house her husband's family had lived in for generations into flats, which she rented out to 'a certain calibre of gentlemen.' There were eight rooms, all of them let. Each room was comfortably furnished in dark colours with overstuffed chairs. She cooked three meals a day and was happy to deliver them on a tray. She took pride in her home. In addition to the lunch, today she brought Thomas a tin filled with fresh scones and a jar of homemade lemon curd. He noticed that she had taken pains with her appearance.

'I'll just come back up and get this in a few hours, Mr Charles,' she said.

'No need, Mrs Billows. I'll bring it down when I go out.'

'I made the lemon curd myself,' she said. She moved towards the second chair in the small sitting area, as if she meant to sit down and visit. Thomas stood and escorted her to the door.

'I'm frightfully busy with work just now, but thank you so much, Mrs Billows.'

'You're very welcome, Mr Charles; if there's anything you need –'

'I know where to find you,' Thomas said. He shut the door behind her and turned the lock. He knew that he was an enigma to Mrs Billows – and the tenants as well – with his well-made clothes, his books, and the unusual hours he kept. He had rented this flat for years and managed to keep his business private, despite polite enquiries.

He ate his ham and potatoes, poured himself a steaming mug of coffee, and contemplated the two dossiers on Michael Blackwell. The thinner one, assembled as a result of Mr Blackwell's vetting and debriefing after escaping the Gestapo, had been singularly unremarkable, and as thorough as could be expected, given the circumstances. As far as Reginald was concerned, Michael Blackwell was just another English citizen who fled Nazi Germany and brought home horror stories of life under the iron-fisted control of the Reich.

Thomas read the file twice and could recite it by memory if need be. One of these days the newspapers would tell the truth about Hitler. Thomas had spent enough time in Germany to see the horrors of Hitler's regime first-hand. Hitler had systematically destroyed all his political opponents, many by execution. After that, he'd set out to strip German Jews of any citizenship rights. The Nuremberg Laws, which were passed in September of 1935, gave the government the authority to seize assets. The Jews who were wealthy enough to leave the country only did so after relinquishing their money to the Reich. And the world stood by, feigning ignorance.

Now Hitler was using every ounce of Germany's resources to build planes and an army, in direct violation of the Treaty of Versailles. Thomas had the misfortune to attend the Nuremberg rally in 1935. He had been sickened by the zealous crowds, so mesmerised by the scrawny little man with the wild eyes. Thomas spent many a sleepless night trying to quiet his mind against the things he'd seen in Germany. Now he hoped that in some small way, he and men like Reginald were helping his country prepare for the inevitable conflict.

He poured himself a small brandy and pushed the thinner file aside. The next file was a complete compendium on Michael Blackwell's entire life. Thomas read about Blackwell's smallpox, his bout of influenza, his years at boarding school, his aptitude for reading and languages, and his struggle – at least until a tutor had been brought in to remedy the situation – with maths. Blackwell enjoyed the privilege of a public school education, and he had travelled the world when he wasn't in school. He learned to ride horses at an early age and tried his hand at breeding dogs. His grandparents on his mother's side were from Germany. Michael Blackwell grew up speaking German – along with French, Italian, and Spanish – like a native. He skied in Switzerland and Austria in the winter and sailed in Cornwall during the summer. He had many friends and seemed to be well liked.

He joined the Royal Flying Corps and fought for his country, earning a Distinguished Flying Cross. In 1920 he returned to England and flailed about with the unsuitable women who lived near or worked for his family's estate in Bournemouth. After that, the information became sporadic. In 1924 he relocated to Germany, and – as far as Thomas could tell – he hadn't been home since. A handful of photos accompanied the documents.

Thomas thumbed through them and almost shut the file in frustration. Because he was thorough, he took a second look through the photos. He noted nothing unusual in the childhood photos. Michael Blackwell had a full head of wheat-coloured hair, a high forehead, intelligent eyes that looked directly at the camera. Thomas surmised Blackwell was a no-nonsense type of man who seized life with gusto. He knew his type. They hunted lions and climbed mountains. Fearless, courageous men, who thrived during wars and suffered during peacetime.

He thumbed through the childhood photos of birthday parties, pony rides, and cricket matches, studying Michael Blackwell's childhood face, taking note as the bone structure solidified into the man Michael Blackwell had become.

The most recent picture in the file depicted Blackwell in his uniform, standing next to an older woman – his mother, perhaps – in front of a rambling house. He turned the picture over and read a typed label '1917 Bournemouth.' Thomas scrutinised the picture, noting the prominent cheekbones, oval face, strong jaw, wide eyes, and full lips. The lips.

His heartbeat quickened. He grabbed the thinner file and pulled out a series of photos taken of Blackwell when he arrived in England, which had been glued to the inside of the file. This man had the gaunt look of the undernourished and sleep-deprived. His hair thinned and receded from his forehead. All of this could be explained by bad diet and lack of sleep, not to mention the added stress of living under a totalitarian regime.

Thomas loosened the picture from the file and set it next to the picture taken of Blackwell in 1917. The man in the recent photo had a round, moon-shaped face – despite the hint of cheekbones – thin lips, and eyes that were just the slightest bit asymmetrical. The line of the brow was different. There was a resemblance, the colouring was similar, but the photos that Thomas stared at depicted two different men. The Michael Blackwell who was living in the Carlisle house was an imposter. Who was he? More importantly, what was he after?

Thomas made a phone call. Ten minutes later, he left the tray of dirty dishes, stuffed the pictures in his pocket, and hurried out the door. He arrived in Piccadilly just as the sun was going down. The tailor shop and estate agent's office were long closed, and the narrow out-of-the-way street that housed the antiquarian bookshop was all but deserted. The closed sign was up, but the door was unlocked. Thomas entered the darkened store.

'Lock that door, will you, Tom?' Sir Reginald called out from the shadowy recesses in the back. 'And come on back here.'

Thomas turned the lock on the door, double-checking the street traffic to make sure no one had followed him, a habit long cultivated and hard to break. He turned and wove his way through the aisles of books to a tiny office tucked in the back of the shop.

Thomas found Reginald there, sitting in the only comfortable chair, his cane – an oak one today with a lapis lazuli handle shaped like a cobra – stood upright between his legs. An old desk with a chair that looked as if it might not support Thomas's weight looked out over a lifeless alley lined with rubbish bins. A single bulb hanging from the ceiling revealed the heaps of books and piles of papers that covered the desk. Thomas wondered how anyone could get any work done in an office so full of clutter. He almost sat in the chair, but decided instead to lean against the windowsill, never mind that his back faced the back alley.

'I'm glad you called,' Reginald said.

'What's happened?' Thomas asked.

He shook his head. 'Mine can wait. Proceed.'

Thomas turned on the brass lamp – tarnished to a shade of sea green from lack of polishing – and removed the two pictures of Michael Blackwell from his pocket. He set them side by side.

Reginald leaned in and scrutinised the pictures, hawk-like. Thomas stepped away from the desk and gave the old man room.

'I'll be damned,' Reginald said.

'Indeed,' Thomas said. 'Can't help but wonder if the imposter is in league with Marlena X. He could potentially have full access to anything Mr Carlisle brings home.'

'She's disappeared,' Reginald said. 'Probably hiding.'

'But if Blackwell – or whoever he is – has a way to contact her, we could use that to our advantage.'

'Agreed.' Reginald didn't speak for a moment.

'Benton Carlisle's been murdered.'

'What?' Thomas searched Reginald's face, trying to gauge his response. 'Murdered? When? How? Marlena X?'

Reginald shook his head. 'Mr Carlisle was cudgelled. Crime of passion. Not Marlena X's line of country, I'm afraid. She'd slit his throat and be done with it.'

'Agreed. She needs him alive, so she can access his work.'

'Unless he caught her trying to access his documents,' Reginald said. 'I doubt she would actually go in the Carlisle house. Why would she? She's got someone inside working with her.'

Thomas said, 'How would you like me to proceed?'

'I'll arrange for you to interrogate Mr Blackwell tomorrow.' Reginald gave a silent nod. 'I suggest that you be as candid as possible with the chief inspector in charge of the case without disclosing Mrs Carlisle's involvement. No need to tell them exactly for whom you work, just hint at the hush-hush nature of Mr Carlisle's work and take it from there. You'll have to play this one appropriately, Tom.'

'Can I tell the police that Michael Blackwell is an imposter?'

'Yes,' Reginald said. 'Chief Inspector Bellerose is the man in charge. Good chap, intelligent. We're going to have to operate with as much candour as possible, I'm afraid. Tell him what you need to, just leave Mrs Carlisle out of it. The last thing we need is for Bellerose to latch on to her as a suspect.'

Thomas sighed. He felt the throbbing at the back of his head. 'If he pushes her, she might tell him –'

'I know,' Reginald said. 'And please don't remind me that she has no training. She has fulfilled everything I have asked her to do with a quiet grace that has impressed me. As I've told you before, she will be of use to us.'

'So tomorrow then?' The walls closed in on Thomas. He was ready to be rid of Reginald.

'Plan on ten a.m. I'll get word to you if the time changes.'

'Very well,' Thomas said. He strode out of the shop, leaving Reginald sitting in the tiny office under the dim light of the bare bulb.

***

The morning after Benton's body was discovered, Cat stood behind the old tree in front of the Carlisle house, spying the place she had called home. Now, the house looked devoid of life, at least from the street. She waited, trying to figure out if Isobel and Marie were home. The curtains in Benton's study and the drawing room that overlooked the street were still drawn. The morning's milk remained on the porch.

She shivered in her aunt's raincoat, crossed the street, and walked up the steps to the front door. Once there, she pressed her ear against the cold wood, listening for any sign of life. Nothing. She reckoned that Blackie had left for work. Isobel and Marie must be busy with arrangements for the funeral. She'd been so preoccupied, she hadn't given any thought to organising Benton's funeral.

She unlocked the door and slipped into the house. She didn't call out to announce her presence. She simply wanted to collect her clothes and her precious books, and slip out of the house unnoticed. If providence smiled on her, she wouldn't see anyone.

The house was cold and filled with a musty smell that Cat hadn't noticed before. The gold mirror that hung in the entry hall – a gaudy piece that Cat loathed – was now covered with a black cloth, an antiquated sign of formal mourning. Isobel would savour the letters of sympathy, the flowers, and the condolences that would come her way. She would bask in the sympathy of others, squeezing every bit of attention out of her grief. Cat tried to feel sorry for her sister-in-law, who would surely be lost now that her brother was gone. She felt nothing. Certain she was alone in the house, she hurried up the stairs, knowing what boards creaked on which stairs and avoiding them without thinking about it.

The door to her room was locked. Cat slipped the skeleton key that opened all the doors in the house out of her purse, unlocked the door to her room, and stepped over the threshold. She cried out when she saw the state of things. The bureau drawers gaped open. A lone stocking hung out of one of them, its mate entangled in one of the tortoiseshell combs that Cat used to hold up her hair while she bathed. One of drawers had been pulled out of the dresser. It lay on the floor, tipped on its side, a myriad of gloves and nightdresses spilled about around it. The bookcase was bare, as each and every one of Cat's books now lay on the floor in a pile of cracked spines and torn pages.

She bit back the overwhelming sense of violation and stayed focused on the task at hand. The sooner she got away from the Carlisles and this house the better. Her suits and dresses had been pulled from the hangers and lay in a tumbled pile on the floor. She spent a few minutes hanging some of the dresses back up. She folded her four best suits and three best dresses. She grabbed three pairs of shoes, two hats, four pairs of gloves, and an extra handbag. She got her coat and her walking shoes and made quick work of folding these items into neat piles on her bed.

The clothes that she didn't take would be sold at one of the second-hand shops. She would have to be prudent with money from now on. She laughed out loud. Given that Benton had kept Cat short of funds since the day they were married, that shouldn't be too difficult. But she had Annie to consider now. She left all but one of her fancy dresses. Somehow Cat didn't think fancy-dress balls would be a part of her new life. She made a mental note to take the quilt from her bed, a cherished gift from her grandmother. Now to fetch a suitcase from the attic. She could pack and slip out of the house, with no one the wiser.

There was only one staircase that accessed the attic. To get to it, Cat had to pass Isobel's rooms. She hurried past the closed door, tiptoed up to the attic, and scurried back down with her suitcase, like a criminal thieving in the night. In the end, Cat opted to only bring one dress and two suits, freeing up room in her suitcase for some of her books. She jammed her clothes and books in – not caring if the clothes wrinkled in the process. She had to sit on the case to shut the latch, but once that was done, she lugged the suitcase down the stairs and set it near the front door.

She went back, fetched her hatbox and purse, and was closing her bedroom door and locking it, when Isobel's bedroom door opened. Cat froze, waited for Marie or worse Isobel. She girded herself for the inevitable confrontation. Light spilled into the dark hallway. No one came. Captivated by the murmur of voices, Cat moved closer to the open door, careful that the hatbox she carried didn't hit the wall and alert Isobel to her presence.

'Freddy's doubled his price.' Isobel's voice sliced through the darkness in the hallway like a razor. 'He thinks I'm going to inherit Benton's fortune, so he's asking for more money.'

'Oh, Izzy,' Marie said.

'I'm going to have to pay him.'

'Give him his bloody money. Once you pay him, we can make plans. I'll arrange a trip for us. It'll be all right. You'll see.' Marie spoke with surprising strength and authority, as though she'd stepped in to be strong for Isobel in this time of crisis. But there was something else there, something that Cat couldn't place. Feeling brave, she stepped closer to the pool of light.

'Benton wouldn't pay. Of course, I didn't tell him that Freddy was the actual blackmailer. He would have been furious. Benton said that once you pay a blackmailer, they never go away. I'd like to know how Freddy managed to take those pictures. He must have been following us. He must have known somehow …' Isobel's voice faded into a whisper.

Cat strained to hear, stepping yet closer to the open door.

'Listen to me, Izzy,' Marie said. 'We're going to pay him. Then we are going to move somewhere so we can have some peace. God knows, I'm ready for it. I'll get the money somehow. Trust me. I'll figure out how to get us out of here. We'll start over. Maybe we'll go to America. We'll get a little cottage by the sea and have a quiet life. How about we pretend we are sisters? No one will be any the wiser.'

'You have such nice dreams, Marie,' Isobel said.

'It doesn't have to be a dream. Once we're gone, Freddy won't be able to find us. He can do whatever he wants with those pictures. We'll be gone. He won't have any hold over us. Not any more.'

The voices stopped.

Cat's curiosity got the best of her. She stepped even closer and positioned herself so she could see into Isobel's room. Marie and Isobel sat next to each other on a sofa that faced the window. Fortunately, the two women sat with their backs to Cat, so she could watch them unobserved. Isobel wore a tattered flannel dressing gown. Her hair fell in a braid over her shoulder, like a silver snake. Marie sat next to her. She put an arm around Isobel's shoulder and pulled her close.

'It will be okay, Izzy. We love each other. That's all that matters.'

'Oh, Marie.' The words caught in Isobel's throat as she faced Marie, pulled the woman into her arms, and kissed her, a long passionate kiss.

Cat put her hand over her mouth to stop herself from gasping, as Marie reciprocated. She watched the passionate intimacy between the women, but couldn't take it in. She stepped away from the door, not quite believing what she had just seen. She blinked her eyes, as if to erase the image of the private moment. She rushed down the stairs, grabbed her suitcase, and hurried away from the Carlisle house, like a thief who had stolen an unwanted secret.

Chapter Fifteen

The morning mist turned to rain just as the taxi pulled up to Lydia's house. From the street, Cat had a clear view of her aunt and Annie through the window. Annie held a paintbrush as she worked at an easel, while Lydia stood behind her, pointing and talking with the unique passion her aunt reserved for anything to do with art. Cat let the taxi go and carried her own suitcase to the front door. She walked into a house redolent with the smell of soup and roasting chicken. Her stomach growled.

'Hello,' she called out.

'In here,' Annie said. She smiled at Cat, and waved the paintbrush she was holding through the air. 'Look, your aunt's teaching me to paint.'

'She doesn't need much teaching. She's really talented. Look at this.'

Lydia turned Annie's easel so Cat could see her work. The canvas depicted a still life of a bouquet of flowers arranged in Lydia's unique style. Rather than paint the flowers in colour, Annie had captured them in black, white, and varying shades of grey.

'This is marvellous,' Cat said.

'Thank you.' Annie smiled with pride.

Cat switched on the lamps and closed the curtains.

'What are you doing? We need the light to work,' Lydia said.

'You're on parade, Lyd. Anyone from the street can see in,' Cat explained.

Lydia cocked her head. She gave Cat a searching look. 'That's never bothered you before.'

'It bothers me now,' Cat retorted. 'I'm sorry. Didn't mean to snap.'

'Annie, if you'll go turn the flame up, we can have our soup. I need to speak to Cat for a moment.' When they were alone, Lydia said, 'What's going on? Are you in some sort of trouble? Does it have to do with Benton's murder?'

Cat wanted to tell Lydia everything. It would have been so easy. But she held her tongue. 'Everything's fine,' Cat said.

'You're keeping something from me, love. Don't think I don't know it because I do. You wear your feelings on your face, despite your aptitude for silence. Never mind. You'll tell me in your own good time. Are you ready for some chicken soup?'

'Yes. But I must make a phone call first.'

'Help yourself,' Lydia said. 'We'll picnic in the studio. Like old times.'

Cat sat down at the telephone desk in the hallway and put her call through to Scotland Yard.

'Sergeant Perkins is with Chief Inspector Bellerose, ma'am,' the man who answered the phone said. 'Can I have him ring you?'

'Either that, or he can come and see me. This is Catherine Carlisle. I found something out …' She didn't know how much she should tell this person. 'It may have to do with my husband's murder.'

There was a pause at the end of the line.

'What did you say your name was?'

'Carlisle, Catherine Carlisle. Please tell Sergeant Perkins I would appreciate it if he could come to see me, or at least telephone. I have some information.' Cat gave the man Aunt Lydia's phone number.

'I'll see that he gets the message, ma'am.'

Aunt Lydia – with Annie's help – had prepared a light lunch of chicken soup, fresh bread and butter, and berry pie for dessert. They ate in Lydia's studio on the floor, picnic style, while the rain pelted the window. Lydia spent an hour regaling Annie with stories of Cat's childhood. Annie ate heartily. Her cheeks were flushed and the dark circles under her eyes had started to fade. The poor girl had been through hell, and Cat couldn't help but feel that she was partially to blame.

After the soup was eaten and the pie reduced to crumbs, Lydia said, 'Let's go make some hot choco –'

A knock on the door interrupted her mid-sentence.

'Are you expecting someone?' Lydia asked.

'Yes. The police.' Cat jumped up and hurried to the door, expecting to see Sergeant Perkins standing outside; instead she saw Violet Havers Green and a fat-lipped man with a big nose covered in an impressive network of veins.

'I've come to collect my daughter.' Annie's mother pushed past Cat and into the house, the fat-lipped man following close behind. 'Your husband's been murdered, Mrs Carlisle. Are you still going to tell me that Annie's better off with you? Don't bother answering. I am taking her home with me right now.'

Cat led them into Lydia's studio, where Lydia and Annie were sitting on the picnic blanket.

'I don't think –' Cat started to say.

'No.' The man shook his head. 'You haven't a say in the matter. She's my daughter, and she's coming home.'

'I am not your daughter. I am not going with you,' Annie said. She and Lydia stood up. Annie faced her stepfather.

'Don't worry, Annie,' Cat said. 'You're not going anywhere.' She turned to Mr and Mrs Green. 'Won't you come in and sit down?'

'We'll stay right here,' Mr Green said. He turned on Annie. 'You get upstairs and pack your things. If you're not ready to go in ten minutes, I'll give you a beating, the likes of which you've never seen.'

Mrs Green's eyes widened. 'Harold.' She placed a hand on his arm. He brushed it off. 'Don't, Vi, this is partially your fault. If you'd disciplined her properly as a child, she wouldn't have run away from you. A child should follow their parents' orders without question. That's how it's going to be from now on, Annie. Do you understand? Get moving, girl.'

Lydia, as was her custom, stood by the mantel. She took a cigarette out of the case, put it in her mouth but didn't light it.

'I am not going to let Annie go home with you,' Cat said.

'You have no authority to keep my daughter from me,' Mr Green said.

'Neither do you, Mr Green. Annie isn't your daughter.'

'Now see here, don't you think you're overstepping the mark?'

Cat turned her attention to Annie's mother, who looked like a trapped rabbit. Her eyes darted around the room, a look of terror in them. 'Your husband wants to molest your daughter, Mrs Green. Surely you're not going to stand by and allow that?'

'You have no proof of that.' Mrs Green's voice was but a whisper.

'I trust Annie,' Cat said. 'She told me that Mr Green came to her room at night while you were asleep. It's obvious she's scared of him. She'll never reside under the same roof as your husband, not if I can help it.'

'Mrs Carlisle, while I appreciate that you are nothing more than a flighty woman with a little too much time on your hands, and while I appreciate what you've tried to do for my daughter, do you think she is safe with you? Your husband was murdered.' Mr Green surveyed Lydia's studio, a supercilious look on his face. 'Are you an artist? Not the best influence for an impressionable young girl.'

Lydia, who had been silent until now, spoke.

'Mr Green, what do you think would happen if Annie went to the police and reported you?'

'It would be her word against mine,' Mr Green said. Warming to his subject, he continued. 'She is a young girl with an overactive imagination. I am a businessman, a pillar of the community. I am good to the children in the neighbourhood. They love me.'

'As it happens, I know about these things, Mr Green. Let me enlighten you. Once the police receive an allegation of any wrongdoing against a child, they would launch an investigation. While they are doing that, Catherine and I would be using our considerable resources and connections to dig into your past and look for any other children you have molested. You see, I understand men like you, Mr Green. I'm sure Annie's not the first child you've toyed with. Trust me when I tell you that I will make it my singular obsession to expose you for what you are. I will go to your neighbourhood and track down every child who has crossed your path. I'm sure one of them will have a story to tell.'

Mr Green's face turned a mottled shade of red. A sheen of sweat broke out on his forehead. Poor Mrs Green seemed to shrink within herself.

'You need a man to knock some sense into you,' Mr Green said.

'Utter nonsense, and you know it. It is time for you to leave my home. You come near Annie again, and I go to the police,' Lydia said.

Mr Green stood up, and moved towards Lydia, his meaty hand clenched into a fist. Lydia, who was faster, grabbed the poker from its spot near the fireplace. She brandished it like a sword. 'I wouldn't mind giving you a beating. God knows, you deserve one. How many little girls besides Annie have you molested, Mr Green?'

Mr Green stopped short. Cat had never seen her aunt so angry. She held the fire poker, her eyes filled with steely anger. Cat's breath caught. She didn't want to be involved in another murder.

'Get out of my house,' Lydia said.

Mr Green eyed the poker and stepped out of Lydia's reach. He grabbed his wife by the arm. Annie's mother – helpless to do anything else – followed behind him. As they turned the corner towards the front door, she cast a helpless look at Cat, her eyes pleading for something that Cat couldn't give her.

'Mum,' Annie cried out.

The door shut. Violet and Harold Green were gone.

Annie stood rigid, her fists clenched, staring at the door. Cat wanted to go to her, but something in Annie's stance told Cat to let the child be. She glanced at Lydia. Lydia shook her head.

'I'm so sorry, Annie,' Cat said.

'I'm worried for my mum, but there's nothing to be done about that,' Annie said. 'She won't leave him. At least not now.'

'I know,' Cat said. 'If she ever wants to leave him, we can try to help her, okay?'

'Thank you, both of you.' Annie went to the blanket and started to straighten up the picnic mess.

'I'll take care of that, love,' Lydia said.

'I don't mind,' Annie said. 'I would rather be busy.'

Cat and Lydia watched Annie as she methodically stacked the plates onto the tray, and carried them into the kitchen.

When she had gone, Lydia turned to Cat. 'Won't you talk to me, love? You look like you're about to snap.'

Cat trusted her aunt more than she trusted anyone. She knew deep in her heart that Aunt Lydia would never betray a confidence. She went over to the drinks trolley and poured two brandies. She beckoned her aunt, and they sat down side by side on the sofa.

'I went to get some clothes today,' Cat said. Her words came out a whisper. She sipped.

'My God, Catherine, what is it? You're scaring me.' Lydia took the unlit cigarette out of her mouth and set it on the table.

'Isobel and Marie,' Cat said. 'They're lovers.'

'Isobel and Marie? Lovers?' Aunt Lydia stared at Cat long enough to be sure that she was serious. She snorted with laughter, tipped back the glass of brandy and drank it in one go. She looked at Cat with incredulity. 'Are you sure?'

'Yes,' Cat said. 'And Freddy Sykes is blackmailing them.'

'You know this how?'

200

'My plan was to start moving my things out of the house. I went today to retrieve some clothes and books. I thought I was alone. I overheard them talking about Freddy Sykes's blackmail scheme. Something made me stop and listen. I heard everything. He has pictures of them in a compromising position. He's blackmailing Isobel.'

'I'll bet she killed him,' Lydia said. 'I'm betting that Isobel asked Benton for the money to pay the illustrious Freddy Sykes. Benton said no. And in the heat of jealous rage, she's offed him.'

'Oh, Lydia, don't make a joke.'

'I'm not, love. Isobel Carlisle has a wicked temper, as you well know.'

'But she loves Benton. She would never harm him.'

'Passion does strange things to a person, Catherine. Never forget that.' Lydia picked up a fresh cigarette and put it in her mouth. 'And if you ever want to talk to me about what's really bothering you, I'll listen. You know you can trust me.'

'I swear, Lyd, you're a witch,' Cat said.

'Before I mount my broom and ride away, we should talk about the elephant in the room, love.'

'What do you mean?'

'You need to go back to that house and get the rest of your things, and you don't need to sneak around Isobel to do it. That house was your home for fifteen years. I'll go with you, if you want, but don't be worried about Isobel Carlisle. Until the will is read, you've as much right to be in that house as she does.' Aunt Lydia took Cat's hand in her own. 'If you let Isobel push you around now, after all this time, you'll never forgive yourself.'

Aunt Lydia's words rang true. What was Cat thinking, skulking around the Carlisle house as if she needed permission to be there? She thought of the books and clothes she had left. She knew she needed to make a clean break of it, go back to the house and retrieve all of her belongings. 'I'll go back tomorrow morning.'

'Do you want me to go with you?'

'No. I need to face Isobel on my own.'

'Good,' Lydia said. 'And once you get things sorted, we'll give you the room upstairs and let Annie have the room off the kitchen. I'll start moving my junk into the cellar. We can paint your room and Annie's, if you want. I'll even treat you to some new curtains and linens. I've been lonely here. It'll be nice to have young people about.'

'Thank you,' Cat said.

Cat settled into the sofa and spent the afternoon reading the *Times*. She checked the personals, but – as was expected – there was no message from Reginald. The rain lulled her. She leaned back, closed her eyes, and napped until the ring of the hallway telephone startled her out of her reverie. She heard Lydia say, 'Of course. One moment.'

'Catherine.' Lydia stood in the doorway, a serious look on her face. 'It's a Chief Inspector Bellerose. He said you called.'

'I'm going to tell him about Isobel and Marie,' she said.

'And the blackmail?'

Cat nodded. 'I didn't love him, Lyd, but I want to find his killer.'

Chief Inspector Bellerose listened as Cat relayed what she had seen and heard at the Carlisle house that day. She gave Chief Inspector Bellerose a verbatim report of all that she had witnessed. When she finished speaking, the silence lay between them, like an empty echo.

202

'Mrs Carlisle, you've given me a very detailed accounting of what you saw today. Would you share any impressions you gleaned, just anything that struck you?'

Cat hesitated, surprised at Bellerose's request. 'There is one thing – it might not be important, but it struck me. Marie is usually so subservient. She kowtows to Isobel in ways that are embarrassing. Not today. Today she seemed as though she were in charge.'

'Do you think Isobel Carlisle could have murdered her brother?'

Cat did not hesitate. 'There's no love lost between my sister-in-law and me, Chief Inspector Bellerose, but personal feelings aside, I do not. Isobel loves her brother. She would never hurt him. Freddy Sykes is a different story. Have you spoken to him?'

'I can't comment on an ongoing investigation,' the chief inspector said. 'Are you planning on going back to the house?'

'Yes, as a matter of fact, I'm going tomorrow to get the rest of my things.'

'Very well. Thank you for calling, Mrs Carlisle.' He hung up before Cat could ask any more questions. She stood in the hallway for a moment. The rain pattered on the roof. Benton was dead. Chief Inspector Bellerose would find out who killed him. Cat felt certain of that. She just wondered at what price justice would be served.

Chapter Sixteen

The rain continued through the night and into the next morning. Rather than leave Annie alone, Cat decided that she would keep the girl with her when she went back to get the rest of her belongings – that way she could keep an eye on her and see that she stayed safe. The visit from the Greens had shaken Annie. She came downstairs for her morning tea pale-faced and subdued. She had borne too much for a child so young.

The events with Mr Green had unsettled Cat. She feared he would return to Lydia's and try to take the girl against her will. When Cat had asked if Annie wanted to stay with her today, Annie's relief had been palpable.

Annie was quiet during the taxi ride. As the cab pulled up to the Carlisle house, Cat vowed to get Annie away from Mr Green's influence, to take her somewhere unknown by him. First she had to deal with Isobel.

A police saloon was parked in front of the Carlisle house. The driver was still inside. A constable was stationed at the front door. He moved in front of it as Cat and Annie approached.

'Good morning,' Cat said. She shook the rain from her umbrella and set it near the door. 'I'm Catherine Carlisle.'

'Yes, ma'am. Chief Inspector Bellerose is expecting you. I'm to tell you that he would like a word with you when he is finished speaking to Mr Blackwell.' The constable nodded and held the door for them.

She and Annie stepped into the house and stood in the dusty hallway. The flowers on the entry hall table drooped. The musty smell had grown worse overnight. Annie ran her finger over the table and examined the grime. 'No one's lifted a finger,' she said.

'Let's move along, Annie. The clothes I want to take are folded on the bed. Remember the quilt. I'll just dash up to the attic and get the trunks –'

'What are you doing here, Catherine?' Isobel stepped around the corner.

'I'm here to get my things.'

'Benton's solicitor is in the drawing room. He's here to read Benton's will. I need access to money, so I can plan his funeral. You may as well sit in. The house is mine now, as well as the contents. When the will is read, you're to leave and never darken my door again.'

'With pleasure,' Cat said. 'But I'll be taking my clothing and books with me.'

'You will not,' Isobel said. 'Those items were purchased with Carlisle money. They belong to me now.'

'I'm taking my clothes, Isobel. Just try and stop me.'

'What are you going to do – physically assault me? Look at you. Look at your face. You're a gutter tramp, Catherine. I rue the day Benton married you. Now you've gone and killed him. As God is my witness, I'll see justice served. I'm going to dedicate my life to proving that you murdered my brother. I won't rest until you hang.'

Cat walked back to the door, opened it, and spoke to the constable. 'Would you come in, please?' The young man stepped into the hallway. 'This woman has been threatening me. Would you please go upstairs with this young lady, and see that no one bothers her while she packs my trunks?'

He eyed the front door.

'I'll speak to Chief Inspector Bellerose on your behalf.'

'Yes, ma'am.'

'Thank you. Annie, just lock the bedroom door while you are packing. That way Miss Isobel won't be able to bother you.'

Isobel turned on her heel and headed towards the drawing room. Cat set out after her.

The housekeeping tasks in the drawing room – where Isobel and Marie spent most of their time – had not been neglected. A cosy fire burned in the grate. The curtains had been pulled against the gloomy rain outside, but all the lamps had been lit, giving the room a soft golden glow. The furniture had been polished to a high shine, evidenced by the smell of lemon oil. Fresh flowers were artfully arranged in a crystal vase and sat on the coffee table, next to a tray with a coffee pot and two cups. Isobel sat down, poured coffee, and handed one of the cups to the elderly gentleman who sat on one of the two sofas arranged around the table.

Seeing that Cat wasn't going to be offered coffee, the gentleman attempted to hand his cup to Cat. 'Would you like coffee?'

'No, thank you,' Cat said, surprised that Isobel would forego propriety in front of a witness. 'I'm Catherine Carlisle.' Cat let her words linger in the air.

'Oh, yes, of course. Bartholomew Owens at your service. I'm Mr Carlisle's attorney. Miss Carlisle asked that I come and read the will.' Mr Owens smiled at Cat, his eyes shining through thick glasses. He had a thick shock of white hair and eyebrows to match. Flakes of dandruff lay like so many snowflakes on the shoulders of his fine wool suit. He sipped his coffee, taking his time as he set his cup back down on the table. He picked up a narrow envelope with the words *Last Will and Testament* typewritten across the front of it, slid out a document, and unfolded it. The task seemed to take for ever.

'Mr Carlisle made this will a year ago. He was very specific in his intentions. Aside from a handful of bequests to various charities, he has left everything to you, Mrs Carlisle.'

'What?' Cat and Isobel spoke at the same time.

'I don't want anything –' Cat said.

'There's been some mistake,' Isobel said. 'My brother would never leave his money and my home to that harlot.'

'Isobel, your brother said that he settled a large sum of money on you when he married Mrs Carlisle, in case you wanted to move house.' Mr Owens set the will down and read from the file, using his fine gold pen as a pointer as he read. 'It says here that he gave you a rather generous settlement, in addition to the trust your parents set up for you.'

Isobel's face blanched white as yesterday's milk. Her breath came in short rasping gasps. Cat wondered if she should summon a doctor.

'I've no husband, no children. I dedicated my life to caring for Benton. When he endowed me with money, I reached out to Lady Montrose. She was so desperate to get her charity work going.'

Cat asked the question, but she already knew the answer. 'Are you saying that you used your settlement from Benton to garner favour with Alicia – Lady Montrose?'

Cheeks flushed, eyes blazing, Isobel jumped out of her seat and moved towards Cat, her hands in fists. Cat jumped up too, an act born out of instinct and resulting from her recent physical altercations with Marlena X. 'I've watched you and Alicia become friends. I don't know why she took to you, but she did. I am the one who has worked tirelessly for her charities. I'm the one who has devoted my life to Benton. You've taken everything from me. My brother, my friendship with Alicia. My life was fine before you came into it. Now I'm in ruins and it's all because of you.'

The walls of the Carlisle house inched ever closer to crushing Cat. Unable to cope with her sister-in-law's embarrassing outburst, Cat turned her back on Isobel and walked away.

'You get back here and face me,' Isobel said.

'I am going to pack my things,' Cat said.

She heard Isobel's footsteps as they hurried after her. Cat ignored them. She couldn't get away fast enough.

'You'd best not steal anything,' Isobel said. 'In fact, I think I'll check your progress to make sure none of my family heirlooms go missing.'

Cat turned around and faced Isobel. Something in Cat's manner gave Isobel pause. She stopped in her tracks. 'Everything in this house belongs to me. You are here at my sufferance. Stay. Away. From. Me.' Cat's words came out in a low grumble, each syllable bursting with a hot potent rage that threatened to explode. She turned on her heels and ran for the stairs.

'Almost ready,' Annie said. Cat stepped into her room, surprised at the neat piles of clothing spread out on her bed, her writing table and on the floor. She hadn't given Annie instructions regarding which clothes to bring and which to leave. Now her bookcase was bare, her wardrobe empty. Two suitcases were shut, ready to be taken downstairs. Annie was industriously folding sweaters and setting them in a third case.

'Thank you, Annie,' Cat said. Within the hour she would walk out of this house for the last time.

'We're going to need one more suitcase, miss, and maybe a box for the rest of the books,' Annie said.

'Would you mind fetching them from the attic? Isobel is busy with the police, so she won't be able to bother you. Can you manage it on your own?'

'Of course,' Annie said.

'Annie?' Cat interrupted her as she headed for the door. 'Thanks for coming with me today. You've been through a lot these past few days. When we figure out where we're going to live, we'll find you a school and arrange some art lessons.'

'Thank you, Miss Catherine. And I'd be happy anywhere, as long as I don't have to go back with my mum and Harold Green.'

Cat looked around the room, now empty of her belongings, the sweet taste of freedom here at last. She picked up a crystal paperweight that Benton bought her on their honeymoon. She set it down and ran her fingers over the silken shade of the lamp on her writing table. The rain stopped. The sun filtered through the mullioned windows, casting beams of light on the threadbare rug.

She walked across the floor to the window, weaving through the suitcases. She wondered about Marlena X and how things would be resolved. Something would have to be done about her. Cat wondered what. She wondered who would help her. Chloe had been less than enthusiastic. Reginald had disappeared and all but abandoned her.

Cat pressed her forehead to the cold glass, a final look at Kensington, with its clean streets and well-manicured inhabitants. She'd enjoyed coming here with her parents as a child. She had fond memories of picnics and trips to the museum, but she had never felt at home here, not like she did at Aunt Lydia's.

People milled along the street. Some stopped to shut their umbrellas and remove their rain hats, while children splashed in the puddles. A dog strained on his leash. And there in the garden square, leaning against the trunk of an oak tree stood Marlena X. Today she had on a raincoat, accompanied by a bottle-green floppy hat that all but hid her face. But Cat still recognised her.

The anger bloomed in Cat's belly. An uncontrollable rage threatened to take her reason. In a spurt of recklessness, Cat ran down the stairs and out the door. So focused was she that she stepped into the street and was nearly run down by a passing car. It skidded to a stop. The driver stuck his head out the window and yelled at Cat. She ignored him. She kept her eyes on the woman, intent this time on having it out with her once and for all. Cat was ready for a fight. She didn't care who witnessed it.

'You there,' she called out to the woman just as she approached her.

The woman tucked herself behind a large tree and buried her face behind a newspaper. She looked up when Cat called to her, registering surprise at Cat's approach.

'I want to speak to you,' Cat called out.

***

A black police saloon was parked one street over from the Carlisle house. As Thomas approached, the driver – a uniformed policeman with hooded eyes and a nasty expression – opened the back door.

'This way, sir. Chief Inspector Bellerose is this way.' He held the door open and glared at Thomas.

Thomas crawled into the back seat of the car. He and Bellerose sat next to each other on the seat. The two men sized each other up. Bellerose nodded, his greeting frosty at best. Thomas didn't blame him. He wouldn't appreciate an outside party participating in the questioning of a suspect.

'Bellerose.' Thomas nodded at the man. Chief Inspector Bellerose was dressed in a finely tailored suit that spoke of financial means beyond those of a Scotland Yard chief inspector. He had a strong jaw and intelligent, questioning eyes.

'Sergeant Perkins is in the front. The driver is Constable Simmons,' Bellerose said. 'Care to tell me why you're interested in Michael Blackwell?'

'No one's briefed you?' Thomas bit back his irritation at Reginald. The old man assured him that all parties had been thoroughly briefed regarding the joint interrogation. Thomas pinched the bridge of his nose, in an attempt to stave off the headache that threatened.

'My superior officers weren't terribly forthcoming,' Bellerose said.

'You're aware of Mr Carlisle's work?'

'Not the specifics,' Bellerose said.

'His firm is furiously working on a project for the Air Ministry. Mr Carlisle's custom is to bring the plans that he's worked on home with him, where he keeps them until they are retrieved by a secure courier and taken to the party who will work on them next.'

'So we have sensitive documents in the Carlisle home,' Bellerose said.

'And we have a long-lost cousin living in the house who claims to have escaped Germany.' Thomas took the two pictures of Michael Blackwell out of his pocket and handed them to the chief inspector. 'It seems that Michael Blackwell is an imposter, Chief Inspector Bellerose. I am not trying to solve your murder, nor would I take credit if I did. My job today is to find out who this man really is and to determine what he's doing at the Carlisle house.'

'Understood,' Bellerose said. 'I need to be in the room with you.'

'Agreed. With the proviso that you don't repeat anything that could compromise the security of my operation.'

'Understood.' The two men shook hands.

The car pulled to the kerb. Chief Inspector Bellerose and Thomas got out of the car. Thomas tipped his head back and stared up at the house, as if inviting the structure to share its secrets.

'Mr Charles?' The other man stared at him.

'Ready,' Thomas said.

A stout woman with a hawk-like nose over thin lips opened the door for them.

Shrew, Thomas thought.

'Miss Carlisle,' Bellerose said.

'It's about time you showed up. Catherine is here. She's upstairs packing her things. Are you here to arrest her?'

'You know I can't discuss an ongoing investigation, Miss Carlisle. I would like a word with Michael Blackwell.'

'Blackie? Whatever for? He hasn't done anything.' Her eyes softened. 'He's not doing well, inspector. Benton's death has shaken him. He drinks too much. He's probably passed out in his room. He needs treatment, poor man.' Her eyes lit on Thomas. 'Who're you?'

Something in Isobel's Carlisle's manner – an underlying aggression – made Thomas want to run. He didn't envy Bellerose having to conduct an investigation with the likes of Isobel Carlisle hovering about.

'This is Thomas Charles,' Bellerose said. 'He is helping me.'

'If you'd do your jobs this would be resolved by now,' Isobel said.

'Where is Mr Blackwell?' Bellerose asked.

'Upstairs, last door on the right. Now, if you'll excuse me.'

Thomas followed Bellerose up the stairs and along the dark hallway. The thick carpet muffled their footsteps. They stopped before the last door on the right.

'Perkins, you stand on the inside of the door in case he makes a run for it. Simmons, you stay out here.' Bellerose knocked.

'Mr Blackwell? It's Chief Inspector Bellerose. Police.' Bellerose opened the door. He and Thomas stepped inside.

The stench of the stale cigarette smoke assaulted Thomas as he and Bellerose stepped into the room. The curtains had been left open. No lamps were lit, and the gloom seeped into every corner.

Michael Blackwell's imposter sat on a chintz chair tucked into the corner. An ashtray filled with dirty cigarettes sat next to him. A tray with a half-full bottle of brandy sat on the table within reach. Michael Blackwell didn't move when the men walked in. His skin was pale and shiny with perspiration, his shirt damp at the armpits and dingy around the collar. God only knew how long he had been sitting there. Thomas wondered if Blackwell's impostor was on a mission to drink himself to death.

Michael Blackwell looked at Thomas with bleary eyes.

'Mr Blackwell, my name is Thomas Charles –'

'You know, don't you? You found out. I killed them.' He ran his hand over his face and took a sip of brandy. 'I'm glad it's over. Relieved.'

Bellerose moved close to Blackwell, as if he wanted to speak to him. Thomas waved him back.

'When's the last time you had something to eat?' Thomas asked.

Blackwell looked at him with bleary eyes. 'Can't remember.'

He opened the door that led to the hallway and said to Constable Simmons, 'Find this man something to eat, will you please? A pot of tea, some bread and butter.'

He stepped back into the room, walked across to the window, and opened it so the fresh rain-drenched air could circulate. Thomas resisted the urge to stick his head outside and take in great gasps of the sweet clean air. Instead, he went to the wardrobe and pulled out a clean shirt.

'Here.' He thrust the shirt at Michael Blackwell. 'Go and have a wash. You can use the bathrooms up here. Wash your face and change your shirt. Get yourself sorted. When you are finished, you can explain who you really are and what you've been up to.'

'I think he might need a doctor,' Bellerose said. 'He seems like he is about to crack.'

'He does. He is. We'll get him seen to. After I speak to him.'

Michael Blackwell came back into the room.

'Have a seat. Get comfortable. Then you can tell me who you really are and why you've impersonated Michael Blackwell.' The impostor sat back down in the chintz chair, while Thomas pulled a chair from the writing table next to him and sat down in it. He leaned back and crossed his legs, settling in to wait. This man would talk; Thomas was sure of it.

'I'll tell you everything. Just don't send me back. They'll kill me if I go back.'

A constable came back with a tray laden with a mug of tea and several slices of bread and butter. The man ate hungrily. After he gulped down the tea, Blackwell poured straight brandy into his teacup and drank it. He sat for a moment, staring at nothing in particular.

'I'm so tired of all the lies. These people have been so kind to me. I'm glad this is over. I don't mind what happens to me, just don't send me back.'

Thomas waited.

'My real name is Dieter Reinsinger. Michael Blackwell was married to my sister, Leni. The Gestapo took them. They're dead. I'm sure of it. It's all my fault. That part of my story is true.'

'Perhaps you could start from the beginning,' Chief Inspector Bellerose said.

Dieter Reinsinger nodded. 'I was an accountant in Berlin. I had a good job, made a good wage, and was able to provide for my sister, Leni. I felt responsible for Leni's welfare. Our parents died, you see, when we were in our early twenties. We only had each other and we were very close. Leni was a beautiful girl with a romantic streak and wild ideas. She kept house, dabbled a bit in the arts. Leni was a romantic, a dreamer.

'She met Michael Blackwell in 1928 at a friend's dinner party. She kept their relationship a secret. They married. We all lived together in my apartment. I hoped my sister would settle down, give up her wild schemes.'

Bellerose stepped close to Dieter, as if he wanted to say something. Thomas shook his head. Bellerose stepped away. They waited.

'I hated him,' Dieter said. 'He was everything I wasn't. He was brave, where I was a coward. He spoke out about the way things are in Germany now. I was too afraid to do so.

'He took my sister away from me. He put her in danger …' Dieter's voice drifted off. Thomas waited.

'I tried to ignore the way Germany changed, as if that would stave off the inevitable. In September 1935 when the Nuremberg Laws were passed, Michael was outraged and he didn't care who knew his feelings.' He looked at Thomas with such sadness, Thomas almost reached out to him. 'I don't know why the Jews are so reviled. I don't understand it. Businesses were seized. Jews were no longer citizens of Germany, but subjects. The laws forbade Jews from practising medicine, teaching at universities, or holding civil service jobs. It's unbelievable that your newspapers don't report on this. And the people in Germany just go along with it. No wonder Michael was so agitated.'

He reached for a pack of cigarettes with a shaking hand. Thomas took the pack from him, put a cigarette in his mouth, lit it, and handed the lit cigarette to Dieter. Dieter took it, nodding his thanks. 'Our next-door neighbours, the Neibaums were the first to suffer. They were quiet people. He was an antique bookseller, who lived a quiet life with his wife. One of their letters was accidentally left in the neighbourhood gossip's post box. She accidentally opened it, and soon everyone on our street knew that Mr Neibaum had inherited a substantial amount of money from a long-lost uncle. He wanted to start an orphanage with the money.

'I was just coming home from work when the men came. They hit him with a stick and told him that if he didn't leave the country, they would take him and his wife to a camp.' Dieter gave a hollow laugh. 'Mr Neibaum lay in his courtyard, his teeth knocked out, his leg broken, his body beaten and battered. Of course, he agreed to leave. Not that he had a choice. But there was a price to be paid for his freedom.'

'What price?' Thomas asked.

'His inheritance. The only way he could get an exit visa to leave the country was to pay the tax – ninety per cent of his inheritance.' Dieter wiped his eyes.

'What does this have to do with Michael Blackwell?' Thomas bit back his impatience.

Dieter flashed an irritated look at Thomas. 'Everything. Michael was an educated man, with a deep knowledge of politics, economics, and history. He and Leni were up to something. I knew it. I'm sure my neighbours knew it. When they went out, I searched Michael's wardrobe and found a box of brochures, innocuous-looking at first glance, entitled *Learn About Beautiful Germany*. I reckoned that Michael – who freelanced as a writer – had written the brochures to sell for the upcoming Olympics.

'Curious about Michael's writing, I opened the brochure. What I saw inside was not information about beautiful Germany. Instead, he had written a scathing indictment of life under the Nazi regime, along with a map of the locations of all the camps. By this time, the Gestapo was watching us. It was just a matter of time before they raided our house. When they found the brochures, they would take us all away.

'I hated him. He put my sister – and me – in danger. I had to do something. You see that, don't you? I couldn't just sit by and do nothing.

'I came home from work one day, just in time to see Leni and Michael loaded into the back of a black Mercedes. Michael struggled. Actually punched one of those Gestapo thugs in the nose. They retaliated by knocking Leni down. I watched from a neighbour's porch, too cowardly to do anything. They weren't supposed to take Leni.' Dieter closed his eyes and bowed his head. The grief emanated from his very essence. 'They shoved them in the back of the car. As the car drove away, I knew I would never see my sister again. I thought about killing myself. I should have.

'I went into our flat and took the money we kept hidden under a floorboard in the kitchen. Michael Blackwell's passport was hidden there as well. As I held my brother-in-law's passport in my hand, I realised that we resembled each other. Our colouring was the same, and the photo was old enough to account for any minor differences in the way we look. I took the passport and the money and went to the British Embassy in Berlin. I told them I was Michael Blackwell, and that the Gestapo had taken my wife and her brother. They managed to get me out of the country.'

'And you came knocking on Benton's door posing as an imposter?' Thomas said. 'Taking a bit of a risk, weren't you? What if they asked about long-lost Aunt So-and-So?'

'I had nowhere else to go. What would you have me do? I knew enough about Isobel and Benton to get by. Michael spoke often of his perfect English childhood. He used to regale Leni and me with stories of his antics with Benton and Isobel when they were young. Swimming, tennis, horseback riding, skiing in Switzerland in the winter. I knew about Michael's father's house in Bournemouth and the ghost stories that he used to tell Isobel when they were children.'

Dieter shook his head. 'Michael Blackwell was a raconteur. When Michael told us his stories, Leni and

I clung to his words, captivated by his life here. Benton and Isobel hadn't seen Michael since he was a boy. Benton – for all his drinking, and the shoddy way he treated his wife – welcomed me with open arms. Of course, Isobel followed suit.'

Dieter took a slice of the buttered bread. While he ate, Thomas moved over to the window. Thomas believed the man's story. This man didn't have the courage to steal documents from Benton and pass them off to Marlena X, nor did he have anything to do with Benton Carlisle's murder. He was too fragile to have killed Benton. Why would he harm the man who had taken him in and given him shelter?

Bellerose stood in the corner of the room. He leaned against the wall. His eyes were hard, his lips pursed.

'Did you steal documents from Benton?' Thomas watched Dieter's face, looking for any sign of duplicity.

Dieter stopped chewing. He met Thomas's gaze directly. 'No. Of course not.'

'Why did you say you killed them?' Thomas asked.

Dieter looked at him, startled at first, then embarrassed.

'You said it was all your fault. What did you mean?' The compassion slipped away from Thomas's face. In that brief instant he saw Dieter's cowardice. He knew what Dieter had done. Now he wanted the man who sat across from him to give words to his betrayal.

'I called the Gestapo,' Dieter whispered.

'You called the Gestapo on your own brother-in-law? Now I know why you stay drunk. I'd do the same, if I were in your position.'

'Don't judge me, sir,' Dieter said. 'I was trying to look after my sister, and my efforts got her killed. I have to live with that.'

219

'We should send you back,' Thomas said. There was a cold edge to his voice. 'Let you suffer like your sister did, like Michael Blackwell did.'

'You gave me your word,' Dieter Reinsinger said.

'I know,' Thomas said. 'I'm now wishing I hadn't.'

Bellerose spoke. 'Is that all, Mr Charles? I'll take it from here, with your permission. Mr Reinsinger needs medical attention.'

Thomas turned his back on them and stared out the window. Outside, the rain had stopped. A woman stepped into an alleyway to put her umbrella down. She shook it before she rolled it up and stuffed it in the shopping bag she carried. Puddles had formed in the street, like small sun-dappled lakes. Two children wearing rubber boots stomped in one, only to be admonished by the nanny who trailed after them.

Another woman loitered beneath a tree at the entrance to the square. She didn't carry an umbrella. Instead she wore a large hat that all but covered her face. Thomas recognised her right away. His heartbeat quickened. Marlena X. Below him, Mrs Carlisle stepped out the front door of the Carlisle house and onto the pavement, hatless, without her handbag or a coat. She walked towards Marlena X, back straight, her steps sure.

'No,' Thomas called out through the open window.

Marlena X looked up at Thomas. She smiled at him, knowing that he couldn't reach Mrs Carlisle in time to save her, knowing that Thomas would give chase, and she would lead him right into her trap. Helpless, Thomas watched as Marlena X turned and hurried away, with Mrs Carlisle in hot pursuit.

Chapter Seventeen

Marlena X stuffed the newspaper in her bag and took off at a quick clip. Without thinking, Cat followed suit, keeping her eyes on the woman as she wove through the foot traffic. They seemed to walk for ever. When the houses gave way to businesses, more people milled along the pavement. Soon Cat found herself stuck in a throng of stationary pedestrians waiting for a traffic light to change. Marlena X hadn't bothered to take off her rain hat. By keeping her eyes focused on it, Cat was just able to see Marlena X standing at the front of the crowd waiting to cross. Cat managed to weave her way through the wall of people, careful not to get too close.

A double-decker bus came barrelling along. Cat saw the rain hat step in front of it. She heard the collective gasp of the crowd. Someone said, 'Foolish woman.'

Marlena X crossed the street, leaving Cat stuck in the crowd, penned in from all sides.

On a whim, Cat backtracked, taking a parallel street that ran the same direction Marlena X was headed. She walked fast to make time. She spied the floppy hat just two blocks ahead of her. Marlena X turned a corner. Cat followed.

The businesses on this street – dress shops, a beauty salon, and a tea shop – were just opening for the day. Marlena X took her hat off and stuffed it into the pocket of her raincoat. Cat ducked into the doorway of a tobacco shop just as she turned around. Cat took a deep breath, counted to five, and peered out at the street. Marlena X was gone. Cat continued down the street until she came to a dress shop, Colleen's Fashions and Accessories. Further along was a tobacco shop, but it was not yet open for the day. The pavement in front of Colleen's had been freshly swept. Inside, an elderly woman walked around the shop with a feather duster.

The bell on the door jingled as Cat went in. She realised that not only was she hatless and gloveless, she didn't have a handbag either. She couldn't very well act as though she were shopping. The shop was a small one, with six round racks of dresses and a selection of shoes on a shelf against one wall. Another wall held drawers that Cat imagined contained undergarments and other unmentionables.

In the far corner of the store, a wooden staircase led to the second floor. Two women, a blonde and a brunette, both in their early twenties and very smartly dressed, folded a stack of women's vests and placed them on the shelf behind the counter. They looked up at the same time and surveyed Cat, who was breathless from the chase.

'Forgive me. My friend just went up. Do you mind?'

'You're a friend of Marlena's? She's just arrived.' The brunette pointed to the stairwell and turned her attention back to her task.

'The other woman is up there already. She was waiting when we got here,' the blonde girl said. 'And mind how you go. There's no light bulb. The landlord's too cheap to buy one.'

Cat took a piece of paper from the stack on the counter.

'Excuse me,' She spoke quietly, just in case Marlena changed her mind and came downstairs. The blonde girl

222

turned around. Cat beckoned her to come close. She whispered, 'This is an urgent police matter. I need you to telephone to Chief Inspector Bellerose at Scotland Yard and give him this address. Tell him that Catherine Carlisle told you to call. Will you do that?'

The brunette spoke. 'Is Marlena in some sort of trouble?'

'She might be,' Cat said.

'Serves her right. She's rotten to the core. I've known it all along.' The woman met Cat's eyes. 'What's happened to your eye? Did Marlena do that?'

'I'm afraid she did,' Cat said.

The woman took the paper from Cat's hand. 'I'll call for you.'

'Is there another exit? Around the back, perhaps?' Cat wanted to make sure that there was no other means of escape.

'No, ma'am.'

Cat crept up the stairs, testing each step for creaky boards. At the top a door had been left open just a crack. A small triangle of light escaped onto the landing, cutting through the murky darkness.

Cat heard movement in the room. She stepped closer and peered through the crack in the door. A tiny bed, covered with a tattered quilt, took up one corner. Next to it was a table with a washbasin and pitcher. A suitcase lay open on the bed. Marlena X moved through the room, gathering her belongings and tossing them carelessly into the suitcase. Cat wouldn't have recognised the woman had she seen her on the street. She was a tiny thing, with a straight back and a long neck that reminded Cat of the ballet dancers she'd loved to watch as a child.

While Marlena X's body was supple and willowy, any grace bestowed on her stopped there. Her face was nondescript and unremarkable. Mousy hair clung to her head in greasy tendrils. Her eyes had the hard merciless look that Cat remembered from the day Marlena attacked her, as if her face froze in that menacing look, galvanising that particular part of her personality. Marlena X was confident, strong, and as terrifying as a poisonous snake.

'I've come for my money. Give it to me now, please. I'd like to leave.' Cat's heart stopped. She recognised the soft-spoken, well-modulated voice. 'You're never going to fit all of those items into that suitcase. Here, let me help you.'

Marie stepped into Cat's line of sight. Not quite believing what she witnessed, Cat stepped further into the shadows. She covered her mouth with her hand before she could cry out. Marie? Cat couldn't believe it. Through the crack in the door, she watched as Marie took several dresses on hangers from Marlena's arm.

Marlena picked up a blue sweater and folded it into a tiny ball. 'I don't know if I should pay you at all.'

'What do you mean? I risked everything to help your cause,' Marie said. 'Now Benton's dead. Isobel is beside herself. We haven't any money and we need to leave. I upheld my part of the bargain, and I expect to be paid.'

'And what will you do if I decide against paying you? Go to the police?'

'You shouldn't have killed Benton,' Marie said. 'You made a mistake – admit it. Murdering him brought attention to us.'

'I didn't kill him,' Marlena said.

'I'm not stupid. Never mind that. When do I get my money? You told me if I got you the documents from

Mr Carlisle, I would be taken care of. I did as you asked. I need to leave now. I can't go back to that house. I'll be arrested. Give me my money and I'll be gone.'

The woman shut the suitcase. The latches snapped shut. 'But you failed, didn't you?'

'I most certainly did not, and you know it,' Marie said.

'You are a fool. Mrs Carlisle was switching the documents right under your nose. All the documents you gave us were useless.'

'That's ridiculous. Catherine? Of course she didn't –'

Marie fell silent. Marlena X stood in the middle of the room. She peered through the crack in the door and spoke to Cat. 'You may as well come in, Mrs Carlisle. I know you're there.'

'Catherine? What – what are you doing here?'

Cat stepped into the room. She barely recognised Marie, who wore a well-tailored, expensive-looking navy suit. Her hair had been properly set and fell in waves around her face. She even wore face powder and lipstick.

'What were you thinking? Taking Ben's documents and giving them to this –' Cat nodded at Marlena, '– spy? She's going to take the information you gave her and use it against our country. How could you?'

'How could I not? I lost my husband and my sons in the war. My whole family. Do you have any idea how it feels to lose everyone you love? I have nothing, no old-age pension, no home, nothing. This country took everything from me. I am owed a little something back, and I don't care how I get it.' Marie's eyes flashed with anger. 'Sanctimony doesn't suit you, Catherine. You're a naive woman who has led a sheltered life. You know nothing of struggle.'

'How could you say that to me?'

'Enough,' Marlena X snapped. She pointed a gun at Marie. 'Mrs Quimby, you have failed miserably.' She turned to Cat and spoke to her as if she were a child. 'In this business, as you will perhaps learn, Mrs Carlisle, it does not do to leave loose ends.'

'Wait.' Cat stepped in front of Marlena X, blocking Marie in the process. 'Just let her go. You're going to leave. No one's going to find you. What do you think Marie's going to do, go to the police and tell them the German agent she was collaborating with left her without paying? There's nothing we can do. I'll see to Marie. I'll give her money to keep her quiet.'

'It doesn't work like that. Now step aside, or I'll shoot you both.'

'The police are coming, Marlena. It's over,' Cat said.

'I don't believe you,' Marlena said.

'I told one of the girls downstairs to call the chief inspector who is investigating Benton's murder. She doesn't like you very much.'

'Marlena, she's right. There's nothing I can do –'

Marlena pointed the gun at Marie. She fired.

'No,' Cat cried out. Her voice sounded as though it were under water. She rushed over to Marie, just as she collapsed onto the ground, a vermillion bloom forming on her shoulder like a poppy opening to the sun. Cat grabbed the pillow from the bed, shook the casing off, and used it to staunch the flow, while Marlena X stood by, a smug look on her face, the hand that held the gun hanging at her side. Marie was alive, white-faced and wide-eyed, but she was alive.

'Marie, stay with me,' Cat said.

'I'm not dying,' Marie said. She looked at Cat with glassy eyes as her breath started to come in rapid gasps.

She grabbed Cat's hand. 'Tell Isobel I love her. Tell her I tried to make things right.'

'Move away from her, Mrs Carlisle. Now. Get away or I'll shoot her again.' Marlena X stepped close to Marie, the gun in her hand steady and sure.

Cat stood up.

'She'll live,' Marlena X said. 'You're a novice at this game, Mrs Carlisle. You've no one to rescue you. No one knows where you are. Stupid of you to follow me, really. Reckless. I've a score to settle with Mr Charles.'

'Mr Charles?' Realisation dawned on Catherine. *So that's why he'd been following me. Does he work for Reginald too?* She hadn't questioned anyone, not Reginald, not Chloe. She'd blindly allowed herself to be used by all of them. She imagined – much like Marlena X was doing to Marie – when they were finished with her they would cast her aside as well.

Marlena's brow furrowed. She cocked her head in question, like a curious puppy. 'You don't know? Your Mr Charles killed my husband. Murdered him in cold blood. So while I was trying to get your husband's drawings – and I admit, you've outsmarted me in that endeavour – my real goal was to settle the score between us. Mr Charles took away the only thing that mattered to me. Now he must pay. You've been used, Mrs Carlisle. They've cast you aside and turned their backs on you. You British have got to be the most gullible fools …'

She moved to the bed, turning her back on Cat to retrieve the suitcase. Cat picked up the closest thing she could find – a heavy wooden chair that was missing a leg – and swung it at Marlena X. It splintered when it hit. Wooden fragments went flying. Marlena X was caught off guard, and when the chair connected with her head, she dropped her gun. It went skidding across the floor, coming to rest just out of Marlena's reach.

'I wonder what Thomas Charles will think when he finds you dead in a puddle of your own blood,' Marlena said in a whisper. She reached behind her and pulled a knife from some hidden place. 'I wonder what Mr Charles will think when I cut your pretty little face to ribbons.'

Marlena advanced. Cat needed to run, but she couldn't move her feet.

'Drop the knife, Marlena.'

Startled, Cat turned. Thomas Charles stood in the doorway, a pistol pointed at Marlena X. The sight of him was so out of context and so utterly surprising, that she forgot about Marlena for just a moment. She stared at Thomas, mouth agape, wondering how he knew where to find her. So focused was she on Thomas Charles that she didn't see Marlena charging towards her until it was too late. In one swoop, Marlena wrenched Cat's arm behind her. She stood behind Cat, the blade of the knife cold against her throat.

'Drop the gun, Thomas,' Marlena said.

'Don't make me kill you, Marlena. Are you ready to die?' The calm in his voice frightened Cat.

'Your silly little protégé will die too. You fire, and I shall slice her throat like a piece of ham. How will Reginald like that? You've botched this one, Thomas. You've failed miserably as a watcher. You've got your new agent killed. Again.' Marlena X laughed.

'I don't care. She's a new agent, untrained. She's replaceable.' He kept the gun trained on Marlena, his hand steady. 'My issue, Marlena, is with you.'

'I told you I would get revenge. You didn't believe me,' Marlena said. 'Now look at me. I'd say I have the upper hand, wouldn't you.'

Marlena X wrenched Cat's arm tighter. Cat cried out. Marlena smelled as though she hadn't bathed in weeks. Her breath, hot against Cat's cheek, smelled of onions and garlic and something noxious. Hate, Cat reasoned. Marlena X smelled of hate.

'Rather unprofessional of you, Marlena. Good spies are not supposed to be emotionally involved. And here you are, settling scores. I believe, dear woman, that you are losing your touch.' Thomas took a step closer and lowered his gun. 'I didn't mean to kill your husband.'

'But you did, didn't you?' Marlena's grip on Cat loosened ever so slightly. Cat stilled her breathing. Thomas Charles was up to something. She watched his face, eager for a hint of what it was.

'Think about it, Marlena. You're the one we were after – there's no hiding that. This job by its very nature exposes you – exposes us – to a certain amount of risk. Your husband was an innocent victim. He wasn't our target in Berlin. You were. You knew we were following you, watching your every move. So why the devil did you lead us to your home?'

'Are you blaming me for my husband's murder?' Cat cried out in pain as Marlena tightened her grip.

'I am. And I can see by the look in your eyes that you blame yourself. You tried to assuage your guilt by killing Gwen. It didn't work did it? What are you going to do, murder every one of my agents? Vengeance won't expunge the demons, Marlena. You and I both know that.'

Marlena pushed Cat so hard she fell to the floor. When she landed on her wrist, splitting pain travelled up her arm to her shoulder. A constellation of stars, a galaxy in its own right, circled behind her eyes. She heard a gunshot. Waited for the pain, for the feel of her lifeblood as it drained out. All she could hear was the deep resonance of her own breath.

'Thomas?' she called out.

'I didn't kill her,' he said.

Cat lay on the floor for a moment, ears ringing, heart thumping. Sirens blared outside. She turned her head and saw Marlena on the floor, clutching her knee. Marie lay still, her shirt sodden with her blood. Cat rolled onto her back. Tears leaked out of her eyes. She felt the hot wetness of them as they slid down the sides of her face.

Thumping footsteps pounded up the rickety stairs. Sergeant Perkins, Chief Inspector Bellerose, and a gaggle of uniformed officers stormed into the room. They broke into groups and rushed over to Marie and Marlena X, blocking Cat's view. Cat pushed herself into a sitting position and watched the chaos around her.

Thomas Charles and Chief Inspector Bellerose stood near the doorway with their heads together. They spoke in hushed voices before they nodded at each other, as if coming to some agreement. Thomas hurried over to Cat. He held out his hand to her. She took it. He pulled her to her feet, but he didn't let her go. Instead he pulled her close and whispered in her ear. 'I'm very fond of St Edmund's pippins.'

Chapter Eighteen

'Are you sure you'll be all right? What if you need something and no one's around to fetch it for you?' Aunt Lydia fussed with pillows, while Annie brought in a tray with a fresh pot of tea and a rack of toast.

'Then I'll simply get off the couch and get it myself. The doctor said bed rest, but he didn't say I couldn't walk to the kitchen for tea.' Cat leaned forward, holding her arm – immobilised in a sling – against her chest, as Lydia arranged her pillows. 'I'm going back to him tomorrow. I'm sure he'll say I'm fine.'

'Are you sure you don't want a powder for the pain?' Annie poured out tea for Cat.

'She's trying to be tough,' Lydia said. 'She's probably concussed, her shoulder's pounding with pain, but she's being stubborn.'

Annie got one of the packets of the powders the doctor had prescribed for pain and set it on the table by the sofa, along with a fresh pitcher of water. 'I'll just leave this here in case you change your mind.'

Lydia looked at Cat with a worried expression on her face. 'Maybe we shouldn't go.'

The altercation with Marlena X had left Cat with a dislocated shoulder and a concussion, but she was on the mend and was craving a bit of time to herself. The doctor had put her under an anaesthetic, and while she slept, he'd popped the shoulder back in place. She'd woken up sore, but had been allowed to go home the next day, provided that she rested until he released her from care.

Since then, Annie and Aunt Lydia had fussed over Cat constantly. She spent the better part of her day on the couch in Lydia's studio, where she dozed and read and listened to Annie and Lydia while they painted. Annie had proven an excellent student. She listened well and asked thoughtful questions. While Cat was grateful for their care, she was craving a bit of quiet. She didn't dare get off the couch while Annie and Aunt Lydia were near. They would flock over like a gaggle of geese, trying to make Cat's convalescence easier, not aware that they were smothering her in the process.

Alicia Montrose also stopped by every day, bringing a different gift with her each time, and staying long enough to visit. The room was awash in flower arrangements, boxes of biscuits and chocolates, and a quantity of magazines – none of which caught Cat's interest.

She questioned the events of the past week, replaying everything in her mind to try to find answers. She hadn't heard from Chloe or Reginald. She didn't expect to hear from Thomas Charles, but surely someone would tell her how things had ended. What had happened to Blackie? Did Marlena confess to killing Ben? And Marie? How was she? Would she go to prison? Cat couldn't fathom all that had happened in the past week. The life she had known in Kensington was no more. She would bury her husband, put her best face forward, and would probably never see any of the well-heeled Kensington set that she and Benton had called their friends again.

'Catherine, are you even listening to us?' Lydia and Annie stood side by side, staring at Cat with concern in their eyes.

232

'I'm not, actually,' Cat said. 'You've both been so good to me, and I appreciate it more than you will know. Go enjoy yourselves for a couple of hours. I'll be fine.' When the door shut behind them, Cat breathed a sigh of relief. Blessed silence. She lay back on the couch. The sun came in the window. The beams warmed her face. Soon she dozed. And dreamt.

The grim reaper was near her, with his long flowing black cloak, the cavernous hood that hid his face and hair. He carried a scythe. In her dream the blade glistened in the moonlight, rapier sharp, as relentless as death itself. She was at a cemetery near a church; fog swirled around gothic tombstones in the exaggerated curlicues of a stage play. Cat walked through the evanescent mist, but every step she took seemed to take her further away from her destination. The reaper's footsteps echoed her own. She stopped and turned to face him. He moved towards her, floating over the ground until he hovered so near Cat she could feel the cold death as it encircled her.

She tried to scream, but no sound came out. She turned to run, but found her feet frozen, stuck to the ground. The reaper's breath came forth in a hypnotic, rhythmic cadence. She reached out her arms and flung the reaper's hood back, the black of it like inky water in her hands. Isobel Carlisle's cold angry eyes stared at her. The knocking sound of death came from somewhere in the distance, soft but relentless. Isobel turned her head in the direction of it and disappeared. The mist disappeared; the cemetery vanished.

Cat woke up and pulled herself out of the darkness of the dream. She sat up, taking in the familiar surroundings of Aunt Lydia's living room. Awake now, Cat realised that someone was indeed knocking on the front door.

'Coming,' she called out. The knocking stopped. Cat stood up, careful to hold the sling that held her arm steady in place. She opened the front door, surprised to see Thomas Charles standing there, holding a large bouquet of yellow roses and a parcel wrapped in gold paper.

'Mr Charles,' Cat said. 'What a surprise.'

Thomas Charles had the good grace to look embarrassed. 'I've come bearing gifts.'

'Come in,' she said. 'I'm in here.'

He followed her into Aunt Lydia's studio.

'Your aunt's studio?'

'Yes,' she said. 'My aunt and Annie have put me up in here, so they can keep an eye on me. They're gone now. Would you like tea?'

'No, thank you,' he said. He walked to the wall where Lydia's pictures hung. While he studied the paintings, Cat studied him. He had the upright posture of a solider or a horseman. She visualised him in an ancient portrait, with a lacy collar round his neck and sword in his belt.

'You can use that chair.' Cat pointed to a maple chair that sat at Lydia's work table. Thomas grabbed it and set it near the couch, while Cat grabbed an empty vase from a shelf and poured water from the pitcher. That complete, she plunked the flowers in the water.

'This'll do for now. I'll trim them up and arrange them later.'

'How's the shoulder? How are you?'

'On the mend,' she said. 'They feared I had a slight concussion. The shoulder was dislocated. It's fixed now. I'm a bit sore, but other than that I'm fine. What's in the package?'

'A small gift for you,' Thomas said. He handed the wrapped package to Cat. 'It comes with an explanation and a proposition. Open it.'

Cat tore the paper away. Inside was a slim book entitled, *A Photo History of Historical Churches and Cemeteries,* by Thomas Charles.

'So you really are a historian,' Cat said. 'I thought that might be a cover for your real job.'

'It is, so to speak,' Thomas said. He stared at the book in her hand, as if deciding just what to say. 'It started out as a cover, but I've actually come to enjoy the research and the writing. That book has garnered me some critical acclaim. More importantly, it has allowed me to travel extensively, under the guise of a mild-mannered writer.'

Cat raised her eyebrows. Mr Charles hardly seemed the mild-mannered writer to her, with his grey eyes and handsome face, with its knowing expression. She had never really studied his face before. Now, in the quiet of her aunt's studio, she saw pain and a fair measure of suffering reflected there. She wondered at the cause of it.

'I can't help but feel that Reginald made use of me,' Cat said.

'Although I don't approve of his noted absence, you shouldn't blame him. There are political machinations in play now. Reginald can't be seen to have any involvement with this. This business doesn't offer a lot of explanations, Mrs Carlisle. If you're going to continue in it, you'll need to learn to work with the information you're given without much question. It's better that way, safer. I will tell you that Marie is recovering. Marlena X claims she didn't kill Benton, and I tend to believe her.

'We've managed to keep Marie's involvement with German intelligence off the front page of the newspapers, thank God. Chief Inspector Bellerose has leads he's pursuing in connection with Benton's murder. He hasn't shared that information with me. He has requested –

235

rather emphatically, I may add – we now leave the murder investigation to him. He will not allow any more interference from me. He's hinted that he's onto a promising lead.'

'Freddy Sykes, I'm sure of it.' Cat said.

'Best not to think about that,' Thomas said. 'I'd like to talk to you about your future. I'd like you to continue with me, if you're so inclined. Your connections could open doors. I assure you that I will make myself more available than my predecessors.'

'I'm interested,' Cat said. She didn't have to think about it. For the first time in her life, Cat Carlisle felt useful. 'Who's "us"?'

'I'll tell you everything in good time. There are procedures to be followed. You're going to have to trust me.'

'Reginald said that,' Cat said. 'Tell me about you and Marlena.'

Thomas stared at her. Cat waited.

'My partner and I were following her. She led us to her room. Her husband was killed. She blames me. She killed my partner and when that didn't satisfy her need for revenge, she vowed to kill anyone I ever cared about …'

Cat wanted to say to something, but she didn't know what.

'Enough of that. Here's my idea: You and I need to concoct a friendship that your friends and family will believe in. I've given you this book thinking you can develop an interest in historical churches and cemeteries. When you're ready, I can offer you a job as my assistant. That will allow us to work together, and travel together, if need be, without raising too many questions.'

Cat took the book and thumbed through it. 'Did you take these pictures?'

'Afraid so,' Thomas said. 'I'm not very good at it.'

'They're not half bad.' She held out her hand. 'I'll look forward to working with you.'

Thomas smiled and shook it.

'One more question, Mr Charles. What's happened to the man who was posing as Michael Blackwell?'

'Dieter Reinsinger? He suffered a complete mental breakdown, I'm afraid to say. He's at a sanatorium having a rest cure. With time, he should recover.'

'They won't send him back to Germany, will they?'

'I don't think so,' Thomas said.

'Why aren't the newspapers reporting on Hitler? I've been reading everything I could find, trying to find some hint of what he's up to. There's nothing.'

'I have no idea, only speculation. Let's not bother with that now.' Thomas said. 'You rest and get better. I'll send you more reading material.'

Cat thought of the day she went to meet Reginald in the park and had asked God for a way out of her life. Cat shook her head.

'What are you smiling at?'

'Not five days ago, I was setting off to meet Reginald. I actually asked for a sign.' She laughed. 'Look at all that's happened.'

'It seems as though your prayers were answered, Mrs Carlisle,' Thomas said.

'Indeed it does,' Cat said.

Chapter Nineteen

Benton Carlisle's funeral took place on a sunny June morning. As was her custom, Isobel made all the arrangements for a private graveside service near the Carlisle plot at Brompton Cemetery, followed by a reception at the Carlisle house after the burial. Cat wouldn't have found out about the funeral at all if it hadn't been for Alicia Montrose, who telephoned Cat and told her of Isobel's plans.

'I've received a card in the mail with the details,' Alicia said. 'So Victorian, I couldn't believe it. I can just see Isobel in black bombazine. I knew in an instant that it would be just like her to plan Benton's funeral and not tell you about it. You must go, darling. They'll talk otherwise. Just make an appearance. Jeremy will escort us. I'll be right there with you – promise. No one will give you any trouble in front of me. Now, do you need to borrow something black? We'll get you a new hat with a veil to cover your bruised eye. What time should I send the car for you?' Cat left the details in Alicia's capable hands, and Alicia came through with a proper suit in black tropical-weight wool, and a hat with a marvellous veil.

Now they were in the back of the promised car – Alicia, her husband Jeremy, and Cat – in their mourning clothes, on their way to the cemetery. Alicia scrutinised Cat's black eye, now faded to a jaundiced shade of yellow. Cat wondered just how much Jeremy and Alicia knew about Benton's death.

Jeremy Montrose worked as an architect at a successful firm with branches in London and Edinburgh, taking over as head of the firm when his father retired, after a long and illustrious career. He designed bridges, so his work took him all over the world. Alicia went with him when she could, but his travel gave Alicia a lot of time to herself. She claimed to treasure the freedom and confessed that time away from each other was the secret to a happy marriage.

Cat had always been amazed at the obvious love the two shared for each other. She and Alicia had conceived children at the same time, an event that had deepened the women's budding friendship. While Cat and Alicia had spent week-long holidays at the Montroses' house in Scotland, shopped for clothes, nursery furnishings, and an appropriate nanny when the time was right, Jeremy hovered in the background, ready to offer his not inconsiderable resources and – his most precious gift – his time. Now Alicia and Jeremy sat next to each other, holding hands like a newly married couple, still in love after all these years.

Jeremy smiled at Cat. 'So I thought I'd give my condolences to Isobel and get the boys, if that's all right with you, Alicia. They could do with some running at the park. I only hope I'm up to the task. You haven't met the boys yet, Cat. They're lovely children, but have a tendency to get a little wild when they are cooped up in my mother's house. I figure I've got two hours before the crystal knickknacks she's got scattered about fall into imminent peril.'

'You think she'd have the sense to tuck them away when the boys come to visit, but she says she doesn't care if the children break things,' Alicia said. 'They'll be glad to get to the country, where they can run wild and play outside until they drop from exhaustion. And you, dear Catherine, can rest. I'm going to return you to London with roses on your cheeks and meat on your bones.'

Jeremy leaned over and kissed Alicia on the cheek. 'I'll leave you with the car and see you at the flat. I figure after time spent with Isobel you'll both want to go have a drink and cry on each other's shoulders.'

'Thank you, darling,' Alicia said.

'I just need to get through this,' Cat said. The limousine rolled to a stop behind a line of cars. Cat slid the black veil over her face. With Alicia on one arm and Cat on the other, Jeremy Montrose led the women along the path that wound through the ancient greying tombstones towards the Carlisle plot. There, near a freshly dug pile of earth, sat Benton's elaborate casket, his murdered body inside.

The graveside service was indeed private. Six chairs had been arranged near the gravesite. Isobel sat in one. A matronly woman dressed in a utilitarian grey coat stood behind her. Cat wondered briefly if Isobel was under the care of a nurse. There was a sadness to Benton's older sister. Despite her thick waist and solid arms, a frailty had come over her. Cat almost felt sorry for her, but the feeling vanished when Isobel took one look at her, rose from her seat, and stormed over to Cat, the matronly woman following on her heels.

'You've no business here,' Isobel hissed. 'You murdered him. Can't you stay away?'

'Now, Isobel –' Jeremy let go of Alicia's arm and tried to situate himself between Catherine and Isobel.

'Isobel,' Lady Montrose said, 'please. Mourn your brother today. For heaven's sake, put your grudge away. After today, you and Cat never have to see each other again. Surely you can find some consolation in that.'

'I'm sorry, Alicia, dear. Cat seems to have put you in the middle of our little family grievance. Never mind. I know that I can comport myself with dignity. I cannot speak for the other party.' Isobel squeezed Alicia's hand. 'Please stay in touch with me after all of this is behind us, Alicia. You're such a good friend.'

In the distance, the vicar headed towards the graveside, his white robes billowing out behind him.

'There's the vicar. Let's be seated and think about Benton, shall we,' Jeremy put a hand on Isobel's back and guided her back to her chair. He sat down next to her, putting a comforting arm around her shoulders.

'My God,' Alicia said. 'I had no idea things were that strained between the two of you. Has it always been like that?'

'Since the day I walked into that house, although it has escalated in the past year or so. She wasn't always so mean,' Cat said. 'Your husband is a saint, and so are you. I can't imagine what she would have said if you two weren't with me.'

Alicia smiled. 'He truly is. Come on, darling. Let's get this over with.'

***

Black limousines lined the street in front of the Carlisle house, while some motorcars stopped just long enough for the passengers to alight. The mourners came alone and in groups, a steady throng of people, clad in black, to pay their respects. A group of drivers – those who had been lucky enough to find a place to park – huddled across the street in the shade of the garden square trees, smoking cigarettes, waiting for their employers to return.

'She's hung black crepe on the door. How surprising,' Alicia said. 'Now, Catherine, darling, I want you to draw on that superior strength you possess in spades and keep your wits about you. They'll all be gawking. The key is to give them nothing to gawk about. I am begging you not to do anything reckless.'

A uniformed butler whom Cat had never seen before held the door open for them. Stooped with age, he looked at them with rheumy eyes and offered a basket of black armbands to Jeremy. Jeremy took one and rolled it over the sleeve of his coat. Cat stepped into the hallway, grateful all of a sudden for the veil that hid her bruised eye. These people gossiped like a sewing circle. Cat's black eye and bruised face would only add to the speculation.

The crowd was gathered in the drawing room, where the two sofas had been arranged across from each other. Isobel sat in the middle of one of them, like a queen on a throne. A dozen silver-framed photos of Benton sat on the table next to her. None of them depicted Cat. The woman who had been with her at the churchyard hovered nearby, an agency replacement for the support Marie had given all these years. The mourners would take turns sitting next to Isobel, offering condolences. Isobel would nod her head and say a few words before she dabbed her eyes and put on a brave face, a martyr to her own grief.

The heavy curtains had been drawn against the sunshine, but extra lamps had been brought in and all of them were lit, bathing the room in an artificial electric glow. Cat thought for a moment about what would happen if she threw open the curtains and raised the windows, so the sweet summer air could circulate in the stuffy room.

Uniformed maids circled the room with glasses of sherry and champagne. A drinks trolley, stocked with every type of liquor, a soda syphon, and a fresh bucket of ice rested along one wall. Friends of the family, many of whom Cat had never met, circled through the drawing room to Isobel. Those who didn't sit next to her leaned over and paid their respects. Benton's close friends, the Bradbury-Scotts, the Rothebys, the Symingtons, the Sykes family – including Freddy and his father – would in all probability stay until the booze ran dry.

When Cat and Alicia stepped into the drawing room, conversation stopped. A collective hush fell over the room as all eyes turned towards Cat. She felt the emotion – sympathy, loathing, and curiosity – of the crowd, tempered by Alicia and Jeremy, whose physical proximity to Cat was the conversational equivalent of a warning. No one would dare disrespect Cat while she was under the Montrose aegis.

'Chin up, old thing,' Alicia whispered.

Cat put one foot in front of the other, aware of Jeremy's hand at her lower back.

Lady Bradbury-Scott and her husband, William, broke the ice.

'Catherine, so good to see you.' They both came up to her, air-kissed her cheek and made the requisite small talk. Cat faced them. 'We were so surprised about all this. How are you holding up?'

Cat's voice came out a whisper. 'Very well, thank you. It's been difficult.' William and Jeremy stepped away from the women and huddled their heads together in quiet conversation.

Lady Bradbury-Scott leaned close to Cat and Alicia and whispered, 'Isobel seems to be enjoying all the attention. We were just leaving, Catherine, but I'm glad we were able to see you. Please ring us. We'll do lunch.'

Cat and Alicia watched as Lady Bradbury-Scott grabbed her husband's elbow and steered him out of the house. They saw one of the drivers disengage from the group across the street and hurry towards the Bradbury-Scotts' car.

'I'll never hear from her again,' Cat said. 'And I can honestly say that I'm not bothered by it.'

'You shouldn't be. I've always found her utterly tedious. All she talks about are her dogs and her grandchildren. But give it time, darling. You never know. Can I leave you alone long enough to get a drink?'

'Of course,' Cat said.

More people arrived, while just as many left. They circled through the house like visitors at a museum, surveying the artwork and the furniture. Cat nodded and said thank you to those who stopped to speak. Waiters wove through the crowd with bottles of champagne, refilling glasses. The conversation grew louder as more drinks were consumed. Cat looked around the room and thought that Benton would be happy to see his friends gathered in his memory. She wondered when her grief – if she had any – would surface.

She grabbed a glass of champagne from a passing waiter and watched as Freddy Sykes sat next to Isobel. He took her hand and leaned close, whispering in her ear. Isobel stiffened. She didn't meet Freddy's eyes. Instead she nodded. Freddy got up and walked out of the room. Cat positioned herself behind a group of men whom she recognised from Benton's work, the perfect vantage point to keep an eye on Freddy. He went up the stairs, turning right at the top, towards Isobel's suite. Isobel got up and walked to the back of the house, towards the stairs that led down to the kitchen. Cat set her champagne down, but rather than follow Isobel, she went up the stairs after Freddy Sykes.

Cat didn't want to run into Freddy on her own. She was in no mood for a confrontation with him. Not on the day for mourning Benton. At the top of the stairs, she turned left and went to her room. The door was shut. She pushed it open and went in. All traces of her were gone. The furniture had been taken away, along with the rug that had covered the floor. The curtains had been taken down; the window was open as far as it could be. The only furniture in the room were two chairs. Sergeant Perkins sat in one of them.

'Mrs Carlisle. What are you doing up here?' He jumped up, startled. The chair he was sitting in tipped over and crashed onto the floor. He walked over to the door, opened it, and peered into the hallway. 'Did anyone see you come up here?'

'I don't think so,' Cat said. 'What's going on? What are *you* doing up here?'

Sergeant Perkins shook his head. 'Not at liberty to discuss this with you, ma'am. I need you to go back downstairs. Now.'

'Of course.' Cat hurried downstairs. Were they going to arrest Freddy Sykes? Whatever the police were doing, Isobel was involved. She went downstairs, just in time to find Alicia and Jeremy at the front door.

'There you are,' Alicia said. She squinted her eyes at Cat. 'What's happened?'

'Nothing,' Cat said. 'When can we leave?'

'As soon as I say my goodbyes to Isobel. I'll say them for both of us, shall I? Jeremy's just off now.'

'My social obligation has been fulfilled. Wild children await,' he said.

'Thank you, Jeremy,' Cat said.

'Glad to be of service.' Jeremy waved and left them.

'Now where has Isobel gone?' Alicia and Cat stood in the hallway, surveying the crowd in the drawing room. Cat scanned the room. Isobel was nowhere to be seen.

'I saw her head towards the kitchen a few minutes ago. Must you say goodbye?' The crowd was getting progressively more inebriated. Before too long, someone would start making speeches about Benton's good character. It would be difficult to leave once the speeches started.

'Of course, we can. I'm ready –' Alicia stared at the stairs. Freddy Sykes walked down them, his hands in cuffs. Sergeant Perkins was in front of him, while another police officer walked behind. Isobel stood at the top of the stairs, her hand resting on the bannister, hidden in the shadows as Freddy sauntered down the stairs, an insouciant smile on his face, as if the whole thing were a game.

Now the conversation really did come to a stop, as all eyes focused on Freddy. People came from the drawing room to witness the spectacle on the stairs. They stood watching, mouths agape, embarrassed but unable to look away. Freddy's father moved to the bottom of the stairs. He faced off with Sergeant Perkins.

'What's the meaning of this? Freddy? What's happened?'

'Your son's under arrest, sir. Now step out of my way,' Sergeant Perkins said.

'I'll not step out of your way. I demand you take those cuffs off him. This instant.' Frederick Sykes, Sr., was an irascible man with a mean temper. Cat, who had spent a laborious evening next to him at a dinner, found him very stupid. She'd expressed this to Benton once – back when they were close – and he'd agreed with her.

'Step aside, sir, or I'll remove you myself.' Sergeant Perkins stood on the last step, and looked down at Mr Sykes.

'Hit him, sergeant. The bastard deserves it,' Freddy said.

Freddy's father stepped away. 'Don't look to me for help, Freddy. I'm finished with you. As God is my witness, I wash my hands of you.'

'Of course you'll help me, Father. You see, I've been blackmailing Isobel Carlisle.' Freddy's voice echoed through the crowd, as clear as if he spoke into a microphone. 'I'm going to insist on my day in court.'

'Frederick –'

'No, Father. I'm going to shine the light on everyone's antics. The newspapers are going to love me! Imagine how scandalised everyone will be when they discover that Isobel Carlisle is a lesbian, who's been carrying on an affair with her secretary all these years.' Freddy laughed, a high wheezing sound that caused his father to recoil. 'Better be careful, Father. Who knows what I'll tell them about you.'

Mr Sykes turned on his heel and walked out the front door, slamming it behind him.

'Let's go, Sergeant Perkins,' Freddy said. 'My cell awaits.'

The silence that followed Freddy pulsed with a life of its own, as though everyone who watched him walk down

247

the stairs and out the front door were breathing in the same rhythm, in and out, one heartbeat. When they had finally gone, the mourners looked at each, incredulous and full of questions.

'Someone refill these glasses,' a voice called out. As if on cue, the talking started at once, the air thick with speculation and astonishment.

'I need a drink. So do you,' Alicia said. She grabbed two clean champagne glasses off the sideboard and hurried after the waiter.

Cat watched as Isobel turned and walked towards her bedroom, her guests forgotten. Without thinking, Cat hurried up after her. Isobel walked slowly to her room, unaware that she had been followed, and shut the door. Cat pushed it open and stepped into Isobel's room. Thick carpets covered the old wood. The room was filled with the finest antiques in the house. Isobel's living suite held a Chippendale mahogany sofa with a shell carved back and matching chairs. A writing desk was situated under the window. A Tiffany lamp sat on top of it, providing the only light in the room. Isobel stood with her back to the desk.

'Why have you come in here? I'm humiliated, Catherine. That should please you.'

'How can you say that?' Cat said. 'I've never wanted to see you hurt. I'm not the one with the hatred here, Isobel.'

'It doesn't matter. Marie's gone; Benton's gone.'

'She loves you,' Cat said. 'She wanted me to tell you that. She said that she tried to make things right. She had her reasons for doing what she did. In some ways she was very brave. Will you go and see her?'

'How dare you speak to me of Marie's love. How dare you try to ingratiate yourself into our relationship.' Isobel looked at Cat, her face filled with deep-seated pain. The anguish flooded out of her pores. 'Look what you've reduced me to, Catherine. You've ruined this family.'

'My God, you killed him didn't you? Did you kill Benton?'

The self-righteous indignation that had propped Isobel Carlisle up for a lifetime slipped away. Her spine went soft. She shrank before Cat's eyes. 'This is all because of you, Catherine. You've ruined my life. I've lost everything I love, and it's all because of you.'

Isobel moved over to the sofa. She stared at Cat with a blank look in her eyes. Her skin blanched to the colour of sour milk. A sheen of sweat glistened on her face. *Is she having a heart attack?* Cat moved towards her.

Isobel got to the sofa just as her knees buckled. She sat, gasping for breath.

'Why don't you leave England, go somewhere like America? Get away from all this. You can have a quiet life, Isobel, pick yourself up, start over.'

'I didn't ask for your advice, Catherine. Now get out of my room. Get out of this house. I can hardly stand the sight of you.'

'Very well,' Cat said. She opened the door and was about to step out. 'I'd tell you to go to hell, Isobel, but you're already there.'

***

Cat slept in the next morning. Alicia had taken her to tea at the Ritz. They'd arrived during a lull and took their time over sandwiches and cakes. Alicia had insisted on champagne, after which they consumed pots of tea and enough food to soak up the alcohol.

Cat awoke with a splitting headache and a grumbling stomach. She dressed and went downstairs to discover a note on the table in the hallway. 'Gone to M. Tussauds.' Cat smiled in spite of herself. Annie had been eager to see a wax replica of Wallis Simpson. Aunt Lydia had pretended to be indifferent, but Cat had caught her looking at the advert in the times.

She made herself a pot of tea and a rack of toast and had just sat down to eat, when a police car pulled up to the kerb. Sergeant Perkins and another man, shorter and wearing a fine suit, got out of the car. Cat opened the door and waited while the two men walked up the path.

'Good morning, Sergeant Perkins,' Cat said. She pointed to the living room.

'Ma'am.' Sergeant Perkins and the other man took of their hats.

'Chief Inspector Bellerose,' the shorter man said.

'Tea? I'll just get cups.'

'No need, Mrs Carlisle,' Chief Inspector Bellerose said. 'We won't be staying long. We've just come to tell you that things have been resolved. Isobel Carlisle confessed to murdering her brother.'

'What? Confessed?' She shook her head. 'I don't believe it.'

The chief inspector stared at her, as if deciding what to tell her.

'She's dead, Mrs Carlisle. Overdosed on sleeping pills. She left a note. Freddy Sykes was blackmailing her. It seems that he had been getting money from her for ages. Got the bulk of her savings. When she told him that she didn't have any more money to give, he told her to ask her brother. Benton refused to pay. She said it was an accident. She argued with her brother. She pushed him; he fell and struck his head.'

'This is unbelievable.' Cat set her teacup down on the tray.

'Will you be all right, Mrs Carlisle? Is your aunt here?'

'No one's here. She and Annie are seeing the wax figure of Wallis Simpson.' Cat looked at Chief Inspector Bellerose. 'What should I do?'

'Nothing,' he said. 'She left specific instructions in her very detailed note about what to do with her remains. You'll need to deal with the house, but that can wait. I hope you don't find me impertinent, Mrs Carlisle, but if I were you, I'd take your family and go on a nice long holiday.'

'We're going to Scotland,' Cat said. 'We're leaving next week. Who knows, we may stay there for an extended period of time.'

She walked the policemen out to their car. After they left, Cat shut the door and locked it. Something whirled in her very being. It wasn't physical, but a rearranging of her heart and soul. Benton was gone. Isobel was gone. All the things that had caused her pain had been removed from her life, like a malignant tumour. An avalanche of grief released into her body. It flowed like a gushing river, a force so strong it knocked Cat to her knees. She leaned against the door as she slid to the ground. Cleansing grief pulsed through her veins.

Years gone by, the death of her parents, her marriage, her unborn children, the death of her husband, her life, reduced to nothing. She bent over and clutched her stomach. The numbness pushed through and faded, leaving Cat with all the feelings she had supressed. Something snapped in her. She wept.

Epilogue

Thomas watched the Carlisle house from across the street. He and Chloe St James were nestled behind the fat trunk of the oak tree in the garden square. Chloe leaned against the tree trunk and used the ember of one cigarette to light another. She tossed the butt to the ground and stamped at it with her shoe. Thomas felt her eyes on him as he watched Catherine.

The time in Scotland had served its purpose. She was suntanned and had put on weight, filling out her cheeks a bit. She hadn't cut her hair and today the ringlets hung down the back of her neck, held in place by a clip of some sort. She moved with the grace of an athlete. He found he couldn't look away.

'Get your eyeful, Thomas,' Chloe teased.

He gave her a look, noticed the smile in her eyes, and shook his head. 'Leave it, Chloe, would you? She's been through hell, you know. Her whole life shredded in the course of a week.'

'She knew what she was getting herself into when she agreed to work for Reginald,' Chloe said.

'Did she? I don't think so.'

'I don't understand the appeal, frankly. She's a privileged housewife who has nothing to offer. She has no connections now. The Carlisles are dead. I'm betting that not one of her old friends reaches out to her.'

'I've a feeling that Mrs Carlisle will be able to insinuate herself into the good graces of society,' Thomas said. 'She's got good instincts, Chloe. You were a novice too at one time, as I recall.'

'Instincts? She's inconsistent and reckless. Her judgement is questionable at best. I can't believe she allowed Marlena X to lead her into her lair. Good thing you were there, Mr Charles, or your protégé might not have made it.'

Thomas ignored her. Two cars pulled up to the Carlisle house. One of them, a blue Vauxhall, carried a man dressed in a business suit and carrying a brief case. The other was a taxi, out of which climbed Alicia Montrose, her blonde hair streaked with sunlight, her arms a golden bronze.

'Ah, the best friend,' Chloe said.

Cat walked down the two steps to the street. She shook the man's hand and nodded at Alicia.

'I admit that Alicia and her husband could help Mrs Carlisle's entrance into the right circles. War's coming, Thomas. We've got our work cut out for us.'

'It's going to be brutal,' Thomas said.

'In any event, Mrs Carlisle is your problem now. Good luck. Until next time.'

Chloe stepped onto the pavement towards the car parked down the street.

The man in the business suit was affixing a 'For Sale' sign to the wrought-iron fence in front of the Carlisle house. Thomas watched as Cat and Alicia stood on the pavement, looking at the house where Catherine had spent fifteen years of her life. Alicia put her arm around Cat. She leaned close and whispered something in Cat's ear. Both women laughed out loud before they got into the taxi and sped off.

Thomas stood for a long time after that. He smoked a cigarette, taking his time with it.

'She's my problem now,' Thomas said to no one in particular. He pushed away from the tree and walked into the square.

Acknowledgements

Historians study and document the past to understand the events that take place in the timeline of humanity and ultimately define our place in the world. My primary goal as a historical novelist is to capture what it felt like to live in a particular era. *The Silent Woman* takes place during the summer of 1937. King Edward had abdicated to marry Wallis Simpson, and England was in the throes of coronation fever as Edward's younger brother, George, inherited the crown. Meanwhile, Adolf Hitler was building planes and conscripting an army—in violation of the Treaty of Versailles—with barely a hint of this activity being reported in the newspapers. England was headed to war, but her citizens didn't know it. An interesting time, indeed! My hope is *The Silent Woman* will transport you back to this tumultuous time for Britain and for the world.

Many people played a part in bringing Cat Carlisle and her story to life. Lisa Ricard Claro talked me off the ledge more times than I care to admit. She has been my friend and colleague since I started writing and has kept me honest (and sane) on this crazy path to publication. The Formally Informal Writers Group, spearheaded by Gina Heron, held me accountable and kept me in the chair writing. They also cheered me on along the way. Heartfelt thanks to Janet Robinson, Angela Baxter, Alix Hui, and Ann Croucher for sharing their sense of place. Thanks to

Kathryn Barbier for her vast knowledge of the state of the world during the time leading up to World War Two. Any errors—historical or otherwise—contained herein are mine.

Thanks to all the beta readers who read rough drafts of this book: Elizabeth Hawkins, Jean Marcus, Pat Murphy, Kim Laird, Jay Reed, and Gloria Bagwell Rowland. I am thrilled beyond measure that you like my books and support me in my efforts to entertain.

A big thank you to Hannah Smith at HQ for encouraging me to write this book, for her excellent editorial feedback, and for giving *The Silent Woman* a home.

Finally, I want to thank everyone who has read my books, been touched by my stories, and taken the time to write reviews. When I sit down to a blank screen and start writing those first words, I have you in mind.